SOLSTICE
OF
DEATH

Also by Laurence Anholt

Art of Death
Festival of Death

SOLSTICE
OF
DEATH

A MINDFUL DETECTIVE MYSTERY

LAURENCE ANHOLT

CONSTABLE

With love for Claire, my midwinter moonchild

CONSTABLE

First published in Great Britain in 2021 by Constable

1 3 5 7 9 10 8 6 4 2

Copyright © Laurence Anholt, 2021

The moral right of the author has been asserted.

*All characters and events in this publication, other than
those clearly in the public domain, are fictitious
and any resemblance to real persons,
living or dead, is purely coincidental.*

All rights reserved.
No part of this publication may be reproduced, stored in a retrieval system, or
transmitted, in any form, or by any means, without the prior permission in writing
of the publisher, nor be otherwise circulated in any form of binding or cover other
than that in which it is published and without a similar condition including this
condition being imposed on the subsequent purchaser.

A CIP catalogue record for this book
is available from the British Library.

ISBN: 978-1-47213-004-4

Typeset in Adobe Caslon Pro by Initial Typesetting Service, Edinburgh
Printed and bound in Great Britain by Clays Ltd, Elcograf S.p.A.

Papers used by Constable are from well-managed forests and
other responsible sources.

MIX
Paper from
responsible sources
FSC® C104740
FSC
www.fsc.org

Constable
An imprint of
Little, Brown Book Group
Carmelite House
50 Victoria Embankment
London EC4Y 0DZ

An Hachette UK Company
www.hachette.co.uk

www.littlebrown.co.uk

Chapter 1

A Deathly Dawn

Snow.

Snow fell.

Snow fell softly on Salisbury Plain.

At first a dusting on frosted grass, then snowflakes like ashes swirling in air. Throughout the night a blizzard swept in from the east, driving sheep to shelter in banks and hedges.

This was the midwinter solstice – a hiatus in time in which the earth seemed suspended in its orbit. When darkness grappled with light. When our ancient ancestors gathered to imbibe their heathen brews. A time of sacrifice and death.

After the snowstorm had passed, only the wind remained. Only the wailing wind and the crows, which circled like ragged witches above a world as white as an unwritten story.

In the oyster-grey light before dawn, a procession set out from the visitor centre towards Stonehenge. Two thousand or more, huddled against the biting wind, led by chanting Druids and assorted New Age revellers. At their rear, tourists in bright cagoules, photographers, and neon-clad officials from English Heritage.

Amongst the multitude was a girl of nineteen named Jojo Bloom, who had arrived in a steam-breathing taxi from Salisbury station dressed in a silver puffer jacket and waist-length braids beneath her fur-trimmed hood. Jojo was here for a mystical experience, but what she did not know was that the solstice would change her life forever.

In their robes, antlers and folkloric costume, the millipede of visitors wound their way through the security barriers, where good-natured guards in balaclavas patted down a few in a search for bottles, knives or spray paint. They were not expecting trouble, and the only arrest was a man with a horse's head and a pocket full of Ecstasy.

As they approached the roofless temple, the air was filled with the *Kra! Kraa! Kraaa!* of the beady-eyed lookouts – the rooks, jackdaws and crows who for centuries had built their tattered nests in the interstices between the upright sarsens and the horizontal lintels.

The temptation was to rush inside the stone circle, but a sense of reverence restrained the visitors. Slowly they formed a girdle around the stones, gazing inward at the virgin quilt of the floor, pockmarked only by the devil's tridents of avian footprints.

When the last stragglers had assembled, the chief Druid raised a hand, red with cold. Broad-bellied. A cumulus of beard about his face. A writhing dragon emblazoned on his white gown. The man was an apiarist in his working life. Now he held aloft a sprig of holly dense with berries, his voice boomed and his words were vapour in the air.

'After the darkness of the longest night, we bid farewell to the Holly King!'

The sprig was offered to his companion on his left – a part-time witch from Aylesbury – and onwards from hand to hand, past the bluestones, past the sarsen trilithons, past the Slaughter Stone and the Altar, returning finally to the Druid himself.

All eyes were drawn to the robed one as he dropped the holly into a cauldron at his feet and bent to retrieve a twig of oak.

'The Oak King of light is reborn,' he thundered above the moaning wind. 'Once more our god and goddess rule together. And light returneth to our lands ... BLESSED BE!'

'BLESSED BE!' echoed the devotees.

Amongst the crowd, Jojo Bloom could barely contain her excitement, for the Druid had timed his ceremony to perfection. At 8.09 precisely, the tip of the sun emerged in the eastern sky. Four thousand hands were joined. And then, to their utter astonishment, a laser beam of sunlight fell like a sword blade along the stone corridor.

There were gasps and sighs, followed by cheers, whoops and ululations, as the moment was recorded on a thousand iPhones.

So many times the dawn had been obscured by a bank of cloud, but today it was naked, and flaming, and red, and glorious.

Now they moved blinking into the embrace of the monument, rejoicing in their proximity to the sacred stones. Hands reached to hug and caress the rough lichen coats of the sarsens.

Some kissed the stones. Some sat in meditation. Spliffs were sparked and mead was supped from horned cups. Flutes were played and guitars strummed in a wild, discordant cacophony. In the heart of the monument, a wild woman beat out a rhythm, her hennaed hands pounding the skin of a tribal drum.

Beneath a mighty trilithon, Jojo Bloom shook free her feathered braids and danced a wild dance of the future. Her body swayed. Eyes closed. Fingers traced animalistic shapes in the glittering morning. Lost in communion with the solstice and the stones.

Down by the Portaloos, police officers relaxed; paramedics shared a flask of tea; security guards petted their dogs. Once more, it seemed, the gods had smiled on these helpless mortals.

At first Jojo ignored the warm drop that landed on her cheek. When it came again, she assumed it was melting snow. But when it traced a path to her lips, she tasted something sweet and metallic. Opening her eyes, she touched the wetness. There was blood on her fingertips, and now her cheeks were smeared with savage streaks. She felt a surge of panic. Had she somehow cut her face?

Staring up at the lintel high above her head, she saw a hand dangling from beneath a mound of snow. A hand unlike any she had seen.

A crowd formed around her, clutching each other in awe. The hand was large. The hand was green. The hand dripped with beads of blood, like berries on winter holly.

And Jojo screamed.

Chapter 2

The Shout

DI Shantala Joyce was balanced on a chair on top of a desk at Yeovil Police HQ. She took careful aim and was about to squeeze the trigger when her phone vibrated in her jeans pocket.

'Jesus, this had better be important, Benno.'

Sergeant Bennett's baritone voice sounded uneasy.

'Busy, boss?'

'I am literally suspended in mid-air.'

'Well this will bring you down to earth. Bit of a shocker for you.'

'Give me a moment, will you?'

Once again Shanti took careful aim, and fired a staple through the paper chain into the polystyrene ceiling tiles. When she was satisfied, she descended carefully.

'Go on, Benno.'

'Right, you know where I live, don't you? Outskirts of Salisbury. Not far from Stonehenge.'

'I'm sure it's lovely. You and Mrs B must be very happy.'

'There's been an incident at the stones,' he said. 'A peculiar one.'

Shanti retrieved her coffee from the top of a bamboo-coloured filing cabinet. She put the phone on speaker.

'What's all that moaning, Benno? I'm having trouble hearing you.'

'That's the wind, boss.'

Although the offices were adequately heated, Shanti felt a chill permeate her body.

'Stonehenge isn't really our ground, is it?' she said hopefully.

'Not as such. But the Wiltshire squad have specifically asked for you and DI Vince Caine. They used that expression again – the one you hate.'

Shanti sighed. 'What expression?'

'Since you cracked the Havfruen and Flynn cases, it seems you're the "go-to team for weird shit in the West Country".'

The coffee was powdery at the bottom. Both bitter and sweet. Not unlike that accolade.

'I'm deeply touched, Benno. But unfortunately they'll have to find someone else – preferably not a single mum in the week leading up to Christmas.'

'I hear you, boss. But I've been on this job all my working life, like my dad and my grandfather before him, and I've never come across one like this. I'm on site now, and I'm telling you there's something ominous afoot. The only team who can handle it are you and Vince.'

She gazed around at the office. Strands of tinsel draped forlornly over desk dividers and monitors. A handful of Christmas cards from local businesses pinned to the noticeboard. From the staff kitchen, the raucous laughter of Dunster and Spalding in manic demob mood. Even the lights of the erratically blinking Christmas tree had been wired to annoy. As Shanti watched, twenty metres of paper chain unrolled majestically from the ceiling and came to rest on the carpet tiles.

'You won't convince Caine, you know that? He's halfway through a midwinter retreat. He doesn't do Christmas. He's a Buddhist, remember?'

'I think you may be wrong,' said Benno.

'Why? Has he converted?'

'I mean he's already in a cab. He'll be with you in ten minutes.'

'Wait. What? How did you speak to him? There's no signal at Caine's cabin. He likes it that way.'

'I got lucky. He was walking to Lyme for provisions. I was as surprised as you, but he seemed pretty excited when I told him the details. Seems Vince is a bit of a Stonehead. That's someone who's mad about Stonehenge.'

'Of course he is,' said Shanti. A picture came to her of her long-haired colleague in full Druidic robes with arms outspread. 'I suppose you'd better fill me in. But I'm not making any promises.'

'Right. You know what day it is?'

'I do indeed. Tuesday the twenty-first of December is Christmas Party Day, and for long-established and deeply sexist reasons, preparations fall on the nearest available female. That's me, Benno.'

'Honestly, boss, I fully intended—'

'Last Christmas – which if you remember was my first in this dismal place – I bought, and even hand-made, Secret Santa presents for the entire team. That's twenty-seven people. Guess what I got in return?'

'Deodorant, boss. You told me.'

'Nicely wrapped, I'll admit. But it was indeed a stick of deodorant. Lynx, to be precise. I carry it everywhere. I take it out and marvel—'

'With respect, this is a lot more important than the office party. Today is the midwinter solstice, commonly known as Yule. Despite the conditions, there was a fair crowd for the ceremony, and at eight twenty-three, a little after dawn, a young lady by the name of Jojo Bloom was dancing beneath one of the trilithons—'

'What's a trili . . .?'

'A stone archway like giant cricket stumps. A drop of blood fell on her face. When she looked up, there was a hand – a large green hand – dangling several metres above the ground. I'm looking at it now; I can see the form of a large male lying horizontal beneath a mound of snow. The only visible part is the hand, which is swaying in the wind.'

'What's with the green thing?' she asked.

'Could be a pagan. There's all sorts here, as you will see – Druids, shamans . . . As we speak, the local team are processing a gent with a horse's head.'

'Hang on . . . you're telling me we have public on site?'

'Around two thousand, at a guess. Normally there would be five thousand, but numbers are down due to the weather.'

'Jesus. Well, is there somewhere to process them?'

'English Heritage have put the entire visitor centre at our disposal. It's a mile or two from the stones, and you'll find the facilities very agreeable. Nice and warm, with a lovely canteen. Free coffee and mince pies if you want them.'

'Sounds like my kind of crime. And we're certain he's dead, are we?'

'He's dead, boss. It was minus nine last night. Though how the hell he got up there is more of a mystery than the stones themselves. I'm not a superstitious man, but it sends shivers down my spine. Why today of all days?'

'There's always a spike at this time of year. Christmas Crime, they call it. Mind you, in my Camden days, it was a festive stabbing, or a nice burglary.'

'I mean the solstice, boss. Round here they believe . . .'

'Go on.'

'The old ones believe that primal forces rise from the funeral mounds on the plains.'

'Yes, but fortunately we're police officers, Benno, so we don't believe in bollocks. Has anyone been up there yet?'

'Dawn Knightly and her SOCO crew have just arrived. Trouble is, Dawn won't allow the climbers to ascend in these conditions.'

'What's she going to do? Wait till spring?'

'She's ordered scaffolding around the trilithon. She wants it tented, too. With a generator and lights. As we speak, there are scaffold poles swinging about like a Buster Keaton movie.'

'Good for Dawn. You can't overrate safety and comfort. How long will that take?'

'Everything should be in place by the time you arrive.'

'Hang on, I haven't said . . .'

She carried the phone to the window, wiped a circle in the condensation and scanned the grey streets for a taxi.

'Can't hear you, boss.'

'I'm thinking.'

What she was thinking about was Paul. The love she had for the boy was a kind of sweet agony, and every day for a month she had ramped up extravagant promises about this most glittering of all Christmases. A murder could be solved, but the conundrum of modern motherhood could not.

'I won't be Mr Popular either,' said Benno, as if reading her thoughts. 'The timing's unfortunate for sure, but there are four days till Christmas. If we make a decent start, we might be able to freeze the investigation for a couple of days.'

'Leave the wordplay to me, Benno.'

Three storeys below, a taxi pulled up by the white-piled kerb. As she watched, a tall man climbed out of the passenger seat, shaking hands with the driver as if they were lifelong friends. He was dressed in a greatcoat, with a battered bag over one shoulder, gloves, hiking boots, a grey scarf and a bomber hat with long flaps like dangling ears, which fluttered in the tail of last night's blizzard.

'Caine's here,' she said. 'We'll be with you in an hour.'

'Appreciate it, boss.'

'In the meantime, you know the drill. Establish a double cordon around the site. I want the contact details of every man, woman and child on the premises, and if anyone witnessed so much as a snowball fight, we'll need a detailed statement. With the exception of SOCO, I don't want a living soul near that jolly green giant.'

'Got it. And by the way . . .'

'Yes, Benno?'

'You'll need to wrap up warm. Hat, thermals, the lot.'

'Jesus, is it that cold?'

'As a penguin's penis, boss.'

She knew he would not come inside – the beige corridors and holding cells were anathema to a man like Caine. She knew he would wait patiently on the steps, as incongruous as an Arctic fox that had strayed from the forest into the concrete edifices of Yeovil.

Perhaps he sensed that she was watching him, because he looked up and raised a hand in greeting. Even from here, she could make out the beguiling smile on his olive-skinned face.

Shanti turned and began stuffing a few essentials into her bag – torch, pepper spray, handcuffs, chocolate. Grabbing her leather jacket, she hurried to the staff kitchen, where half a dozen uniforms were sharing cracker jokes.

'Sorry to spoil the fun, but the party's off.'

'Aw, boss!'

'Suspected homicide at Stonehenge. I'm heading over with DI Caine.'

'You're not going to cancel leave?'

'Possibly. Probably. We'll see how it goes. You need to stand by. So stay sober, Spalding.'

'Why me, boss?'

"Cos you're the one concealing a bottle of Skol up your sphincter.'

Chapter 3

A Karmic Cop

Tyres squealed as Shanti reversed out of the parking space, pitching the Saab down the icy ramp to the street.

'How are you, Shant?' asked Caine, rearranging the detritus of toys, folders, books and wrappers at his feet. 'You look . . .' he gazed at her softly, 'radiant.'

The man had a peculiar aroma about him – something you couldn't buy in the shops. Pine trees. Incense. Earth.

But she was not going to do this. She had a job to do and a son who needed her home. Emotions were utterly superfluous. The fact that Caine had emerged from the Undercliff wearing that Zen-like smile and three days of stubble on his angular cheekbones was of no relevance.

When she spoke, her words were staples from a gun.

'Right. Quickest route to Stonehenge, Caine? Benno says most of the minor roads are impassable.'

'Up the A359 to Sparkford,' he answered as if reciting a poem. 'Then east on the A303 towards Andover. Forty-five minutes max.'

Although it was not yet 9.30, the pavements were thronged with shoppers – normal families doing normal things. A netted forest of Christmas trees added to Shanti's shame.

'You can take it off now,' she said.

'Take what off, Shant?'

'The hat, Caine. I feel like I'm in a Beatrix Potter story.'

As he shook free his hair, the car was filled with a fleeting aroma of lemongrass shampoo.

The thing that Caine could never comprehend was that a crime scene was a war zone. Right now, Shanti was strapping on her armour. Emotions off. Logic on. This karmic cop was way too soft.

'Spit it out, then,' she said. 'Why you were so keen to come on board. In all my years, I've never met a more reluctant cop, but Benno tells me you practically dived into that cab.'

She didn't need to turn to picture that affectionate smile. The oil-well eyes.

'I'll admit he got me intrigued. A body on a trilithon at Stonehenge. On the night of the solstice, Shanti. How on earth would you raise a body seven metres in the air?'

'I've already sussed that. A cherry picker or a forklift.'

'It's possible. But then there would be tracks in the snow. I suspect it's far more mysterious than that.'

'You can't fool me. I know your real motive.'

'You do?'

'Admit it, that winter retreat business is a bit sad, isn't it? Billy No-Mates all alone in his woodland shed while the rest of the world is celebrating.'

'Meditation is neither happy nor sad, Shanti.'

'Like you, Caine. You're neither happy nor sad. Just annoying.'

13

The city was busier than she'd expected. She thought about blue-lighting it, but the roads were dodgy. Hit a patch of ice and you'd have pedestrians tumbling like chocolate Santas.

'But you're right,' Caine was saying. 'There is another reason. I like working with you. You know I do.'

'Right. We can cover this topic very briefly indeed. I'm sure you remember the rules. It's awfully simple. Imagine a thin blue line between us . . .' She indicated a boundary along the hand-brake. 'On one side there's the job in hand – the valiant fight for justice. On the other side, there's . . . other stuff, which is not germane to proceedings.'

Jumping the red light at the top of the hill, she swung sharp right onto the A359, which was banked with dirty drifts. The roads had been gritted out here, and she began to weave expertly in and out of slow-moving vehicles, attracting a few hoots and enraged expressions from other motorists.

'You're driving very fast, Shanti.'

'I'm highly trained, Caine. Advanced Driver of the Year, if I remember correctly. I expect you did the cycling proficiency.'

'You're a brilliant driver, and I know time is of the essence – the golden hour and all that – but not to put too fine a point on it, everything at the stones will be frozen, so perhaps we have a little longer than normal.'

'You sit quietly like a good boy and leave the driving to me.'

She had whacked up the heating, and Caine began to wriggle out of his greatcoat, which he folded carefully. As he stretched to place his scarf, coat and hat neatly on the back seat, Shanti made the classic error of glancing at his midriff, exposed between T-shirt and jeans. Clearly that retreat diet was insufficient. For some reason, the random word 'washboard' came to mind.

Refastening his seat belt, Caine gazed out at the countryside, where snowy fields swept like laundered sheets to the horizon.

'Look at it, Shant – the solstice light. Isn't it extraordinary? You should have seen the Undercliff this morning, it was like another world.'

He was right. The icing-sugar landscape was bathed in luminosity so intense it made your head ache.

'Tell me about Stonehenge,' Shanti said. 'Benno says you're a bit of an authority.'

'I wouldn't say that, but I was pretty fascinated as a teenager.'

'Poster on the bedroom wall, was it?'

'Well, I . . . How did you know that?'

She half hated the sarcasm in her tone.

'Just a hunch.'

'Want to know what got me interested?'

'I sense I'm about to find out.'

He turned to her enthusiastically. 'Do you remember *Neolithic Neighbours*?'

'Citation required.'

'It was a fabulous TV show when we were teens. You'll definitely remember the theme tune . . .' He began to hum a strange dirge, until Shanti glared at him. 'It ran for about ten years,' he continued, 'and I remember being bereft when it finished. The premise was that a group of experimental archaeologists lived together as a tribe near Stonehenge. There were three or four families, including kids of my age. The community built roundhouses and dressed in skins and furs exactly like our ancient ancestors. Every week they learned a new skill – foraging, body art, flint knapping . . .'

'Indispensable in Camden Town.'

15

'And you know what, Shanti? I still have my *Neolithic Neighbours* books and – keep this secret – I was planning to give one of them to Paul for Christmas.'

Jesus! Why did he have to do this? A memory came to her of Paul following Caine along the coastal path, lost in sunshine and happiness as they tracked wildlife, collected firewood, sharpened sticks . . . The boy idolised him.

'Give me facts,' she said tersely. 'Not too many.'

'Right, well, Stonehenge is a complex ring of standing stones built around 3000 BC. The thing that blew my mind as a young-ster was that those colossal stones were transported from many miles away – some as far as the Preseli Hills in Wales.'

'So, a ring of old stones that came from somewhere else.'

'Magical stones, Shant.'

'Word rejected.'

'Deeply mysterious, then. You feel it internally somehow.'

'Like period pains.'

That tender smile again. He reached to the floor and col-lected some Lego bricks. 'Maybe it's because the technology seems so anachronistic,' he said. 'The incredible thing is that the trilithons are interlocked like giant Lego bricks. A carpenter's mortise and tenon, in fact. It's extraordinarily sophisticated.'

'I suppose they didn't have much else to do.'

'But this was the Stone Age, Shant. All they had were antlers and flints, and that stone is tougher than granite. It makes you wonder about so many things . . .'

'If you mention UFOs, I shall exit the vehicle.'

He placed the Lego tidily in the glove compartment.

'You wait till you're standing there – it's impossible not to be affected by the place.'

'But what's it for, Caine? I mean, what's the point of it?'

'That's the intriguing thing – no one knows for certain. But one thing I learned from *Neolithic Neighbours* is that Stonehenge was a celestial calendar – a Stone Age computer, you could say. And the most significant event of the astral year is right now . . . today.'

'The midwinter solstice is the shortest day, right?'

'Yes. It's the moment when our part of the planet is tilted furthest from the sun. The truth is, it's all about sex.'

'No it isn't. I've sat in traffic jams for hours staring at those stones, and there is nothing sexy about them.'

'Our ancestors would disagree. They saw this as a moment of celestial ecstasy when Mother Earth was impregnated by the Sun God. You see, the midwinter solstice falls exactly nine months before the harvest.'

'Jeez. Give me strength.'

'I suppose it represented a glimmer of hope in the hunger months. Imagine it! There would have been feasting, hallucinogenic dancing and even . . . I hardly dare to say it . . . human sacrifice.'

'Wait a minute. You're not saying . . .?'

'The body on the stone? I've no idea. But we're about to find out.'

Shanti overtook a hulking truck, which splattered the windscreen with sludge, forcing her to drive blind until the wipers did their thing.

'Yeah, about that, Caine – we've got three days to find out, four at the most. I know your diary is pretty quiet, but I've got issues at home.'

'Ah, Shant, I'm sorry to hear that. I know how hard it is for you. Do you want to talk about it?'

'Not particularly, no,' she said, but she told him anyway. 'Paul's dad has been on about having him for Christmas, but he only does it to get under my skin. He offers Paul all kinds of things that I can't match. But it isn't good for him, that's the point. Whenever Paul goes to visit, he comes back all unsettled, and it takes me and Mum ages to steady him. That's why ... that's why I made a stupid promise, which I'll never be able to fulfil.'

'What kind of promise?'

'Oh, I don't know. I think I promised him the best Christmas of all time.'

'That's wonderful. What a fabulous mum you are.'

'A fabulous mum? You must be kidding. Paul's friend Sienna is literally on her way to Lapland with her mummy and daddy to meet Santa Claus. They're going on an actual reindeer ride with tinkly bells, and where are we, Caine? Heading east out of Yeovil on the A303.'

'But that's just it – Paul's mum is the lead officer on a major investigation. She's like Superwoman. Paul's mum is *you*!'

'Oh Caine!' A tear welled in her eye. 'Why do you put up with me?'

'I'll tell you why, Shanti. Because the universe has thrown us together. It's because you are the only person who makes me feel—'

She lurched around a gritting lorry and around the subject.

'Look. We must be getting close.'

Half buried in a snowdrift at the roadside was a sign showing the familiar portcullis motif of English Heritage.

'I was remembering a quotation in the taxi,' said Caine. 'A clever person once said that every generation gets the Stonehenge it deserves.'

'So what does our generation deserve?'

'Regimentation, I suppose. You queue for tickets within an allotted time slot. You take a shuttle bus to the monument and you circulate clockwise behind ropes.'

'Benno told me there were people dancing amongst the stones this morning.'

'Ah, yes. Today is an exception. Managed open access, they call it. At the spring equinox, the summer solstice, the autumn equinox and today, the midwinter solstice, the rules are relaxed and visitors are permitted to enter the monument itself. I think they even waive the entry fee. I suppose it's a nod towards respecting the religious rights of those who consider Stonehenge a sacred space.'

'Like who?'

'Wiccans. Pagans. Druids.'

'Druids aren't really a thing, are they?'

'They certainly are.'

'So I'm getting a picture of historic tensions involving disparate groups?'

'Exactly right. The stones have always been a lightning rod for conflicting factions – archaeologists, environmentalists, landowners, travellers, the military, politicians, the tourist industry, pagans … Just look at the controversy over the proposed road tunnel. Depending on your point of view, Stonehenge is a vital spiritual hub belonging to the people; or a fragile archaeological treasure that needs protection by the authorities.'

'I'm with the second lot.'

'Hmm. I'd say it's a delicate balance between the two. But in general, I come down in favour of freedom and fundamental human rights.'

'That's because you are fundamentally an anarchist. You're in completely the wrong profession, did you know that? Your career adviser should have been sacked.'

'You're absolutely right, Shanti. There isn't a day when I don't think about handing in my badge.'

'Ah, yes. This is the bit where DI Caine starts fishing for compliments about his intuitive investigative skills.'

'Inuit skills might be more useful today.'

'But thankfully we've arrived, so you can put your fox hat on. We've got an appointment with a green cadaver.'

Chapter 4

Killer in the Crowd

Stonehenge Visitor Centre was a modernistic affair, perched like a heron on the wind-blown plains, with outspread wings of glass and chestnut. To Shanti, the place seemed more redolent of an airport than the prehistoric monument that lay unseen two miles to the east.

As they approached the security barrier by the car park, a pack of newshounds surged towards the car, yelling and thrusting cameras at the windows in the most alarming way.

'Jesus, how long have they been there?' said Shanti to the armed uniform who examined their warrant cards.

"Bout forty minutes, ma'am,' he replied through his balaclava. 'There's more arriving by the minute.'

Dependable as ever, Benno had reserved the last parking space with a cone. Shanti eased between two squad cars and killed the engine. The car park was crammed, not only with the cars, battered vans and motorbikes of the solstice visitors, but also with emergency vehicles, SOCO vans and a couple of olive-green military trucks.

As they stepped into the dazzling morning, they were buf-
feted by a brutal wind, which made Shanti gasp and steady
herself against the car. Turning up the collar of her jacket, she
staggered to the rear of the vehicle, where she strapped on hiking boots, wrapped a scarf around her neck, and pulled on gloves
and a mauve hat that her mum had knitted many years ago.
Even then, the double bobbles had seemed gratuitous.

'Not a word, Caine,' she hissed.

Supported by a forest of steel struts, the undulating roof of
the visitor centre seemed to groan beneath its load of snow. The
DIs entered a wide passageway dominated by a ghostly bank of
unmanned ticket booths. Up ahead, the passageway opened into
the shuttle bus terminal, which was swathed in sparkling ice. To
their right stood the museum and the Stonehenge Experience.
To the left, the gift shop, crammed with Stonehenge paraphernalia – tea towels, posters of the monument and a row of snow
globes. Why had she never brought Paul to this place? There was
nothing he would not love about the experience. Perhaps they
sold *Shit Mum* T-shirts inside.

Benno's burly form stood sentinel inside the huge glass-
fronted café. As the doors glided open, Caine and Shanti entered
a noisy interior like a vast fish tank, populated by a throng of
thousands.

It took a full minute to unscramble the chaotic vision. Pagans,
witches, knights, tourists and shrill students huddled around
chunky designer tables. Some appeared to be in shock or suffering from hypothermia; a few were weeping shakily. They were
attended by a team of paramedics and army cadets, who bustled
about dispensing hot drinks and space blankets. At the far end
of the slush-covered floor, a band of robed and tattooed Druids

sipped tea in front of motorcycle helmets on the tabletops before them.

Benno came to greet them, red-faced with cold and concern. For reasons Shanti had never fully understood, the veteran sergeant venerated Caine, and now he nodded respectfully at the younger man.

'Thanks for getting here so quickly,' he said.

'Seems the press beat us to it,' said Shanti, pulling off the woollen hat and stuffing it into her bag. 'How did that happen, Benno?'

'You won't like this, boss – it seems we've got social influencers and local journos right here in the crowd. They are literally live-streaming an ongoing investigation. Hashtag Stonehenge is already trending on every platform.'

'That's all we need,' said Shanti, shaking her head in dismay.

'I suppose it's the perfect seasonal story,' said Caine.

Shanti surveyed the bedlam. What was lacking was decisive leadership. In the basement of her mind, she booted up *Senior Investigating Officer.*

'Right, Benno, all this reinforces the need to process this lot as soon as humanly possible. I'm sure they don't want to be here either.'

'We're making progress,' he said. 'See the evidence gatherer over there? She's got everything on video. We're also collating contact details, plus corresponding vehicle registrations, for every individual on site. Trust me, no one will disappear on my watch.'

'We trust you completely,' said Caine. 'And as a local, I wonder if you recognise any of these people?'

'One or two. I've come across the bikers before, and I know a few of the army officers.'

'Yeah, tell us about that,' said Shanti. 'What's with the squaddies? I didn't ask for them.'

A group of ridiculously young cadets were shifting furniture and offering support to the elderly under the watchful eye of a suave officer in combat fatigues.

'English Heritage have a long-standing relationship with the local barracks,' said Benno. 'They couldn't be more obliging. I'll introduce you to the major . . .'

'Maybe later,' said Shanti. 'I don't want to seem ungrateful, but this is a police matter. If we're short-handed, we'll call in the Yeovil squad – I've already cancelled the party.'

'They won't be happy, boss.'

'Happy? This isn't a Pharrell Williams song. How soon can we get to the scene?'

'Dawn knows you've arrived,' said Benno. 'She'll call the moment they're ready. In the meantime, I thought you'd like coffee.'

A large lad reversed out of the kitchen with a trolley. Benno handed a cappuccino to Shanti, tea to Caine. There was even a miniature pot of local honey, called Henge Hives.

'Is there anyone else we should register?' said Caine, stirring a spoonful into his tea.

'See the young lady down there? Next to the fellow with a white beard.'

'Everyone's got a white beard,' said Shanti. 'It's like Santa's grotto.'

'Silver puffer jacket and braided hair. That's Jojo Bloom. She's the one who spotted the body.'

The silver girl was ashen-faced and strangely immobile, as if frozen. A young female police officer kneeling at her feet attempted to comfort her.

'She looks traumatised,' said Caine, with pained compassion on his face.

'Yeah, she's a bit shaken,' said Benno. 'We questioned her comprehensively, but there's nothing to glean. Wrong place at the wrong time is all. Her mum's on the way. That's my new intern with her now.'

'Do we have any indication as to the identity of the victim?' asked Shanti. 'Any reports of missing persons?'

'Not a squeak. But I suppose most people are still in bed.'

'Yeah, I remember bed,' she muttered. 'Listen, Benno, we're going to need an incident room. Is there somewhere we can use?'

'Now that you mention it, there are folding screens down there. We could shift the Druids and divide off the far end of the café. It'll give us a decent base. I think I spotted a projector screen too.'

'See to it, will you? Caine and I will deliver a team briefing as soon as we return from the scene.'

A look of mild panic crossed Caine's face. He was not a natural public speaker.

'How's the coffee?' asked Benno. 'There are croissants if you want them. That canteen is on a different level.'

Shanti had missed breakfast and the aroma of pastry was intoxicating. But a sense of urgency drove her on.

'Another question, Benno,' said Caine. 'I've attended the solstice a few times, and I'm sure I arrived cross-country on foot. How can we be sure that people haven't slipped away?'

'Fair point,' the sergeant replied. 'It's the one positive about this weather. As you say, visitors normally drift in from every direction using minor roads and footpaths, but after last night's blizzard, the security team decided to restrict access to the main gate only. That means everyone arrived the same way as you.'

'So the perp could be right here amongst us?' said Shanti.

'It's possible,' said Benno.

'The killer in the crowd,' she mused.

They watched the uniforms working systematically through the room. The elderly and those with children were interviewed first and allowed to leave. Then the uppity ones – the belligerent and the entitled, who were always too important to wait their turn.

Benno took a brief call, zipping his jacket as he spoke.

'That was Dawn,' he said. 'She had a few issues with the lighting, but the tower is up and SOCO have started a fingertip search. So as soon as you're ready, I'll drive you down. She thought you'd want to observe the excavation.'

'Excavation?' said Shanti warily.

'From under the snow, boss.'

An aversion to death is a primal instinct, which manifests as trauma, fear, anxiety or revulsion to the point of nausea. These responses are nature's way of avoiding disease, contamination and threats to our own mortality. Perhaps one in a hundred people can learn to override them – surgeons, soldiers, morticians, pathologists and investigating officers. Shanti's secret, which she could barely reveal to herself, was that she was not immune. The dead man who waited for her on the plains filled her in equal measure with fascination and stone-cold dread.

Chapter 5

The Winds of Time

Wedged between ropes, shovels, traffic cones and a fat red battering ram, Caine surveyed the landscape from the back of Benno's Land Rover. He noticed that in distinct contrast to the wet black roadway, the pristine plains were unmarked by a single footprint.

The voices from the front of the vehicle sounded remote and mesmeric, like long car journeys as a child.

'This is the same route the shuttle buses take to the stones,' Benno was telling them. 'And it's where every one of those visitors walked this morning.'

The solstice had always affected Caine strangely. It was something ineffable, to do with the suspension of time. Like the state of *bardo* that the old Buddhists talked about. Between death and rebirth.

'Can you recall any previous incidents at the stones?' said Shanti distantly.

'Nothing significant,' replied Benno. 'Not since the eighties, anyway. There used to be a thing called the Stonehenge Free Festival ... naked revellers dancing on the stones ...'

'That wasn't you, was it, Benno?'

'A little before my time. But I remember Dad coming home very shaken. There were terrible clashes between the authorities and the travelling community.'

Caine hauled himself back into the parallel world of police procedure. 'The Battle of the Beanfield,' he said.

Shanti turned round. 'I thought you were asleep.'

'It was a seminal moment in policing history,' he continued. 'You can still find videos on YouTube.'

'It wasn't our finest hour,' agreed Benno.

'Talking of video footage,' said Shanti, 'there must be CCTV here. What do we have from last night?'

Benno steered down the centre of the roadway, which was long and straight and completely deserted.

'Good and bad news on that front. There's a live-feed camera called Stonehenge Skyscape. It's solar powered with a two-hundred-and-twenty-degree fisheye lens, so theoretically you can watch the stones round the clock, from anywhere in the world.'

'I sense a but,' said Shanti.

'But unfortunately last night's footage is mainly white.'

'You mean snow blocked the lens?' said Caine.

'You've got it. You see the blizzard coming in around five p.m. Soon after that, snowflakes begin to settle on the lens. After that, it's a white-out.'

'Very convenient,' said Shanti. 'Where I come from, a spray can did the job.'

'But there must be other cameras?' said Caine.

'Plenty at the visitor centre, but unfortunately the security team locked up early because of the weather. After that, there's no activity whatsoever.'

'You haven't told us about the security team,' said Shanti.

'The job is subcontracted to an outfit called GoodGuys from Salisbury. They're decent lads. A couple are ex-cops, so you won't be surprised to know they were pals of my dad. Normally they patrol the stones all night, especially just before the solstice.'

'What an amazing job,' said Caine. 'But they weren't around last night?'

'One of the lads admitted that after a couple of hours sitting in a van, he and his mates went home. It was well below freezing and they figured no one would be out and about in that weather. Besides, it was quiz night at the Stonehenge Tavern.'

'Jesus. So when was the last time someone had a proper view of the stones?' said Shanti. 'I mean, before the visitors this morning.'

'GoodGuys are a hundred per cent certain there wasn't a body up there when they knocked off. My new intern is a whizz at research and she managed to pull some nice images off social media from daytime yesterday – taken by tourists mostly. There was clearly nothing untoward on that trilithon, morning or afternoon. Which suggests the incident took place late last night or in the small hours of this morning.'

'In essence,' said Shanti, 'a murderer rocks up in the middle of a snowstorm and hauls a bloody great green man on top of a tricycle.'

'That's a trilithon, boss.'

'I wonder if it's a little early to assume murder?' said Caine.

'Yeah, he probably felt poorly and went for a lie-down.'

LAURENCE ANHOLT

Out here, the plains had a different quality. An openness. A bareness. A timelessness. After a few minutes, Caine leaned forward and squeezed Benno's shoulder. 'Could you drop us here?' he said.

'Feeling carsick?' asked Shanti.

'You know how I like to do things, Shant. I need to get a feel for the place.'

'You're telling me you want to walk?'

'It's less than half a mile.'

'Half a mile? Are you out of your tiny Buddhist mind? Time is of the essence, Caine, and besides, it's bloody freezing out there.'

'I could meet you at the stones?'

She knew when a battle was lost. She also knew that this Arctic fox needed to sniff around. Caine had already climbed down, and now he was prowling, getting his bearings. Smelling the air.

'OK, thanks, Benno. Could you collect us in, what, fifty mins?'

'No probs, boss.'

'Don't send another driver. I want you to look at the body yourself. Maybe you've met before.'

'Understood. I'll get those visitors processed.'

'And the incident room – don't forget the incident room. I want the whole team present for a briefing.'

When the Land Rover had retreated towards the glow of the visitor centre, Shanti joined Caine on the tarmac, where the beast from the east clawed at their clothing, searching ruthlessly for chinks.

30

Caine was rotating slowly on the spot, with coat tails and earflaps billowing, and arms outspread like a circling bird. 'Look at this place!' he yelled. 'Those hillocks are funeral barrows, Shanti, and that's the Greater Cursus. Normally the whole place would be teeming with tourists, so this is a one-off opportunity.'

'You're damned right,' she shouted back. 'I'll never work with you again.'

'You can almost feel the millennia flowing through you.'

'What I feel is a howling gale flowing through my thermals.'

She set off briskly, body bent against the wind, one arm encircling her face. 'Now where are these stones, Caine? Over this ridge? Oh! Oh, good grief . . .'

She halted abruptly and stared in wonder at the spectacle below.

Chapter 6

The Portal of the Dead

If you've never visited Stonehenge, you might picture a Stone Age Manhattan. Concentric rings of brooding boulders, at once primitive yet sophisticated. At once vast yet tiny beneath the upturned bowl of the sky.

All around the perimeter, blue and white police tape fluttered frantically. Within the monument, a white-suited swarm of SOCOs were going about their business on hands and knees, like a strange tribe of snow people.

Each rugged lintel wore a drooping cap of snow, and in the centre of it all, Dawn's nylon-clad tower rose like a vast stack of sugar cubes, or a modernist sculpture by Christo.

'All right,' said Shanti. 'I'll admit that's quite a sight.'

'It's awesome,' sighed Caine as they approached the barriers. 'You know what I liked to imagine when I was a young man?'

'Did it involve Raquel Welch in a fur bikini?'

He grinned at her.

'I liked to imagine how this place must have appeared to

visitors of the time. You see, the stones we see today have weathered over thousands of years, but when Stonehenge was built,
these sarsens would have been gleaming white. Imagine that,
Shanti! Pilgrims to this place would have been confronted by a
dazzling temple. A tribute to the gods, but also a massive status
symbol for those who built it. It makes you wonder ...'

'It makes you wonder why they didn't think of a roof. Look,
that must be the CAP at the side.'

The common approach path was a single access point for all
personnel arriving at the scene of a crime. It was designed to minimise disturbance and was generally meant to be the route least
likely to be used by a suspect. Here, that was irrelevant, as the
slushy ground might have been trampled by a herd of reindeer.

At the cordon, an armed officer checked and double-checked
their warrant cards.

'Suggest you stick to the walkway, chief,' she said, gesturing
towards a galvanised track. 'There's a rope to hold onto if you
need it ... Nice hats, by the way.'

And now they entered the temple itself, and it felt to Shanti
as if they were stepping into an operatic stage set, built to a stag-
gering scale.

'Jeez,' she said. 'That murderer gets top marks for imagination.'

As she spoke, the stocky white-suited form of Senior Forensic
Investigator Dawn Knightly emerged like a Michelin man from
a tent. When she saw the DIs, she waved a tubular arm. There
had always been a mutual affection between Shanti and the
older woman – the respect of one mother to another, and a
shared gallows humour.

'Happy Christmas, Shanti,' she yelled. 'I can't give you a hug
– cross-contamination, you know.'

'Reminds me of the early Covid days,' said Shanti.

'Ah, that's not even funny,' said Dawn in her soft Somerset tones. 'Come on, let's get out of this damned wind. You'll need to get togged up anyway.'

Checking that Caine was out of earshot, Shanti said, 'Listen, Dawn, I'm not brilliant with heights. How high is this tower of yours?'

'About seven metres. But trust me, I wouldn't work up there if it wasn't safe. You'll be fine. Come on.'

As Caine joined them, they entered a rippling SOCO tent, where an officer handed over Tyvek suits and asked them to sign a clipboard.

'So, what are your first thoughts?' asked Caine.

When she lowered her mask, Dawn's round face was flushed with excitement.

'It seems a bit contradictory, Vince. The crime scene has a primitive quality, and yet it feels staged somehow.'

'What's that mean?' said Shanti.

'I can't quite put my finger on it. The incident was brutal. Frenzied almost, so you'd expect clues everywhere. But so far we've found nothing. My gut tells me that whoever did this was a professional. It's almost as if they were DNA-aware.'

'A cop, you mean?' said Shanti.

'Who knows?' said Dawn. 'But one poor bugger's Christmas is ruined, that's for sure.'

'And the family too,' said Caine sadly. 'For them Christmas will never be the same.'

'Benno said you had a few technical issues,' said Shanti, wriggling into her suit.

'A problem with lights melting the snow. Had to switch to

LED. All good fun, though. Guess what we found when we got up there?'

'Erm, was it a dead man?'

'Crows, Shant. Or damned ravens or whatever they're called. Hopping about on his chest. They'd been sort of . . . picking at him.'

Shanti had noticed the creatures ogling her from behind the stones. Like vaudeville villains in capes.

'Is this going to be a nice case?' she asked. 'I mean, season of goodwill and all that.'

'A murder of crows,' muttered Caine.

'Do you want him?'

'I wouldn't mind,' said Dawn, eying Cain approvingly.

'I believe Stonehenge has a whole corvus colony,' he continued. 'Ravens, rooks and jackdaws too. They've been here for generations. They're highly intelligent creatures. Apparently they can remember human faces.'

'So you'll be interviewing them as witnesses?' said Shanti.

'All I know is they give me the willies,' said Dawn. 'And they made a right mess of my cadaver.'

'Jeez,' sighed Shanti. 'Most people are in the pub.'

She sat on a folding chair and pulled on elasticated overshoes.

'Trust me, Shanti. You wouldn't want to miss this one. Weirdest case I've ever attended, and I've done a few. He's a big fella, and from what we can tell, he's covered in green body paint. There's a prominent beard under there too.'

'Everyone round here has a prominent beard,' said Shanti. 'I think I'm growing one myself.'

'Anyway, get your kit sorted and you'll see for yourself. I'll meet you at the top.'

When Dawn had gone, Shanti pulled on double nitrile gloves, while Caine handed his coat to the safety officer and slid into his suit, pulling the elasticated hood over his fur hat.

'Strong look,' said Shanti.

'There are hard hats if you want them,' said the officer, pushing forward two yellow shells.

Caine declined, but Shanti removed her bobble hat and placed the helmet over the nylon hood, then followed Caine into the icy squall.

When they reached the tower, a uniform held the flap so they could enter the blindingly bright canopy that enclosed the great trilithon. Galvanised stepping plates had been laid across the ground, which was a mulch of mud, chalk, ice, grass and the sticky red oxide of blood. All around, the floor was marked with yellow numbered evidence plaques.

The ingeniously constructed scaffold rose more than three times Shanti's height, with ladders and trapdoors connecting the three decks. As Shanti stared upwards, she had the impression that the structure was dissolving into the dazzling ether.

Within the framework, the ancient columns appeared as massive petrified trees. Up close, the roughly hewn stone was caked with orange and ochre lichen, and smattered with the guano of those ominous birds.

At the foot of the first ladder, Caine stood aside to let Shanti pass; but she prodded him forward to lead the way. Vertigo aside, she had a profound aversion to being followed upstairs.

Caine was as nimble as a cat. Despite the baggy oversuit, he hauled himself rapidly upwards, while Shanti clung to each icy rung as the walls trembled around her.

When she arrived at the first deck, she found Caine leaning forward, waving one arm vertically in the narrow gap between the columns.

'It's a doorway,' he said, staring at her with raven's eyes.

'If you say so, Caine.'

'But a doorway that is too narrow for a person to pass.'

'Yeah. They should have thought of that.'

'It's a portal for the dead,' he whispered.

At the top of the third ladder, he turned to help her through the final trapdoor, but she brushed him aside.

When he had swung himself upwards, Shanti found herself alone. In her peripheral vision she became aware of a gently swaying object. With a rush of alarm, she realised that this was the hand – the oversized green hand that Benno had described – sealed now within a polythene bag; neatly labelled and secured around the wrist with cable ties. From the green nails of the two longest fingers, globs of rust-coloured blood had oozed into a congealing pool at the base of the bag.

Horrified as she was, the professional within her began to theorise: the extreme cold would be a factor, but if the blood was only congealing now, then death had occurred recently – a few hours ago at most.

As she emerged at last into the upper section of the tower, Shanti's gaze came level with eight white overshoes belonging to Caine, Dawn and two of the SOCO team, who patrolled the top deck like the crew of an Arctic submarine.

'Welcome to my world,' called Dawn cheerfully.

Chapter 7

Beautiful Ritualistic Murder

The dead man reclined long and broad like a stone knight beneath his white quilt.

Dawn had mentioned the birds, but that did not prepare Shanti for what she saw: the snow around the upper chest was a scarlet bib, tossed and trampled by those rummaging corvids, whose distinctive footmarks were everywhere. And deep within the snowy crust, she made out silvery coils of beard.

'Right, here's the plan,' said Dawn. 'I'm going to remove the snow from the face, then I want to take a careful look at the upper torso.' She waved a probe towards the wound. 'I don't want to spoil your lunch, but I reckon those birds were attracted by a very nasty injury.'

They watched in trepidation as she selected an assortment of scopes and trowels and began to painstakingly remove the snow from the top of the head, depositing each scoop carefully into a steel tray, where it was examined for trace evidence. At their side, the photographer recorded the scene from every conceivable angle.

'Is he wearing something on his head?' asked Caine.

'A wreath, by the look of it,' said Dawn. 'A floral crown, perhaps?'

As she picked the snow from the foliage, a mane of silvery hair came into view. Discoloured in places by a green wash, it cascaded to the man's shoulders, over green-tinted ears each pierced with a silver ring.

'I'm going to tackle the face,' said Dawn. 'So I'll ask you to step back to give us room.'

They did as they were told, huddled in the numbing cold at the rear of the platform as Dawn and her assistants hunched over the body. Millimetre by millimetre, the glacial excavation continued, and as she worked, they heard Dawn mutter, 'Strewth!' 'That's unusual.' 'Never seen that before.'

At last she turned. 'I hope you're ready for this,' she said.

Shanti and Caine stepped forward.

'Jesus,' breathed Shanti.

'May he be at peace,' said Caine.

It was the powerful face of a man in his late sixties, the labyrinthine wrinkles accentuated by a green patina, so that he seemed to radiate humanity. The countenance was benevolent and almost regal – the face of a man who had lived a long and extraordinary life.

But what made Shanti reel were the eyes.

Under frosty eyebrows, the green king stared to the heavens. But where pupils should have been were frozen white orbs.

She liked to tease Caine about how unsuited he was for this work, but at moments like this, Shanti doubted everything about the job. She wondered what these situations did to her mental health. She questioned whether she had the fortitude to withstand such scenes again and again – sights that regular people would never imagine in their darkest dreams.

'I suppose it was well below freezing,' said Dawn, by way of explanation.

Shanti felt vulnerable. For once she was glad to have Caine at her side. What kind of human would do that to another? And then the harsh reality descended – the killer was still at large. Perhaps they should wear stab vests or something.

Dawn was made of tougher stuff. With a sable brush, she flicked the last scraps of snow from the bulbous nose. As she moved down to the upper body, she began to work faster, removing large scoops of snow with a steel trowel, to reveal a barrel chest and portly belly.

It was clear now that the dead man was dressed from head to foot in sodden green garments – a lime-green jacket over a viridian shirt; olive corduroy trousers and oversized pea-green boots. And on top of the silver mane was that holly crown – sharp, crisp and garnished with berries like rubies.

'And now,' announced Dawn, when the photographer had done her work, 'it's time to scrutinise that injury.'

With latex fingers she raised the beard, and Shanti inhaled a gasp of icy air. The wound was brutal – a zigzag gash across the throat, like a ragged furrow in a field.

'Gaping incision to larynx,' muttered Dawn into her recording device. 'Approx one-fifty by twenty-seven mils. Suspected laceration of trachea and jugular.'

'So, the dripping hand . . .?' said Caine.

'Nothing wrong with the hand,' replied Dawn. 'From what I can tell, the blood channelled downwards from the throat, along the arm.'

'That looks like an unusual wound, doesn't it?'

'Yeah. I agree. There's something mighty fishy here. It's an uncommonly crude laceration, and far wider than you'd expect from an orthodox blade.'

'Meaning what?' said Shanti.

'Meaning I have no idea. A rough bit of metal, maybe? I've never seen anything quite like it.'

'No chance of self-harm?'

'Forget it. You'd pass out long before you could finish the job. In any case, why do it up here?'

'An accident, then?'

'Nicked himself shaving, you think?'

'We have to exclude all possibilities.'

'Hang on ... I think I've spotted something.'

Dawn leaned in and, with the aid of a hand lens and tweezers, extracted three or four minute particles from the wound, which she deposited into an evidence bag.

'What have you got?' asked Shanti.

'Too small to say.' Dawn held the bag up. 'We'll get it to the lab asap.'

'Could I make a couple of observations?' said Caine quietly.

'Be my guest.'

'He's going to say something clever,' warned Shanti.

'Well, he was lying beneath a heavy blanket of snow ...'

'We spotted that.'

'... but there's also a thin layer of compacted snow *beneath* the body.' Kneeling beside the cadaver, Caine looked up at his female companions. 'I'm suggesting that the formation of snow will help us to calculate the time the body was put in place. The thin layer beneath the body suggests that it had been snowing for a short time when he arrived. Whereas the heavier layer on top means that he was here throughout most of the blizzard.'

'Yeah, you're right,' said Shanti. 'My instincts say four a.m. – maybe a little later.'

'But there's another thing,' said Caine. 'He's a big man, isn't he?'

'Around six foot three,' said Dawn. 'That's upwards of a hundred and ninety centimetres.'

'And yet despite the horrific injury, there's little sign of a struggle. Why didn't he put up a fight? That's what I'm wondering. He gives the impression of being peacefully asleep.'

'Drugged?' suggested Shanti.

'That's definitely possible.' Caine stood upright. 'I'm beginning to suspect he was dead on arrival.'

'How could you know that?'

'Well if he died *in situ* – here on the lintel – his body heat would have melted the snow beneath him, and probably some of the snow on top.'

All the while, Shanti tried not to meet the dead man's gaze. Those frozen ponds were an image that would return in the night.

'I think we've got as far as we can up here,' said Dawn. 'We'll lose all daylight by four, so what I need to do is rig up a pulley so we can deliver him to the morgue for autopsy.'

'You're brilliant, Dawn,' said Caine.

'And just to be clear,' said Shanti. 'The assumption is . . .?'

'The assumption is murder. Beautiful ritualistic murder.'

Chapter 8

Then Comes the Naming of the Dead

They heard ladders clatter and the sound of laboured breathing, before Benno emerged through the trapdoor. As he hauled himself red-faced onto the deck, the sight of the dead man stopped him in his tracks.

He stared for a moment. Then stared again.

'I think I know him, boss.'

'You do?' said Shanti.

'I think so. What happened to his eyes?'

'Frozen solid. Forget the eyes. Forget the green paint. He's six foot three, Benno, with silver earrings and shoulder-length white hair. He's pretty distinctive, I'd say.'

'I think this is the man known as Finch. And if I'm correct – if this really is Finch – then this case is about to blow up bigger than you would believe. In fact, it's absolutely bloody nuclear!'

'You're being cryptic. What are you saying?'

'I'm sorry. Finch is a member of the local aristocracy. He's considered an eccentric, I suppose. We've had a few dealings over the years – minor breaches of the peace, trespass, that sort of thing. What else? Oh yes, he usually has a couple of huge dogs with him. He's known to the local force as an environmental activist. But I've always thought of him as a decent sort. In any case, he didn't deserve . . . this.'

'You said this could be nuclear?'

'Finch is short for Hector Lovell-Finch. And if that name sounds familiar . . .'

'Which it does.'

'. . . it's because Hector Lovell-Finch is the father of someone very famous indeed . . . someone notorious, in fact. I think you know who I'm referring to.'

'Oh Jesus,' gasped Shanti. 'What have we got ourselves into?'

Chapter 9

The Biggest Story Since
the Nativity

In the visitor centre car park, where the last of the visitors were leaving, it was snowing again – as softly as a slow-motion pillow fight.

The Druids fastened their helmets and revved the engines of Triumphs, Nortons and Harleys before steering warily across the mushy ground.

In the incident room that Benno had established behind screens at the far end of the café, Vincent Caine alone noticed the chiaroscuro masterpiece reflected across the vast windows – thirty or so cops leaning against walls or perched on tables, many swathed in scarves, gloves and balaclavas. At the centre of the composition, Shanti Joyce paced back and forth in the beam of a projector.

'It's Christmas,' she told them. 'And I'm as keen as you to get home. However, we are, as of now, dealing with a major homicide of a spectacularly brutal nature. There is a murderer out there, ladies and gents, and not just a common or garden Saturday-night brawler. What we are dealing with here is a deeply disturbed individual. Or individuals, perhaps.'

On a table in front of her, some forward-thinking officer had placed a scale model of the monument, with a cut-out cardboard figure indicating the position of the fatality on the relevant stone. To the side, Caine watched with undiluted admiration as Shanti warmed to her theme.

'Which brings me to my next point. In case you hadn't noticed, there's an ever-increasing horde of international journalists outside the gates who are ... what's the word? ... *slavering* for a juicy Christmas story. And this, ladies and gentlemen ...' she paused theatrically, 'is the biggest story since the Nativity. Please be aware that these journos will use every trick in the book to get on site. Not only will that be prejudicial to the case, but it may also deprive the victim's next of kin from hearing the tragic news in the sensitive manner to which they are entitled. In addition, it denies us the crucial opportunity to gauge their response. So the key word here is *confidentiality*.'

She paused again, partly for dramatic effect and partly to sip from a mug of marshmallow-topped hot chocolate.

'That's the polite term. A more realistic way of putting it is to say that if anyone in this room breathes so much as a word about this case over a glass of sherry to their mum, then they will be queuing at the job centre faster than you can say "Ho, ho, ho!" Do I make myself clear?'

It seemed she did.

'This is a fast-developing investigation, and we are currently pursuing various leads relating to the identity of the victim, which I would prefer to keep under wraps until we have confirmation. What I will say is that the deceased was a distinctive gentleman, well over six foot tall, in his late sixties. I'm sorry for being reticent, but what I will say is that we believe he was a local man who was well known in the vicinity and beyond.

'I'm going to show you a few images.' She raised a remote control and half turned to the screen. 'You'd better brace yourselves. I'm afraid this isn't easy viewing. The purpose of the exercise is to ensure that we are all fully aware of what we are dealing with. If you think you recognise this man, then please refrain from discussing it with your colleagues. Just make yourself known to Sergeant Bennett or another SIO immediately after the briefing.'

Officers with a few cases under their belt pride themselves on maintaining a cool demeanour, but the pictures of the green king laid out on the trilithon, with the holly crown, swirling beard and ice-pool stare, elicited gasps and audible intakes of breath.

'We believe that the unfortunate aspect of the eyes was simply caused by the sub-zero temperatures during the night. What is more pertinent is the fact that the throat has been opened with an instrument unknown. Once again, these images are upsetting, but it's important that you appreciate the particularly heinous nature of this crime.'

As Shanti revealed the injury beneath the swirling beard, several officers exchanged glances or shook their heads in awe.

'As we speak, our forensics team, ably led by Senior Investigator Dawn Knightly, is preparing to transfer the body to the morgue, and we're hopeful that pathology will uncover further evidence. At this point, I'd like to hand over to my colleague, DI Caine . . .'

For a moment, Caine seemed dazed. Eventually he rose awkwardly to his feet, still dressed in the greatcoat and the bomber hat with the dangling flaps. As she handed over the remote, Shanti thought she noticed a few smirks amongst the male officers in the room. This was the man known as 'Veggie Cop', who did not drink or share their locker-room banter and yet, to their consternation, seemed to have a mesmeric effect on women.

Caine was oblivious to all of this, but against her nature, Shanti felt a surge of protectiveness towards her colleague.

'Er, just a moment ... I'm sure you are aware that DI Caine is an expert on unusual crimes of this nature – perhaps the best detective in the force – so you will want to pay the utmost attention. Is that clear? Right, carry on, Caine.'

Caine seemed a little surprised by her introduction, but he smiled gently at his audience and waited ... Waited for silence. Waited for calm. Waited just a little longer than was necessary. At last he spoke, softly and soothingly.

'I often think that the hardest part of this job is informing relatives of the death of a loved one. Sadly, that's what DI Joyce and I will be doing later today. I'm sure we are all sensitive to the fact that this is a human being. A man who lived and loved and breathed. That's what we need to keep uppermost in our minds. An elderly man – like your own grandfather, perhaps – who was probably adored by his family.

'Now, in my opinion, the place and time of the incident are critical. It goes without saying that Stonehenge is one of the most iconic locations in the world, and this horrid incident took place at the precise time of the midwinter solstice, which is a seminal moment in the astrological calendar. For me, that's beyond coincidental.

'I'd like to bring your attention to his green attire …' he flipped back to the appropriate slide, 'the body paint and the evergreen wreath. He is dressed, I believe, as the Holly King – an aspect of the Green Man – who is honoured at the winter solstice. So I would suggest that we are looking for a perpetrator who is informed about this kind of thing – possibly someone with an interest in the mystical world.'

Again Caine paused. As if waiting for inspiration.

'I don't know what you think about this, DI Joyce, but it seems to me that this crime has a theatrical quality. Could it be that this murder was carried out by someone who was seeking the limelight? A person who sought to be noticed in the most public way possible? Someone who was, quite literally, seeking a platform?'

'A massive extrovert, you mean?' suggested Shanti.

'Or the opposite,' said Caine cautiously. 'A person who feels disempowered or insignificant.'

In the ensuing silence, it was unclear whether Caine had finished or if he intended to speak further. A kind of collective embarrassment filled the room, until Shanti stepped forward, took the remote from his fingers and switched off the projector.

'Right, useful observations, DI Caine. Thank you for that. In addition to those reflections, I'd like everyone to consider three key questions. One: who murdered this gentleman in such a bizarre way? Two: *why* did they murder him? And three: *how*? How on earth did this extremely large person materialise on that trilophone without any witnesses at all?

'It's the twenty-first today, and I know we're all anxious to be home with our families. Unfortunately, murderers do not respect holidays. But if we work together as a team, I am confident that a disturbed and dangerous offender can be swiftly brought to justice. Are there any questions?'

'Was this a sacrificial murder, ma'am?'

'I'm not a fan of that term, but I am cognisant of various pagan elements operating in the vicinity, so I'm not ruling anything out. As DI Caine says, we will be conducting some significant interviews today, so it's likely that we'll be able to confirm the victim's identity before the close of play, at which point you will understand why a degree of discretion is necessary.

'I'd like to leave you with one final thought: as we speak, a killer is at large. If DI Caine is right and they are seeking attention, they may be feeling extremely pleased with themselves right now. Perhaps they are identifying their next victim, and it is us who will be held accountable. I want each and every one of you to be *terrified* of that possibility. And I want you to understand that time is slipping through our fingers like ... like melting snow.'

Chapter 10

The Solstice Files

'That was brilliant, Shanti,' said Caine when the team had left the room. 'That's why I leave that stuff to you. I don't have that kind of authority.'

'To be fair, you raised a couple of decent points,' said Shanti as she examined the scale model of the monument. 'What was that about the green outfit?'

'Ah yes. I'm pretty sure that Finch was dressed as the Holly King, who is a pagan representation of the earth itself.'

'And there's me thinking Mother Nature was a woman.'

He was standing just a little too close. Gazing at her just a little too softly.

'I appreciated what you said about me.'

'What did I say?'

'You said I was the best detective in the force.'

'I don't think I said that, Caine. It's not the sort of phrase I'd use.'

They were joined by Benno, carrying a stack of newspapers and with a concerned expression on his face.

'We had four,' he announced.

'Four what?' said Shanti.

'Four officers who recognised the deceased from the slides. I'm as sure as I can be that Finch is our man.'

'Jeez. OK. And can we rely on those cops to keep shtum?'

'I think they understand the score. I don't want to add to your worries, but you might want to look at these . . .' He dumped the newspapers on the table.

'What . . .? How . . .?'

'Long lenses from the A303 by the look of it. Maybe a drone – although it's very windy. Anyway, I've dispatched a couple of constables with cones.'

Shanti stared in dismay at the photos of the monument, looking fabulously picturesque in the sparkling sunlight. There were the inevitable headlines: SOLSTICE SLAYER. BLOOD IN THE SNOW. A CHILLING KILLING. There was Dawn's tower. There were the white-clad SOCO officers on hands and knees across the site. There was Caine with earflaps blowing. There was Shanti herself directing operations in that ridiculous double bobble hat. She tossed the papers back to Benno.

'Not exactly flattering, are they?'

'It's those bunny suits, boss – they always make it look like you've had an early Christmas dinner.'

'Thanks for that. Right, I'm determined that we inform the relatives in the appropriate way, so we'll take ten minutes for lunch then we'll hit the road. All right with you, Caine?'

'Always ready,' he said.

'That's debatable.'

'I'd like you to meet young Masako before you go,' said Benno. 'I let her in on the probable identity of the victim – in strictest confidence, of course – and she's already started to put together a dossier on the Lovell-Finch family. It contains some pretty fascinating insights into the relationship between Finch and son.'

As they passed into the main canteen, Shanti almost stumbled over a group of squaddies who were busily mopping the floor on the other side of the screens.

'What's going on?' she hissed. 'I thought we talked about this.'

'I conveyed your message, boss. But they're so keen to help. They've done a brilliant job, as you can see, and to be honest, we need all available hands.'

It was true. Every surface of the canteen gleamed, and each chair and table had been arranged tidily on the spotless floor.

'But that team briefing was incredibly sensitive,' she said. 'There's zero soundproofing in these screens.'

'Apologies, boss. It was an oversight.'

'I think Benno's got rather a lot on his hands,' soothed Caine as they took their trays and joined the queue at the servery. 'And you had the foresight to withhold names, Shanti, so I'm sure there's no damage done.'

'It looks like they've finished anyway,' said Benno. 'Here comes the major now . . .'

A man was marching towards them, all smiles and salutes and camouflage clothes.

'Major McAble,' said Benno. 'I'd like to introduce DIs Shantala Joyce and Vincent Caine, who are leading the investigation.'

Caine observed a heavy auburn moustache, which the major stroked lovingly like a favourite pet. He shook hands warmly with Shanti, but Caine was apparently invisible to him.

'Shocking business,' McAble said. 'Glad to have played our part.'

The accent was English public school braggadocio, but Caine detected an undercurrent of something more unusual – Glaswegian patter, perhaps.

'We could spare a little more time tomorrow,' the major went on. 'All good training for the recruits.'

'Er, hang on,' said Shanti. 'There's clearly been a misunderstanding. We appreciate your work, Major Mac . . .'

'McAble.'

'. . . but I was just telling Sergeant Bennett that I'd prefer to keep this as a police matter. We have our own ways of doing things. I hope you understand.'

'Of course. Absolutely. The last thing we want is to be in the way. We'll withdraw immediately.'

'Nothing personal, you understand,' said Shanti. 'We all have our own methods; I'm sure you wouldn't want my team turning up at a military event.'

'Quite so. Delighted to have met you, DI Shantala Joyce. And your colleague too. Best of luck with the inquiry, and, er . . . bon appétit.' Another genial grin. Another swift salute.

When the major had rounded up his team and they had filed through the sliding doors, the room lay empty except for a scattering of cops, security personnel and English Heritage staff eating at tables.

Through the panoramic windows, the youthful squaddies could be seen hauling themselves into military vehicles; in the eddying landscape, they might have been troops in a Siberian war zone.

Benno, Shanti and Caine carried their trays to a table in a

discreet corner of the incident room – large, medium and small portions respectively.

'I've been trying to sort your accommodation,' Benno told them. 'I'm sure you'll want to be as close as possible to the scene of crime. The trouble is, every hotel and B&B within fifty miles is booked solid, and prices have practically doubled. Lady told me she could have sold each room five times over. You know why?'

'It's Christmas,' said Shanti drearily.

'That's not it.'

'Well what, then?'

'Those journos, boss. Every newshound on the planet is heading this way.' He took a humongous bite of cheeseburger.

'If I'm honest, I'd rather head home,' said Shanti.

Caine dipped his spoon into his bowl of minestrone soup.

'Of course you would,' he said sympathetically. 'But Shant, it's nearly an hour to Yeovil at the best of times, and look outside . . . there's a lot more weather on the way.'

'Fine. You sort it out with Paul,' she said.

'Why don't I see what's available?' said Benno. 'Then we can review it later.'

They were joined by the young intern, with her laptop and a stack of files.

'Masako, I'd like you to meet DIs Shanti Joyce and Vincent Caine. As you know, they're the SIOs on this case.'

'So,' Masako said, eyes sparkling with genial intelligence. 'I'm already a fan. I'm currently dedicating a chapter of my thesis to you guys.'

'You what?' asked Shanti.

'Well, the Havfruen and Flynn cases in general. But it's DI Caine's left-field approach to crime-solving that intrigues me.'

'Sorry to disappoint you,' said Shanti. 'But this case is all about good old-fashioned policing protocol – logistics and pragmatism. Now then, Masako, Sergeant Bennett has been singing your praises all morning, so pull up one of those nice chairs and let's see what you've got. My left-field colleague and I need to be out of this door in five minutes.'

A sense of efficient determination radiated from the young woman as she distributed neatly printed documents.

'So, as you haven't chosen a code name, I've gone with Operation Solstice for the time being. I hope that's OK?'

'Nice,' said Caine.

'I'll get back to you on that,' said Shanti. 'It's traditional to use something more random.'

'I've been researching the Lovell-Finch family, and there's plenty out there. You'll see that pages 1 to 7 of my report contain a synopsis of my findings. The subsequent pages are more detailed, but I imagine you'd prefer to study those at a later stage. By the way, I'm available day or night if you have any queries. My contact details are right here.'

'Thank you,' said Caine. 'This is incredibly helpful.'

Shanti's steaming Stonehenge Hotpot was unashamed comfort food, but by God, she needed comfort today.

'So, I've made a visual comparison between the SOCO images of the deceased and some recent snaps of Hector Lovell-Finch, harvested from various sources. I think the resemblance is evident.'

'That's our man,' agreed Shanti.

'No mistaking him,' added Caine.

Finch was a polar bear of a man, at once rugged and aristocratic. He appeared affable, with his silvery beard and shoulder-length hair. In two of the images, he was accompanied by an enormous pair of identical shaggy hounds, and from the way he was embracing them, it was clear that he adored them.

'Fine dogs,' said Caine. 'Irish wolfhounds, right?'

'Their names are Ganesh and Albion,' Masako said. 'You'll find more about them on page 17. From what I gather, Finch and the dogs were a familiar sight, striding across the plains.'

'I wonder where those dogs are now,' mused Caine. 'There were no canine footprints beyond the stones.'

Shanti had turned to another image. 'What's going on here, Masako? He's holding a metal detector ...'

'Yes, Finch was a detectorist and a keen amateur archaeologist. But above all, he was an environmentalist who was passionate about all things green.'

'Ha, I see what you did there!'

Masako flashed the faintest of smiles.

'The national database shows police records for Hector Lovell-Finch dating back several decades for minor infringements such as obstruction and breach of the peace.'

'And that's how you came across him, Benno?' said Caine.

'Yeah, he was usually amongst a group of much younger activists at anti-war or environmental demonstrations. But like I say, we always found him cooperative.'

'So now I'm going to tell you a little about the family background,' continued Masako. 'Hector Lovell-Finch was the twelfth earl of Lovell Court. The picture labelled LF/17 shows the ancestral family home, which is less than ten miles from here.'

'Jeez,' said Shanti. 'What a pile!'

'That photo is a few years old, and I gather there have been a few changes since then.'

'What sort of changes?'

'I'm not entirely sure,' Masako admitted. 'I think it ties in with an almost Damascene moment in Finch's life in the 1980s.'

'A what?' said Benno.

'An epiphany,' said Caine. 'A transformation.'

'Up until then, he had been a conventional member of the landowning aristocracy,' continued Masako. 'But in the eighties, he turned to left-wing politics and eco-activism, which horrified the Lovell-Finch dynasty. It was a dramatic change and I haven't fully ascertained what initiated it. What I do know is that in 1986, the gossip columns became obsessed with his highly acrimonious divorce from his first wife, Tiggy Antrobus-Lovell-Finch, who was a socialite and moderately successful actress. There are clippings on pages 23 to 25.'

'Never heard of her,' said Shanti. 'Is she still alive?'

'She is,' said Masako. 'But unfortunately she resides in a nursing home now, following a cryptogenic stroke soon after the divorce. It's all in the file.'

'And then Finch remarried?'

'Yes. Within a couple of years he had married a Brazilian woman named Constanza, who is considerably younger.'

'Now there's a surprise,' said Shanti. 'Money equals eligibility, you know.'

'Finch and Constanza have a fourteen-year-old daughter.'

'But Finch was in his late sixties, wasn't he?'

'Sixty-seven.'

'That's late to have a child.'

'So, I'm still looking into this, but as far as I know, the daughter lives at Lovell Court with her mother.'

'Hmm, OK. This is good stuff, Masako. But you've left

something out – something nuclear, as Sergeant Benno so elegantly described it.'

'You're referring to Finch's son from his first marriage.'

'I am indeed.'

They studied a picture of the reedy MP, with his sallow complexion, luxuriant eyebrows above owlish glasses, and thin hair slicked across a large balding scalp.

'I can't stand the man,' blurted Benno, as if unable to contain himself.

'I'm surprised at you, Sergeant Bennett,' said Shanti.

'You know me, I treat all people the same …'

'A man without prejudice,' agreed Caine.

'… but if there's one thing I despise, it's poncey members of the aristocracy with twenty-seven hyphens in their name who talk like they've got their heads up their arses.'

'To be fair, he only has one hyphen,' said Caine.

'And one arse,' said Shanti. 'I'm sure I don't need to remind you that as police officers, we leave our politics at home.'

'It's not to do with politics, boss. It's to do with being a self-righteous bigot—'

'We'll stick to the facts, shall we? Carry on, Masako.'

'So, we're looking at the renowned Conservative MP Quentin Lovell-Finch – Finch's son from his first marriage.'

'Colloquially known as the Honourable Member for the Underworld,' added Benno.

In the photo, the MP was probably in his late thirties, but he presented as an elderly gentleman from a different era – older, almost, than his own father.

'So can we assume that Quentin is the heir?' asked Caine.

'I think that's probable,' said Masako. 'Although it's no secret that he hadn't been on speaking terms with his father since his parents' divorce in his teens.'

'I'm with the father,' muttered Benno.

'And where can we find Quentin Lovell-Finch?' asked Shanti.

'So, normally he'd be at Westminster, but Parliament is in recess right now, so there's a good chance he's with his wife, Petronella, and their children at their country retreat.'

'Which is where?'

'The Old Vicarage is less than ten miles from here and only about five miles from Lovell Court.'

'That's odd, isn't it?' said Shanti. 'Finch and Quentin couldn't stand each other, but they lived virtually side by side.'

'Perhaps the Old Vicarage is part of the family estate,' Masako suggested. 'Anyway, I guessed that would be your first point of call, so I tracked down a phone number. Would you like me to set up an urgent appointment?'

'Oh, good grief, no!' said Shanti. 'That's not the way we do it at all. My left-field colleague and I will drive over immediately. It's all about observing the spontaneous response. Right, Caine?'

Caine paused thoughtfully. 'Look, I wonder if it might be better if you and Benno visit Quentin, while I head over to Lovell Court to talk to Constanza and her daughter. From what Masako says, Finch was a lot closer to them. They'll be devastated, I imagine, but they'll probably have seen him more recently.'

'Nice try,' said Shanti. 'Let's be frank, none of us are fans of Quentin Lovell-Finch. But the poor man has just lost his father in the most atrocious way, and you know what he'll have to do later, don't you?'

'Formally identify the body,' said Benno.

'Exactly. Which is a tough call for anyone. So it's our duty to break the news as gently as we possibly can ... and to tactfully interview him, of course. You're good at that stuff, Caine, you know you are.'

Caine warmed visibly. He had finished his soup and was dividing an apple into perfect geometric slices.

Shanti rose to her feet. 'Benno, I'd like you to send a couple of uniforms to Lovell Court to notify the widow and daughter. Someone sensitive.'

'Not Dunster and Spalding, then?'

'Exactly. Family liaison officers, if that's possible.'

She pulled on her coat and hat, and shoved the file into her bag. 'Good work, Masako. It won't go unnoticed.'

'My pleasure,' said the fresh-faced intern. 'It's incredible to see how you guys operate. Oh, and by the way, I've made a start on Quentin's financial profile. It's pretty covert, but I've already flagged up a number of queries about offshore accounts, links to oil firms, and government defence contracts. It also seems that he lobbies on behalf of various obscure private companies.'

'I wouldn't expect anything less,' said Shanti.

'I'm sure it's all legitimate,' Masako added, 'but it might be relevant. So, you'll find details in the last pages of the Solstice Files.'

'Excellent. Are you ready, Caine? Or are you performing an autopsy on that apple?'

Chapter 11

The Honourable Member for the Underworld

The windscreen of the Saab was filled with the frantic, flattened, gurning faces of the world's media. To one side, a news anchor was crushed underfoot by the stampeding horde, emerging with broken glasses and a bloodied nose.

'Jesus, they're wild!' gasped Shanti. 'How will we get through?'

'Maybe we should give them a statement,' said Caine.

'I'm not going out there.'

'I'll do it then.'

'We'll do it together. But keep it vague, Caine. No names.'

As they stepped cautiously from the vehicle, they were confronted by a bristling wall of cameras and microphones and a barrage of shouted questions.

'Who's the mystery man, DI Joyce?'

'Do you have an identity, DI Caine?'

'Ladies and gentlemen, please!' shouted Shanti. 'If you all yell at once, we can't hear what you're saying . . . Thank you. Now, you will understand that we are at the earliest stages of this inquiry. For operational reasons, we are limited in what we can tell you—'

'Who discovered the body, DI Caine?'

'Is this a Satanic cult?'

'All we can tell you is that we are investigating the unfortunate death of a gentleman in his sixties. For reasons we don't yet understand, his body was discovered early this morning on one of the lintels at Stonehenge.'

'We know that. How did he get there, Inspector?'

'Did the murder take place up there on the stone?'

'How did he die, Inspector?'

'Look, I think we're going to have to make some kind of a deal,' said Shanti. 'If you allow us to go about our duties, we guarantee that you will be the first to hear of any significant developments in the case.'

'In the meantime,' added Caine, 'we implore you not to speculate or jump to conclusions. You will help us greatly by asking your audience to come forward with any information that may assist our inquiries, no matter how trivial it may seem.'

'That means information about anything suspicious they might have witnessed last night – before or during the snowstorm,' Shanti put in.

They retreated into the vehicle, and as Shanti accelerated steadily forward, the throng slid and tumbled and jostled on the verges at their side.

When they reached the main road, she hit the accelerator and the car lurched forward.

'My God! I've never seen anything like it. When they point those lenses, it's like guns aiming at you. Look at me, I'm actually shaking.' She held out her hand, which Caine squeezed briefly. 'Just wait till they realise the victim was a Lovell-Finch ... They're not following, are they?'

He turned and peered through the back window.

'I think we're OK. Take it steady here, Shanti. There should be a narrow turning. Yes, over there on the left.'

'A few signs would be handy.'

She swung the car into a steeply sloping lane bordered by high banks thick with tangled roots. Overhead, branches bowed beneath the weight of snow, so that the Saab ducked and weaved through translucent subterranean burrows.

'They were like wolves, weren't they?' said Caine. 'Benno told me that the old folk believe primal forces are unleashed at the midwinter solstice.'

'He told me the same drivel. But let's be clear, this is a murder investigation, not a teenage zombie movie. Now keep your eyes open for this house. Jeez, the Lovell-Finches certainly keep themselves tucked away.'

'The Old Vicarage should be at the foot of this hill, and the big house, Lovell Court, is a few miles beyond. You must admit, Shanti, these lanes are beautiful, and they're a haven for wildlife – look at all the tracks.'

'Save it for your nature diary, Caine.'

Half hidden in the foliage, Shanti saw a faded sign for the Old Vicarage. She hit the brakes, but the car slid gently on like a boat before coming to rest by a pair of stone gateposts.

'No sign of the media yet,' said Caine. 'But someone has been out this morning. Fresh tyre tracks, see?'

They entered a short driveway lined with snow-capped laurels.

'Now listen,' said Shanti. 'These are influential people, at a uniquely distressing time.'

'I know that.'

'So you won't mention primal forces? Or human sacrifice?'

'I'll do my best,' he said.

'Try not to be left-field, Caine.'

It was a classic Gothic rectory, with brick elevations swathed in ivy. A fine dwelling for a country vicar perhaps, but relatively modest for descendants of aristocracy, which they knew this couple to be.

As he climbed out of the car, Caine noticed that a large bank of snow had slid from the roof into a flower bed. Three vehicles were parked inside an open-fronted oak garage to one side of the turning area – a white Mini, a silver Mercedes, and a highly lacquered maroon vintage car, glimpses of which could be seen beneath a tarpaulin. It was the Mercedes that had been used that morning; the tyre treads were jammed with snow.

As the chimes of the doorbell fell away, they waited in the elaborately decorated porch. Shanti took in the glass baubles and satin-bowed wreath on the brass knocker – the sort of decorations sold only in Harrods.

'Thanks for being here, Caine,' she said unexpectedly. 'Sorry for being crabby.'

'There's nowhere I'd rather be,' he said softly.

The door was opened by a full-figured woman with a profoundly anxious expression on her pale face, whom Shanti took to be Petronella Lovell-Finch, wife of the MP. She held a fat, bonneted baby in her arms, and a flock of equally pale children clung to the hem of her floral dress. There was something outmoded about their clothing, which included a great deal of velvet and tartan.

Shanti offered her warrant card and the appropriate concerned tone. 'DIs Joyce and Caine. We're very sorry to call unannounced, madam, but we need to speak urgently to you and your husband – that's Quentin Lovell-Finch, I believe. Is he at home?'

Ignoring her completely, Lady Lovell-Finch turned and called loudly, 'Quinty, there are police people iteside. Shall I send them rinde the back?'

'I'm on the telephone,' came the irritable reply from upstairs. 'Tell them I'll be dine shortly. Tell them there's a draught coming into the hise.'

Like a shepherdess with her flock, Petronella led the DIs along the passage – all opulent reds and greens, trimmed with gilt picture rails and framed photos of Quentin Lovell-Finch with various politicians and dignitaries, including members of the royal family.

Near the door to the drawing room, one of the children turned to Shanti and stuck out a long pink tongue. He was about Paul's age, but a whole lot uglier. Petronella ruffled his hair and smiled wanly. 'Remember, Victus, manners maketh man.'

In the early days, Shanti had enjoyed this aspect of the job – visiting an array of homes and premises the like of which she would never otherwise have seen. She remembered describing them to Mum, and to Paul when he was little. She loved to watch their expressions of wonder.

This was a fine room all right, with a vast Christmas tree, oak bookcases crammed with ancient tomes, and even a handsome rocking horse. But once again, Shanti noted that it was relatively modest. It seemed that Quentin and Petronella had fallen on hard-ish times.

'Help yourself to sherry,' piped Petronella. 'Quentin will be with you shortly. Run along, children.'

When they had gone, the drawing room fell silent, apart from the crackling of the fire and the bored tick-tock of a grandfather clock, which waited like a manservant by the wall.

Shanti took a seat on a double stool at the grand piano, from where she surveyed the beautifully wrapped presents beneath the sumptuous tree. She became aware of a tiny voice – her anxious inner child – reminding her that she, the working-class daughter of immigrants, had no right to be here. She had strayed where she did not belong: the inner sanctum of her wealthy and educated betters. Classic imposter syndrome, she realised.

But with it came a counter-voice: she had raised her son to be comfortable in his own skin. She would be intimidated by no man.

In the meantime, her vigilant colleague was prowling the room, ever alert for clues. Behind the tree he spotted a sideboard laid out with framed photos. Alongside more pictures of Quentin with political luminaries were several washed-out images of a beautiful starlet with vast eyelashes in Biba-style clothing, whom he took to be Quentin's mother, Tiggy, in her prime. Tucked away at the back of the collection he found a group shot of jocular public schoolboys. The youthful Quentin Lovell-Finch was easily identifiable by his lanky height and thick-lensed spectacles. Raising his phone, Caine took a number of photos.

After ten full minutes, they heard footsteps descending the staircase and a muttered conversation between Petronella and Quentin. Then the door opened and they were joined by Quentin Lovell-Finch, looking every bit as cartoonishly familiar as he did on the evening news. Although he was not much taller than Caine, his stooped slender frame and large head made him appear like a giant. There were the abundant eyebrows, proliferating over thick lenses. There was the sallow skin and, in abundance, the haughty manner.

'*Quis custodiet ipsos custodes?*' he trumpeted.

'I beg your pardon?' she said.

'No need to beg, dear lady. It is how I greet the constables at Westminster. My little jest. It means: who will guard the guards themselves?'

'Right. I bet that gets them laughing.'

The MP patted the rocking horse and sauntered towards a drinks trolley, where he began to peruse the bottles on display. Shanti noticed that the ubiquitous pinstripes had been replaced by burgundy slacks and an ancient sweater with a reindeer motif.

'Sir, there's no easy way to broach this . . .' she began.

He barely turned his head.

'You've come about my father,' he said.

'You . . . you know?'

'Your tact is marvellous, dear lady, but I am well aware that my father passed away in the early hours of this morning. Typical of him to choose this time of year to create maximum havoc.'

He selected a decanter and removed the stopper. Shanti watched his nostrils quiver as he inhaled.

'But . . . I mean, how could you possibly know?' she said.

Now he gazed at her haughtily –

'I have – to put it simply – contacts in places where you will never tread.'

'You mean contacts in the police? At . . . at English Heritage? Or the army, perhaps?'

He poured a generous measure into a tumbler.

'Correct. I have contacts in all those places.'

There was something unusual about the shape of his head,

Shanti realised. It was lozenge-shaped, so that the back protruded far over the collar, sending strands of oiled hair plummeting suicidally like a waterfall.

'I'm astonished,' she said. 'But if you don't mind me saying, you seem remarkably unfazed. Do you realise that his death may not have been accidental?'

'*Morte magis metuenda senectus*, as they say.'

'They didn't teach Latin at my comprehensive.'

'Fear old age rather than death.'

'I fear murder, Mr Lovell-Finch.'

'Quite so. Let justice be done.'

'Justice will most certainly be done,' she said quietly. 'Which is why we require your full cooperation.'

With silver tongs, Lovell-Finch fished ice from a bucket.

'Dear lady . . .'

'That's Detective Inspector.'

'. . . for three hundred and twenty-eight days per annum, I serve my constituents in every conceivable manner. But at Christmastide, I selfishly seek a little respite in the bosom of my family – we have a baby daughter, not three weeks old. But even then, it seems, I am obliged to deal with police officers, and no doubt journalists and assorted members of the hoi polloi.'

When he turned at last to face the room, he noticed Caine as if for the first time.

'What about your long-haired companion? Doesn't he speak?'

'He listens, Mr Lovell-Finch.'

The politician carried the tumbler across the room, scrutinising it all the way as if it were a fine diamond. When he was settled in an armchair, he said, 'I'm afraid we'll have to keep our meeting brief. In the light of what has transpired, I have arranged a visit from my solicitor – that was him on the phone when you arrived. Lord knows the shambolic state of Father's will, so I thought it best to get the legal wheels in motion before the holidays. I can spare twenty minutes and no longer.'

Shanti bristled. 'I must respectfully inform you that we have the authority to question you for as long as necessary. Under caution at the station, if required – in which case that solicitor might come in handy.'

He gazed at her sternly. 'Do not make an enemy of me, dear lady. As the bard once said, "I would challenge you to a battle of wits, but I see you are unarmed!"'

Shanti opened her mouth to retaliate. Checked herself. Then said, 'Isn't it rather early to be discussing the terms of the will?'

'When one has been banished for as long as I, it is not a moment too soon.'

'You hope to inherit Lovell Court?'

'That, frankly, is none of your business.'

'Oh, but frankly it is. You see, my long-haired colleague and I are the senior investigators in this case. All things Lovell-Finch are our business.'

'Your manner borders on impertinent.'

'And your manner borders on obstructive, Mr Lovell-Finch, and if I may say so, just a tiny bit entitled.'

'Entitled?' he brayed. 'Dear lady, I am *literally* entitled. My father ... my late father was the twelfth earl of Lovell Court. Ergo, I am the thirteenth. I can trace my lineage to the twelfth century and beyond. Is that something you can do?'

Caine stepped into the centre of the room, his voice calm and measured.

'All right, Shanti,' he said. 'I think it's possible that the sad news hasn't quite sunk in.'

'Like Caliban, he speaks!' snorted Quentin, rising from his chair.

Both men were tall, but whereas Caine was athletic, the gangly politician carried his height like an unwelcome legacy from his father.

'It's like this, Mr Lovell-Finch,' said Caine. 'In our job, motive is crucial. That's why matters of inheritance are relevant. It isn't personal, I assure you. We will be making similar enquiries of everyone involved. It is our understanding that there was some . . . ill will between you and your father?'

'Tell me, Detective Caliban, have you visited Lovell Court?'

'We hope to visit tomorrow.'

'Then you will see with your own eyes.'

'See what, sir?'

'Why I harbour a degree of antipathy. My home has been . . . vandalised.'

'You disapprove of the furnishings?'

'The furnishings? Lovell Court has been laid to waste! Desecrated! Violated! I do not use these terms lightly.'

'I'm sorry to hear that,' Caine said. 'But I suppose the upkeep of an estate like Lovell Court must be colossal, and I understand the divorce from your mother was costly. Perhaps your father didn't have the funds?'

'What a lot of digging you have been doing! Perhaps my father should have returned Lovell Court to the family. We would never have neglected it so. But he was always stubborn. You wait till you see the squalor.'

'The thing that confuses us is that you seem more upset about the state of a house . . .'

71

'Not just a house – one of the finest stately homes in England!'

'. . . than you do about the death of your father.'

There was a long pause, during which Lovell-Finch prodded the fire with a poker and the clock ticked like prayer beads on a chain of time.

'If you sit down, Detective Inspector, I will attempt to elucidate.'

'Oh, I wish you would,' said Shanti.

Caine took a seat beside Shanti on the piano stool. She relocated swiftly to a chaise longue.

'I realise that the familiar cliché of the heartbroken son would be reassuring for you,' said the MP. 'Of course I regret my father's death, but as we barely exchanged a word in twenty years, I find it hard to be deeply affected. You talk about justice – well, for me, justice will be achieved when Lovell Court has been restored to her former loveliness and I take my rightful place as the head of the household. Ergo: when that woman has been expelled, along with the grubby people who are squatting there. If Father's death brings that about, it will not have been entirely in vain.'

'You are referring to your stepmother, Constanza Lovell-Finch?'

'Is that her name? I am in no way related to this person.'

'And these grubby people?' said Shanti.

'*Hostis humani generis*. Which means, to the unschooled, enemies of the human race. My father ensconced himself within a nihilistic tribe of degenerates – environmentalists, they call themselves, yet they know nothing of the countryside. I truly believe that when he met these individuals, he went utterly mad! Like King George – growing his hair and beard, painting his face, and so on. It broke my poor mother, and Lord only knows what our forebears would have made of it. Did you know that these squatters are even attempting to change the name of my ancestral home?'

'To what, Mr Lovell-Finch?'

'I know not. I care not. The house has been Lovell Court since its erection, and I would rather die in a ditch than call it by another name.'

'And this is why you and your father became estranged?'

'Correct. I have not the slightest interest in his brand of New Age claptrap, and he had no truck with my politics.'

'Yes, your own political opinions are a matter of public record,' said Caine.

'Call me old-fashioned, but I believe that some people are born at the top of the pile, and it's a natural drip-down effect . . .'

Shanti shifted uncomfortably. 'Look, we're not here to discuss politics. The only relevance is that your father appeared to revise his political stance at a particular moment in his life, and that created acrimony between you. Is that a fair summary?'

'I am *seething* with acrimony, dear lady. I'm not sure whence your family hail, but since time immemorial, we Lovell-Finches have owned half this county – including the edifice known as Stonehenge.'

'Your family owned Stonehenge?'

'Mummy's family, actually. Her people were Antrobus. Look it up if you don't believe me – there are encyclopedias on the shelf. You'll find it under A.'

'I'll google it later.'

'I wouldn't be surprised if a primordial ancestor hadn't commissioned the dratted thing, thereby giving employment to legions of labourers.'

'Tell us about your mother,' said Shanti. 'Lady Tiggy Antrobus-Lovell-Finch. She was a debutante, and a well-known actress in her day?'

'Tiggy is ite of bindes.'

'As I have explained, there are no bindes ... I mean bounds to our investigation. Your mother is in a nursing home, I believe?'

'Not that it is in any way germane to the proceedings, but your information is correct. When my father took his extraordinary turn, Tiggy suffered a cruel stroke, which put paid to her career. She has subsequently required care for her most basic needs, something that I – due to my constitutional duties – am unable to provide. Mummy is ... how should one put it? Flummoxed. Befuddled. Discombobulated. Nonetheless, my wife is very Christian about these things, and Tiggy has always been welcomed for Christmas at the Old Vicarage. The children adore her. I will collect her tomorrow, and I suppose the irksome task of informing her of Finch's passing, will fall to me. Not that poor Mummy will understand.'

'I'm sorry,' said Caine.

'Quite so. Now, I'm afraid I will have to curtail this jovial exchange. As I said, I am expecting my solicitor.'

'We've almost finished, sir,' said Caine. 'It's only a formality, but I wonder if you and your wife are able to account for your movements last night. Specifically, the early hours of this morning.'

'Am I being asked to provide an alibi, like a common criminal?'

'It would be most helpful.'

'Well, as a matter of fact, Petronella and I slept badly. It was a wild night, and in the small hours, a large bank of snow slid off the roof. We were also woken repeatedly by Velveteen.'

74

'Velveteen?'

'The new baby. She has colic, and Nanny was in and out of the nursery throughout the night.'

'I see. And could we have a word with, er, Nanny?'

'It's Christmas. Nanny has returned to her family in ... wherever she lives. I drove her to the station this morning.'

'Could I ask which car you used?' said Caine.

He stared as if at a simpleton. 'The Mercedes, if you must know.'

'Thank you,' said Shanti. 'An officer will be in touch to obtain contact details.'

'Petronella will deal with it,' said Quentin, heading for the door. 'Now, I'm quite sure you will be needed on the beat or something.'

'Yes, on the beat,' said Shanti rising to her feet. 'I'd like to say that we won't disturb you again ...'

'*Gratias, Dominus.*'

'... but unfortunately, our inquiries have barely begun. Before we leave, I wonder if I might trouble you with one more impertinent question.'

'I am on tenterhooks, dear lady.'

'Did you murder your father, sir? Cut his throat and place him on top of a triloplane?'

Quentin Lovell-Finch almost choked on his Scotch.

'Or cause another to do so on your behalf? It's just that if you are complicit in any shape or form, we will find out, Mr Lovell-Finch. It would make things very much more convenient if you could let us know. Preferably this side of Christmastide.'

Magnified by dense lenses, those great eyebrows fluttered like pigeons in a trap.

'You will leave the premises before I call . . .'

'Before you call who, sir?'

'Damn you. Damn you to hell.'

Shanti and Caine followed his elongated occiput along the corridor as he marched to the living room door.

'As DI Caine says,' said Shanti, 'we will be visiting Lovell Court tomorrow. Perhaps you have a message for your step-mother and your half-sister?'

Quentin paused for a moment –

'Yes. Yes, I do have a message for those individuals. Kindly inform them that things are about to change. Tell them to round up their uncouth acquaintances and pack their shabby things. Tell them to expect a visit from Lord Lovell-Finch, thirteenth earl of Lovell Court. The door is thither.'

They were guided briskly through the porch and into the bitter wind outside. At the top of the steps, Quentin Lovell-Finch sniffed slightly.

'When you have seen for yourself what they have done to my childhood home, perhaps you might empathise a little more with my circumstances.'

'DI Caine does the empathy,' Shanti replied, unlocking the doors of the Saab. 'I do the impertinent questions.'

He glared at her. 'And in answer to your vulgar inquiry, it is there that you will meet those hoodlums.'

'Which hoodlums, sir?'

'The hoodlums who murdered my father.'

He turned and retreated into the house, followed closely by the back of his head.

Chapter 12

Unfuckingbelievable

'Unfuckingbelievable,' said Shanti as they returned along the snowy tunnels.

'Don't take it personally, Shant.'

'*Dear lady, I am* literally *entitled . . .* I almost vomited into his grand piano.'

'He was rather infuriating.'

'*I would challenge you to a battle of wits but . . .* What was it?'

'*But I see you are unarmed.* He was wrong, though, that isn't Shakespeare, although it's often misattributed.'

'Well why didn't you tell him? I'd have loved to have seen his snotty little face—'

'Because I'm not interested in playing intellectual games, and besides, he's just lost his father.'

'Ooh, bring me my tiny violin. The man is a grade A socio-path . . . or a murderer. Jesus, I'd love to cuff those skinny wrists and bang him in a cell – I'd visit every day just for the fun of it. The way he bragged about being a member of the elite, whilst we

– the hoi polloi – give up our holiday to resolve his father's murder!'

'I suppose he works hard . . .'

'But he's doing the wrong sort of work. Don't you see that? He spends his days shovelling money out of the Poor People's Pot and into the Rich People's Pot. Well, I'll tell you what, soon there won't be anything left, then where will his kind be?'

'Let it go, Shant.'

'The irony is that it's him and his public school chums who have cut police funding to the bone. And not just cops – teachers, nurses, prison staff, social workers, firefighters, librarians . . . AAARGH! I could scream!'

'You just did. Listen, I agree with everything you say, but it was you who talked about leaving politics at home. I was so impressed when you said that.'

'But he treated us with contempt. What was all that Caliban stuff?'

'Caliban is a reference to *The Tempest.*'

'I know that. We actually studied Shakespeare at my inferior school. But the way he spoke to you . . . I could have strangled him.'

'That makes me happy. You were so cross with me earlier.'

'Well, you're my mate. Sort of. That man puts everything into perspective. People like him inhabit a different universe from you and me. A different century. You're more interested in enlightenment than entitlement, and I respect that.'

'That's really very good, Shanti.'

'And why does the back of his head stick out so far?'

'You can't blame him for that. Maybe it's where he stores his ancestry. Could you slow down just a little?'

'You what? Oh Jeez, I'm sorry. He got me so wound up. As

far as I'm concerned, Quentin Lovell-Finch is my number one suspect. I'm going to crawl through his life. Find out everything about him. I also intend to visit his mother in the nursing home – Tiggy or whatever her name is.'

'I agree. But in the meantime, can I remind you of a Buddhist teaching?'

'Is this to do with embracing uncertainty?'

'That's the one. You know, I wonder if Quentin's arrogance might be a mask for childhood trauma. I had a troubled relationship with my own father, so I know that pain can manifest as childish outbursts.'

Shanti's phone buzzed in her jacket pocket. She pulled it out, glanced at the screen and tossed it into Caine's lap.

'It's Mum. What am I going to do?'

'Speak to her, of course.'

'You do it, Caine. I'm driving.'

'I can't do that. Here – I'll put it on speakerphone . . .'

Amma's voice filled the car.

'Shanti? Shanti? Is that you?'

'Hi, Mum. It's not the best time . . .'

'I've heard the news . . . Are you at Stonehenge? It's the main story on every channel. They're saying there's a body on top of one of the stones. That's a joke, isn't it? Tell me it isn't true?'

'You know I can't talk about work.'

'Not even to your mother?'

'I'm sorry. It's a difficult case.'

'Are you working with Vincent Caine?'

'What's that got to do with anything?'

'That makes me happy, darling. You know how much I like Vincent. I always thought that you and he—'

'Hello, Amma,' said Caine.

'Vincent. How are you?'

'Jesus, Mum! Please!' said Shanti.

'What time can we expect you home?' asked Amma.

'I'm trying to explain – I may have to stay a night or two. But we will have Christmas together, the three of us. I promised Paul and I promise you.'

'The trouble is, Paul is saying he wants to spend Christmas with his father after all.'

'Oh no. No, Mum. Please back me up on this. My job is hard enough without feeling guilty all the time. You're on my side, aren't you?'

'Of course I am. But Paul is eight years old. He doesn't understand why you can't be here. He says all his friends are doing Christmas things. I told him I'd take him to buy a tree this afternoon. The artificial ones are very good these days. They don't drop needles and they last for years.'

'Get a real tree, Mum. Even if it's a small one. Look, I need to go. Let me have a quick word with Paul.'

'I'm sorry, darling. He's being difficult. He won't come to the phone.'

'Please, Mum. I beg you. I want to say one thing.'

She drove silently for a minute or so. Then she heard her son's voice. Faint. Moody. Reluctant.

'What?'

'Paul, listen, sweetheart – you know about Mum's work, right? You always say you're proud of me. So you need to understand that it's not quite the same as other people's jobs ... Now don't say that, honey. It's not my fault if a case comes up without warning. Please don't be cross. I promised we will have a brilliant

Christmas. You, me and Amma. And I always keep my promises, don't I?'

'No.'

'OK, to prove it, I promise that if we don't have the best
Christmas ever, then . . . then . . .'

'Then I can go to Dad's place, every holiday, forever.'

'Well, I . . .'

'You see. You don't mean it.'

'OK. OK. I promise. Best Christmas, guaranteed. I have to
go. I love you, Paul. To the stars and back.'

At the visitor centre, Shanti went into the toilet block and took
a moment to centre herself. By the time she had joined the
others in the incident room, Caine had briefed Benno on their
peculiar encounter at the Old Vicarage.

'Sounds like Lovell-Finch Junior lived up to expectations,'
said Benno, pouring her a mug of tea.

'I just don't get it,' she said. 'When my dad died . . . Jeez, I was
shattered for more than a year. Even if he despised Finch, you'd
think there would be some emotion.'

'He was very difficult to read,' agreed Caine. 'The truth will
emerge, I'm sure of it.'

'In the meantime,' said Benno, 'I'm pleased to say that I've
found you somewhere to stay. It's not ideal, I admit, but at least
you'll be close to the scene of crime. My niece works at the
Stonehenge Tavern. With a little persuasion, I managed to
reserve a single room, but unfortunately . . .'

'Here it comes.'

' . . . unfortunately, you'll be directly above the lounge bar,
which may be busy tonight, and it's also booked for a private

function tomorrow. I'm sorry, boss, but it was literally the last room in the county.'

'All right, thanks. And what about Caine? No room at the inn and all that.'

'Ah,' said Benno. 'Well, this is going to sound very irregular, but my contact at English Heritage has offered you a bed right here at Stonehenge.'

'Amazing!' enthused Caine.

'Hang on, you haven't heard the details yet. If you go round the back of the exhibition area, you'll find a very authentic recon- struction of a Neolithic village. I understand those roundhouses are surprisingly comfortable, and you're welcome to stay there.'

'It gets better all the time,' said Caine.

'You're probably too young to remember, but those buildings were occupied by a "time team" of archaeologists and crafts- people as part of a long-running TV show. Practical ethnography, they call it.'

'*Neolithic Neighbours!*' exclaimed Caine.

'You remember it,' Benno said, his face lighting up. 'We were big fans in the Bennett household.'

'This is extraordinary,' said Caine. 'I was telling Shanti about it only this morning.'

'Can I work with someone normal now?' muttered Shanti.

'All but one of the original team have moved on,' Benno con- tinued. 'So the only occupant is the team leader, Professor Ned Tull. When the series ended, English Heritage allowed him to stay on and continue his studies.'

'Neolithic Ned!' said Caine. 'I don't believe it!'

'From what I gather, Professor Tull is recognised as a world authority on Stonehenge.'

'He certainly is. Ned was almost a mentor when I was growing up.'

'Right,' said Shanti, rising to her feet. 'It looks like you boys have plenty to talk about, so I'll say goodnight. I need a hot bath and an early night. Where do I find this Stonehenge Tavern?'

'Two miles down the A303, not far from Everkill barracks. You can't miss it – they've built a mini concrete Stonehenge out front. The locals call it Clonehenge.'

'I'm getting pretty tired of those stones.'

'You'll like it there, boss, I promise. They have an excellent carvery. Good beer, too.'

She drained her tea and started fastening her jacket.

'What about you, Benno? Are you heading home?'

'I've got one more thing to do, boss – I'm going down to watch the body being dispatched to the morgue.'

'I'm sure Dawn can handle it.'

'Call me sentimental, but it's something I like to do – it feels like seeing the last guest safely into a taxi after a party.'

'You big softie,' said Shanti. 'Right, I'll see you both here for breakfast at six thirty. I hope your hut lives up to expectations, Caine.'

'Have a good rest, Shanti.'

She wound her scarf around her neck.

'You know what would make me sleep like a baby this Christmas? To see that Quentin Lovell-Finch up before a judge.'

Chapter 13

Major McAble

Darkness had fallen like a velvet hood. As she headed slowly along the A303, Shanti's mind spun with relentless questions. Who had killed the Holly King, and why?

As if to drive the riddle from her brain, she scrolled through various radio channels – cheery seasonal panel shows, jolly Christmas jingles, dreary carols and, on Radio 4, a depressing monologue from a cardinal about evil forces in the world, and how the birthday of our Lord had been sullied by the unholy incident at Stonehenge. He asked the listeners to pray for the emergency services and police, who were working tirelessly to bring the perpetrator to justice.

Tirelessly? Shanti felt frazzled. Frozen. Famished. Fatigued, not just by this epic case, but by the impossible juggling act of motherhood and career.

On the snow-piled verge to her left, she saw the row of traffic cones that Benno had authorised to deter photographers. On an impulse, she pulled into a lay-by, nudging three cones aside with the front of the car. The temperature was well below freezing, but she climbed out and found a spot where the snow-capped hedge was low enough to provide a clear view across the plains.

From here, she could see the monument surprisingly clearly. There was Dawn's tower, illuminated by arc lights and the pulsating strobe of emergency vehicles. It was apparent that Dawn had successfully rigged up the winch system, because as Shanti watched, a large black body bag was lowered cautiously on a stretcher down the outside of the tower. At ground level it was met by many outstretched hands and positioned on a waiting gurney. An open-doored ambulance reversed to the barrier and the stretcher was swallowed inside. A moment later, the black-windowed vehicle took off in the direction of the visitor centre, until all that could be seen were waves of blue light across the plains.

What brought Shanti out of her reverie was a rumbling – an ominous convoy of twenty or so motorbikes approaching along the road behind her. They were powerful machines – Harleys and Gold Wings. Some with sidecars. And they were driven by helmeted riders in leathers, with scarves around their faces. As they passed, the bikes emitted an aggressive roar and she felt a splatter of sleet against her cheek. At last the night riders were consumed by darkness, leaving nothing but the interwoven threads of tail lights.

At least the brightly lit facade of the Stonehenge Tavern seemed welcoming. Good old Benno, he always looked out for her. The car park was filled to capacity, but she managed to pull up on the verge by the mini-henge, where each lintel was topped with snow like its mighty twin on the plains.

Frozen through and aching in every limb, Shanti hauled her bag from the boot. Crunching across the snow towards the large pebble-dashed building, she squeezed into the public bar, which was crammed wall to wall with journos. As her ears adjusted to the pounding music and raucous laughter, she realised she was being addressed from every side.

'Here she is, everyone!'

'Got a word for us, Inspector?'

'Are you staying here, DI Joyce?'

Ignoring their incessant questions, Shanti used her bag as a battering ram and barged between backpacks and beer bellies towards a reception desk at the end of the bar, managed by a crimson-faced girl with tinsel in her hair.

'You should have a bed for me?' she yelled. 'In the name of Bennett?'

'Benno's my uncle,' the girl said. 'Sorry, it's a bit squashed in here, but the lounge bar is being prepared for a private party.'

Of course it was. That was what people did at Christmas.

'Here's your key. Up the stairs, fourth door on the right. Not our best room, I'm afraid, but I gave it a quick wipe-over. You can get a complimentary drink if you want one.'

'Ah, no thanks,' said Shanti with regret. 'Bit shattered.'

As she scribbled in the register, she felt a presence behind her – one of the paps was pushing his belly into her back, so that she could smell the beer, crisps and tobacco on his breath.

'Ted Carpenter, *News of Britain*,' he hissed. 'Could I buy you dinner, Inspector? In fact, *NOB* would be happy to cover all your expenses in return for a short—'

Shanti seized her key and attempted a swift exit towards the stairs. But these boys had travelled a long way, no doubt disrupting their own Christmas holidays, and they were hungry for a story.

'Could you give some details about the deceased, DI Joyce? Large, small? Black, white?'

'Any distinguishing features?'

'Can you confirm this was a particularly brutal murder?'

'How much blood are we talking about?'

Shanti spoke loudly and firmly. 'Excuse me, ladies and gentlemen. I appreciate you lot have jobs to do, but I have just finished an extremely long day and I am knackered. So I will not be answering any questions tonight.'

Cameras flashed and mics waggled like so many thrusting appendages. The scrum would not let her pass. Shanti felt a surge of panic. An involuntary memory came to her of a horrible countryside holiday before her divorce. She had been pushing Paul in a buggy along a rural footpath when she found herself surrounded by bullocks. The more flustered she became, the more the inquisitive brutes pressed in, with their rough tongues and psychopathic eyes. Paul became hysterical. A hoof buckled a buggy wheel, and then ... what had happened then?

In the public bar of the Stonehenge Tavern, the man named Ted Carpenter had pushed his way to the front of the herd and was shoving a wad of banknotes in her face. 'Five hundred for an interview. A thousand for exclusive rights.'

'Are you offering money to a police officer?' she demanded.

In that instant, she remembered how the bullock incident had ended – she had taken control. Nothing would threaten her son. In the stinky corner of the stinky field, a kind of superhuman strength had overcome her. Yelling at the top her voice, she had lifted the bawling boy in the broken buggy high over the heads of the astonished herd, and as they stampeded in every direction, she had fled to the gate. Now she employed the same tactics with the paps. She raised her bag above her head and yelled at the top of her voice:

'THAT'S ENOUGH! DO YOU UNDERSTAND?'

All but Mariah Carey were silenced.

'The next person who harasses me will be arrested on the spot for obstruction of a police officer. Is that perfectly clear? Any of you want to test that?'

There were no volunteers. Instead they backed slowly away and Shanti found herself alone in a deserted semicircle as tranquil as a woodland glade.

Alone but for two people.

'Awesome!' said Benno's tinsel-headed niece behind the bar.

'Respect!' said a man on a barstool in front of the bar. He was tall and well built, and he was slow-clapping like a seal.

'I'm sorry you had to put up with that,' he crooned, relaxed and faintly amused. 'But you handled it marvellously.'

Unlike the shabby journos, this man was dressed in the height of fashion – or at least the height of fashion in 1987 – all tight-fitting denims, Timberland boots and an oatmeal cashmere sweater that clung snugly to his toned torso. In the warm light of the bar, he might have been one of Mum's stars of the screen.

Shanti stared in bewilderment. The lustrous yellow moustache. The hint of a Scottish burr.

'I see you don't remember,' he said, drawing up another stool. 'We met this morning.'

She had seen a lot of men that day. Some of them were dead.

'McAble's the name,' he reminded her. 'Major Troy McAble. And you, if I remember correctly, are Shantala. She was a goddess, wasn't she?'

'I'm sorry?' said Shanti, simultaneously furious, flabbergasted and just a tiny bit flattered.

'Shantala. Another name for the love goddess Parvati, if I'm not mistaken?'

'Yeah, well, no one calls me Shantala. Shanti's fine by me.'

Was Cashmere Man flirting with her? His questions seemed absurdly inappropriate, and yet ... and yet there was no denying it: beneath the men's magazine cover, McAble was devilishly handsome.

'Right. Well, nice to see you again, Major,' she said.

'Troy,' he purred. 'Look, by a stroke of luck I've managed to get my hands on a surprisingly decent Glenkinchie.' He rolled his mouth around the syllables. 'You can almost taste the heather.'

As he poured the amber liquid into a glass, Shanti noticed an odd detail – the self-confident soldier had tremulous hands.

She assessed the situation. Yes, she was tired. But work came first in everything, and the major might have intel. Besides, what harm was there in a nip of Scotch and a nibble of eye candy to raise the Christmas spirits?

'A small one then,' she said eventually, taking the weight off her walking boots.

'Ah, Troy's a lucky boy.'

He raised his glass in a toast, holding eye contact for a second longer than felt comfortable. She was not usually a whisky drinker, but this was a warm flame in her frozen belly.

'I should probably apologise for being scratchy this morning,' she said.

'I like a woman who scratches,' said McAble, flashing the whitest of smiles.

Shanti almost regurgitated the Glenkinchie.

'Pepper spray's more my thing,' she replied.

'Touché,' he said, caressing his moustache.

Pretty or not, his communication skills were Neanderthal.

'Major ... Troy ... I think I'm right in saying that your garrison ...'

'Everkill.'

'... that Everkill garrison has a historic connection with English Heritage?'

'Yes, the military has used the plains for training purposes for as long as anyone can remember. The Romans probably. In return, we give them a hand whenever things need lifting.'

'So you know the area well?'

'As well as anyone.'

She lowered her voice. 'Could I ask you something? In strict confidence?'

He leaned in a little too close.

'You'll have to speak up. I suffer from tinnitus. Hazard of the job. Explosives, you know.'

Shanti glanced furtively over her shoulder to make sure no paps were near. Throughout the day, she had lectured everyone, including Caine, about confidentiality. But sometimes a calculated risk was in order. Besides, it was only a matter of time before the world discovered the identity of the Holly King.

'Does the name Hector Lovell-Finch mean anything to you?'

'Ah!' said McAble, a little too loudly. 'You're referring to the old tree-hugger? Finch, they call him. Hang on ... you're not saying ...? Christ almighty! Was that Finch on the stone?'

'I'm afraid so. But if this lot find out, Armageddon will break loose. So please keep your voice down.'

He stared in a kind of joyous disbelief, then refilled his glass and downed it in one.

'Sweet Jesus, the donkey and the whole Bethlehem massive! You know who he is, don't you?'

'We have some idea.'

'And his son? You know about the son?'

'You know the family?'

'Well, not intimately, but I've had a few close encounters with Finch. I'm afraid he was a figure of fun in the mess. Anti-war. Anti-meat. Anti-every-bloody-thing.'

'Right. This is interesting. I'd like to talk further.'

'Oh, so would I, Shantala. I can't remember the last time I had so much fun. Look, I'll make a deal with you.'

'What kind of deal?' she asked cautiously.

In answer, he tossed a gold-edged card onto the bar top. Shanti picked it up and peered at the elegant lettering. It was a formal invitation.

Everkill Garrison requests the pleasure of
your company at the annual

Officers' Christmas Ball

Drinks and dancing to the soothing sounds of the
Flirty Fusiliers

At the Lounge Bar, Stonehenge Tavern, Everkill, Wilts.
Wednesday 22 December
Eight till late

'It's always a riot,' promised McAble. 'And no journalists either. I've got a team setting up the stage now. It's all in aid of charity.'

A party? In what possible way was a party useful to her?

'Major McAble, you don't seem to understand. I'm not here for fun. The only reason I find myself in this ... hostelry is because I am trying to solve a murder.'

'Precisely. You accompany me to the ball tomorrow night, and I will dish the dirt on Finch.'

She gathered her bag and stood up.

'It's late, Major McAble. But if you have any information that might advance my inquiries, then I would certainly like to talk to you.'

'I'll take that as a yes,' he said, pushing the invitation towards her with shaky fingers.

Shanti forced a smile and slid the card into her bag.

'Thanks for the drink, and I appreciate your discretion over what I've told you.'

McAble tapped the side of his elegant nose.

'Mum's the word. See you on the dance floor, Goddess Shantala.'

Heading wearily up the narrow staircase above the bar, she located her room halfway along the landing. Her heart sank at the sight of the lonesome single bed and the antiquated radiator, which seemed pathetically inadequate against the blasting biblical blackness beyond the ill-fitting window. There was a tired table, a sticky stool and a worn-out wardrobe containing a lopsided hanger and a full-length mirror. The only consolation was the tiny bathroom, with a tub like an iron tug, which belched out scalding water.

Back in her room, she made a short call to Mum – more guilt, more hollow promises – before easing her aching body between the chilly sheets.

She thought of Caine. What on earth would he make of an unreconstructed man like Troy?

The perpetual pounding from downstairs was subsumed into her sleeping brain and she dived deep into a nightmare of circling birds and eyes like frozen pools.

Chapter 14

Neolithic Ned

Turning up the collar of his greatcoat and yanking down the ears of his hat, Vincent Caine stumbled into the blustery night. It was bitingly cold, and the swirling sky obscured the stars.

Entering a quadrangle at the back of the visitor centre, he spotted a fresh trail of snowy footprints across the ground. They were about the size of his own feet – made by a largish man, in other words – but there was something abnormal about these prints. It was a detail that would have eluded many, but to Caine's eye they lacked the distinctive patterned treads of trainers or hiking boots. Furthermore, the indentations were rounded at the edges, so unless the mystery man had been walking in his socks, Caine deduced that his feet were bound in some manner of soft material.

As he walked, Caine experienced two subtle sensations. The first was a faint whiff of woodsmoke. The second was a flurry of sparks, like tiny fireflies, which scurried past his shoulders.

Following the tracks in the direction of the smoke, he came

across several domes, like igloos beneath their caps of snow. He felt a weird sensation of déjà vu. There was no doubt that he was standing in the very place that had featured so often in his childish imagination – the hand-crafted hamlet that had been the setting of *Neolithic Neighbours.*

All but one of the roundhouses seemed uninhabited, their doorways banked with snow. But thin smoke drifted through the thatch of one building, and the trail stopped at its door. Pulling off one glove, Caine touched the daub wall, which was warm and curved as the belly of a cow.

Seeing no knocker, he called out a greeting, but he was met with silence from within. He seized the handle and shoved the wooden door.

As he stooped beneath the low portal, it felt to Caine as if he were stepping back through the centuries to a wiser, simpler age of firelight and shadows. The circular floor was made of pummelled chalk, and a fire at its centre threw dancing shadows on the hemispherical walls.

Beyond the flames, a figure wavered like a mirage. A wild man squatting in skins and furs. His face was greasy and weathered. His long grey hair and beard were plaited and tied off with decorative beads. He looked up at Caine with tragic eyes.

'Professor Tull?' asked Caine.

'Who wants to know?' grunted the man.

It was him all right – the one they called Neolithic Ned. The host of Caine's favourite Sunday evening show. But the cheerful enthusiasm that had defined him had vanished, and in its place was an older and . . . yes, profoundly sorrowful man. There was a story, Caine sensed, behind the decline of his childhood hero.

'My name is Vincent Caine,' said Vincent Caine.

'Police?'

'Yes. We're looking into—'

'I know what you're doing,' growled the wild man. 'There's been enough of you about today.'

As Caine pulled shut the door, he found the air so smoky that his eyes began to stream.

'I apologise for the intrusion. I was told I might be able to stay in one of the empty roundhouses for a few nights.'

For the first time, Tull smiled, showing a set of blackened teeth.

'You like the cold, do you, Vincent Caine?'

'I'm sorry?'

'Listen,' he said. 'These buildings are chalk daub. Now, the good thing about chalk daub is it holds the heat – better than your modern under-floor heating system. The bad thing about chalk daub is it takes a day and a half to get up to temperature.'

'Oh. I see,' said Caine.

Despite Tull's truculent manner, Caine was fascinated by a man who believed that the way to comprehend your ancestors was to immerse yourself fully in their ways. Dress in Neolithic clothing. Eat Neolithic food. Embrace Neolithic technology. And this he had done for twenty years.

'Well,' Tull said grudgingly, 'as you're here, you'd better sit by the fire. He pointed towards a sheepskin on the floor. 'You'll have to forgive the smoke. Normally it filters nicely through the thatch – kills the insects, too – but I can't get much of a blaze today. Last night's storm has thrown everything out of kilter. Can't remember anything like it in five thousand years.'

Caine settled cross-legged on the manky fleece and warmed his hands at the fire.

'*Neolithic Neighbours* was a big part of my childhood,' he said. 'I even wrote to you a couple of times.'

'Did you now?' said the old man, looking at him for the first time with something approaching interest.

'Things were tricky at home,' said Caine, building on the rapport. 'I suppose I thought of you as a father figure. An elder, you might say.'

Tull gazed at him as if staring into the past.

'Want some tea?' he said. 'It's nettle and cleavers.'

'You know what?' said Caine, pulling off his hat and grinning broadly. 'That would be wonderful. Should I call you Professor ... or Ned?'

'Call me anything you like.'

With the aid of a forked antler, Tull placed a pot on the fire. And as he busied himself with dried herbs, Caine took the opportunity to survey the interior of the dome. On rough-hewn shelves an assortment of timeless objects had been arranged: clay pots, bone spoons and a variety of beautifully worked tools of wood, stone and antler – spears, arrows, needles, hide scrapers, and blades of many kinds. A pair of hazel slat beds stood on either side of the door – one bare, one piled with furs. Up in the roof, a flayed rabbit hung by its feet, which disturbed Caine's sensibilities.

With great dexterity, Tull poured steaming water into two finely decorated bowls, and handed one to Caine.

'I put a little rosemary in there,' he said in an almost affable way. 'Cowslip, too.'

'Thank you,' said Caine. 'That wouldn't be honey in that jar, would it?'

Tull passed the clay jar across the flames. With a twisted stick, Caine dropped a globule of the nectar into his tea.

'I can't abide uniforms,' said the old man, his haggard face illuminated by the glowing fire. 'But you seem different.'

'I'm not keen on uniforms myself,' said Caine, finding a simple comfort in the way in which his hands enfolded the warm cup. 'Nonetheless, I will need to ask a few questions.'

'Thought you might. How's the tea?'

'Like summer meadows,' said Caine.

'Flatbread here if you want it.' Tull tore off a chunk and tossed the rest across the fire.

Caine ripped the unleavened bread with his teeth and dunked a piece in his bowl.

'You told me you'd seen events unfolding today, but I didn't notice you.'

'I see you, but you don't see me. I keep a low profile.'

'Did you attend the solstice ceremony this morning?' Caine asked.

'I didn't,' Tull replied. 'Haven't been part of the ceremony for years. But I heard what happened. It's an inauspicious beginning to the year, that's for sure. An augury, some might say.'

'How did you hear?' asked Caine.

'GoodGuys Security. Folks at English Heritage. I've lived here for decades, Vincent Caine. I know everyone, and I hear everything that goes on.'

'So you knew the man on the stone?'

'Finch? Yeah, I knew him. And I'm sorry about what happened. Hope you catch the bastards.'

'Would you describe Finch as a friend?'

'We weren't buddy-buddies, but I met him sometimes, walking with those hounds.'

'Albion and Ganesh.'

'Finch took an interest in my work. I think he attended a couple of my ancient craft workshops over the years. He was always pleasant enough, and there's a shared affinity between those who revere the stones.'

'If you revere the stones, why stay away from the ceremony?'

Tull's mournful eyes stared through the smoke. Eventually he said, 'The solstice has become a circus. Too many tourists. I prefer to mark it in my own way. Besides ... I'm on awkward terms with the Druids.'

'You are?'

'They don't like me because I tell the truth. As I have said in lectures and interviews time and again, Stonehenge was built thousands of years before Druids were even invented.'

'Now hang on,' said Caine. 'Surely the Druids are the guardians of the stones? They preserve the spirit of solstice, don't they? If anyone has a right—'

'Oh, they have a right. Everyone has a right. But some of them aren't *authentic*, if you see what I mean. They live on housing estates. The chief Druid runs a local apiary. Some of them drive around on motorbikes – off-road too, which is a disgrace on sacred land.'

'I've always thought of Druids as gentle pagans who venerate nature.'

'Maybe some are. But you can't get away from the fact that it was Neolithic people like me who built Stonehenge, not the bloody Druids. Authenticity is everything, Vincent Caine.'

'I'm sure you're right. Tell me about your relationship with English Heritage.'

'They've treated me well enough. When *Neolithic Neighbours* ended, I thought I'd be asked to move on, but we found ways to make it work. I give talks about the monument and occasional walking tours, and in return they let me live here. I run the odd workshop – curing skins, flint knapping, cheese-making, pottery, that sort of thing. I don't like it much, to tell the truth, but I have to earn a crust.' Tull ripped off another scrap of flatbread. 'The main thing is, I get special access to the stones, and that's the most important thing in my life.'

'Ah yes, I understand. Do you have any idea who would want to hurt Finch?'

'That's your job, isn't it? Now listen, I'm an old man, and I follow the circadian rhythms, if you know what that means.'

'The natural rhythms that govern sleep.'

He nodded. 'By rights I should have been tucked up long ago. But what are we going to do with you? Like I say, the other dwellings will be perishing.'

'I don't know,' said Caine. 'Perhaps I could find a corner in the visitor centre. It's warm over there.'

Tull rose wearily to his feet, as if aching in every joint. For the first time, Caine saw the toll that time – or misfortune – had taken. He was still an impressive man, but so gaunt that the leathery tendons and bones were exposed within his furs, like an anatomical study by da Vinci.

'I suppose you could sleep here,' he said reluctantly. 'If it's only for a couple of nights.'

'Oh, I wouldn't want to impose . . .'

Ignoring Caine's protests, Tull began to make up the other bed, laying skins and furs across the wicker frame.

'My missus and the kids used to live here,' he said sadly. 'But something happened to my boy . . .'

'I'm sorry.'

'Then Pamela upped and moved into an apartment in Amesbury. I have a daughter, too, and grandchildren. We're all on friendly enough terms, but I suffer from a thing called electro-sensitivity. Decades of Neolithic living has left me with an aversion to artificial lights and central heating. Now I've got a dilemma, because they like me to stay with them to celebrate Yule, but I go a little mad in that apartment.'

'I sympathise, Ned. I live off-grid too.'

'An off-grid detective. There's a thing.'

Tull rolled a fleece around a wooden block to form a pillow.

'I'll tell you something interesting,' he said, brightening a little.

'Go on.'

'Neolithic couples slept in separate beds. Guess how we know?'

'I've absolutely no idea,' said Caine, wide-eyed like the boy he had been.

'During excavations, we find traces of phosphorus. Know why?'

'I haven't a clue.'

'Wee.'

'I'm sorry?'

'Not very politically correct, but the women slept with the youngsters, and the little ones would wee in the bed.'

'That is fascinating.'

'I'm glad you think so. Pamela wasn't so impressed. Anyway, you can have her bed if you want it, and her skins.'

'You're a hospitable man,' said Caine. 'I hope I'm not being insensitive, but you mentioned your son. Only, I think I remember him from *Neolithic Neighbours*. A fine-looking lad with long black hair? We would have been about the same age.'

A poignant pause.

'You remind me of him a little, Vincent Caine. It's why I invited you in.'

Caine touched the old man's wiry arm. 'Would you like to talk about him?'

'I would not,' he said.

In silence, they prepared for sleep – raking the ashes, scrubbing teeth, stepping outside to piss in the snow. As they sat on the low beds to remove their footwear, Caine was gratified to observe that Tull was untying the criss-cross laces of the hand-stitched boots that had made those distinctive treads in the snow. That cured hide rubbed with pig fat was as waterproof as wellingtons, and soft as slippers.

When they had climbed beneath their furs, they lay listening to the night. In the moments before sleep, the old man muttered, 'I live a lonely life, Vincent Caine. All I have is the monument. I think of each stone as a family member. More so since I lost the boy ...'

But his words were swallowed by the spitting fire and the howling wind.

Chapter 15

A Bloody Blade

'How was the sweat lodge?' asked Shanti, loading her fork with the perfect fusion of toast, egg, bacon and ketchup.

'It's a roundhouse,' said Caine. 'The professor is very particular about that. It's surprisingly comfortable in there, but I didn't sleep too well, since you ask. I had the weirdest dreams and I was disturbed by the wind.'

'You can get tablets for that.'

'That's really very funny, Shanti.' He sliced a banana into his yoghurt and sprinkled it with granola. 'I can't wait for you to meet Ned. He's a minefield of intel.'

'A POI, you mean?'

'Ned wouldn't harm a fly, as you'll find out for yourself. He's agreed to meet us at the Stonehenge Experience tonight, and he'll happily answer your questions.'

They were joined by Benno and his young intern, making corrections to a document as she walked and looking annoyingly fresh-faced. If the first word she spoke was 'so', the whole investigation was off.

'Morning, boss,' said Benno, laying an affectionate hand on Caine's shoulder and placing bagels and coffee on the table.

'Is it my imagination,' said Shanti, 'or are the kitchen staff packing away? There seems to be a lot of cleaning going on.'

"Fraid so,' said Benno, pulling up a yellow designer chair. 'Everyone will be heading home for Christmas except a skeleton crew from GoodGuys . . . and the journos, of course.'

He nodded towards the panoramic windows. In the blackness by the gates, Shanti could see the familiar forms of Spalding and Dunster, on early guard duty beneath an arc light. Everything about their demeanour suggested a reluctance to be there, as they remonstrated with a persistent TV crew.

'To be honest, I'm under a bit of pressure at home too,' continued Benno. 'Family coming to stay, you know. But I won't let you down, boss, you know that.'

'Right,' said Shanti dismally.

'In the meantime, Masako's been busy again. Why don't you show us what you've got?'

'So,' said Masako. 'Everything I've found confirms the picture of Finch as a passionate and unconventional man, who rebelled against his aristocratic roots and wasn't afraid of getting into conflict over his beliefs. But here's the amazing thing – I went to school with Sky.'

'You went to school with sky?' said Shanti. 'It's still early. Could you unpack that for me?'

'Ah, OK. You remember I mentioned Finch's daughter? She was a late addition in his life. Her name is Sky Lovell-Finch.'

'That isn't a name, it's a weather report.'

'Well, it turns out we went to the same school, although she's several years younger than me, of course.'

'Of course,' said Shanti, picturing an infant school.

Masako passed around a set of printouts featuring a blurry headshot of a skinny mixed-race teen with gleaming black hair, high cheekbones and remarkably large eyes.

'She's fourteen now. But even back then, she had quite a reputation.'

'What kind of reputation?' asked Caine.

'I'm not sure how to describe it – older than her years, I guess. She was into veganism and radical politics and all kinds of ser- ious issues. So, I spoke to some friends last night and they all remembered this fiercely intelligent kid with a kind of hippie vibe. Apparently she organised a couple of climate strikes at school. Some people recalled her beautiful Brazilian mum and a much older father, to whom she was devoted. It's fair to say she left a vivid impression on everyone she met, and according to the headteacher, she's a sort of wunderkind.'

'Translation?'

'A prodigy,' said Caine. 'A wise child. Under different circum- stances, it would be amazing to meet her.'

'Under different circumstances, it would be amazing to be in bed,' muttered Shanti.

Caine gazed sympathetically at the photo. 'Prodigy or not, fourteen's a shocking age to lose your dad. How did she take the news?'

Benno pulled out his notebook. 'The liaison officers used the words "calm" and "detached". That's not unusual, but the mother, Constanza, was the opposite – angry, wailing, tearing her hair, vomiting even. Medical intervention was sought.'

'Awful,' said Caine.

'They're expecting you at nine thirty,' Benno confirmed. 'And

I'm trying to arrange an appointment for you with Finch's first wife, Tiggy.'

'Quentin's mother,' said Shanti.

'Right. But it's not easy. They have strict rules at the nursing home. I'll message you when I get it sorted ... Oh, and I asked the kitchen to prepare packed lunches ...'

He handed over two paper bags, one labelled 'V' for vegan.

'Thanks, Benno,' said Caine. 'You think of everything.'

'So, I don't know if you had a chance to read the Solstice Files?' said Masako.

'Just working my way through it,' said Shanti. 'It's fascinating stuff, but there is ... er, quite a lot of it.'

'It's just that the section on Tiggy Antrobus-Lovell-Finch might be useful before you meet.'

'I'll try to fit it in.'

As they talked, Benno took a brief call. He rose to his feet with a concerned expression on his face.

'Sorry, boss, need to dash. There's been a development at the scene of crime. Dawn's on her way to see you now.'

When Benno and Masako had left, Shanti gazed through the window at the fat snowflakes tumbling in the eerie morning light.

'Did you ever feel like the last human after the zombie apocalypse?' she said.

'I'm here for you, Shant. Right to the very end.'

'I think I'll take the zombies,' she said. 'What's going on at the stones?'

'We're about to find out,' said Caine. 'Here comes Dawn now.'

A volley of camera flashes heralded the arrival of a SOCO van, which hurtled into the car park from the direction of the stones. Dawn Knightly stepped down, dressed in white togs and carrying a grey plastic suitcase. Even from a distance, the acute anxiety of her demeanour was apparent.

A moment later, the doors at the far end of the canteen slid open, and she walked briskly into the incident room, her face etched with alarm.

'What's up, Dawn?' said Shanti. 'You look terrible.'

'Jesus, guys. I can't get my head around it . . . You won't believe what happened.'

Caine put an arm around her shoulders and guided her to a chair.

'What can I get you?' he asked.

'If you haven't got whisky, a cup of that tea would go down nicely.'

Caine handed her his own cup as Dawn placed the suitcase on the table in front of her.

'Jeez,' said Shanti. 'You're all shaky. I've never seen you like this.'

Dawn looked about anxiously. 'I think I've been targeted,' she whispered. 'I think the perp is out there right now, watching me at work.'

'You mean you were attacked?'

'As good as. I'd better show you . . .'

She took a large swallow of tea and pulled on a pair of latex gloves. Then she unclipped the case and lifted out a transparent evidence bag, which she held to the light.

'What the hell is that?' said Shanti.

Caine was staring at the object in the bag as if transfixed.

'It's a hatchet,' he said. 'A flint hatchet.'

'I'm going to need a little help with this,' said Shanti.

The colour had drained from Dawn's normally ruddy complexion, and she was struggling to find words for what had occurred. She took another long guzzle of tea, then stared at the DIs with wide eyes.

'Remember those particles I took from the throat wound? OK, well the lab have confirmed they were minute flint chips.'

'Interesting,' said Shanti. 'But I don't see—'

'About half an hour ago, I came down from the tower and went to the van, which was parked in the turning area for shuttle buses, by the Portaloos. That's when I found this ... present, waiting for me on the footplate. I damn nearly stepped on it.'

'You're saying someone placed this object on the footplate of the forensics van while you were, what, ten metres away?'

'That's exactly what I'm saying. Of course, all hell broke loose. The local team are running about like blue-arsed flies, combing the area with dogs. They've got drones up too, but they couldn't even spot a footprint out there. Whoever did this simply disappeared. It's really shaken me up.'

'I'm so sorry,' said Caine, squeezing her arm. 'But I doubt it's personal, Dawn. It's just meant to ...'

'Meant to what, Caine?' said Shanti. 'What exactly are they trying to do?'

'I'm not entirely sure,' he admitted. 'Warn us off? Heighten the dramatics? Do you have any more gloves, Dawn?'

'What? Oh, yeah.' She handed him a box. Caine slipped his hands inside some nitrile gloves and carefully took the evidence bag. He held it at eye level and studied the contents carefully.

The implement had a triangular flint head that was jammed into a split wooden shaft, lashed in place with thin strips of hide.

'It's beautifully made,' he said. 'Is that blood on the blade?'

'Almost certainly,' said Dawn. 'I'm sending it to the lab asap.'

'You mean you think this is the murder weapon?' gasped Shanti.

'It seems highly possible,' she said, still deathly pale. 'The minute I set eyes on that jagged wound to the throat, I knew it had been inflicted by an unconventional weapon. This ticks every box. My team have made a comparison between our photos of the injury and this . . . thing, and it's a very credible match.'

'But you can actually see finger marks on the haft,' said Caine in amazement.

'What's a haft?' asked Shanti.

'A handle,' said Caine.

'Yeah, it's covered in greasy black prints,' agreed Dawn. 'You can almost read them with the naked eye.'

'But you said the perp was a pro,' said Shanti. 'You told us they were DNA-aware. You thought they'd left the crime scene completely clean.'

'I suppose I was wrong.'

They stared reverentially at the bag, as if it contained a sacred relic.

'What would you call this thing anyway?' said Shanti after a while. 'Is it an axe?'

'I'd say it was a knapped flint hatchet, or an axe hammer,' said Caine.

'Right. But it's hard to believe it's sharp enough to do the job.'

'Knapped flint is as sharp as steel,' said Caine. 'Don't forget, an implement like this was originally designed to butcher meat and prepare skins.'

'Yeah, we didn't come across many knapped flint hatchets in Camden Town.'

'You still look a little shaky, Dawn,' said Caine. 'Perhaps you should take some time out. You've had a horrible morning.'

'You're a very sweet man, Vincent Caine,' she replied. 'But it's my last day and I've got to sign off the scene of crime before I leave. I'll be OK. I'm made of strong stuff. I wanted to update you on this development and get this off to the lab before they shut up shop. I have a feeling this hatchet has quite a story to tell.'

'I'll just grab a couple of images before you go,' said Shanti. She located her phone and photographed the implement from every angle.

When she had finished, Dawn replaced the bag in the case, as gently as a baby in a cot.

'Thanks for the tea and sympathy,' she said to Caine. 'Not entirely sure about the honey, though.'

Once she had gone, Shanti stared at Caine across the table.

'A criminal psychologist would have a field day with this maniac,' she said. 'It's as if he's relishing the whole thing.'

'Like a staged melodrama,' agreed Caine.

'Tell me about the weapon,' she said. 'Presumably it's ancient?'

'Well, it's a replica of an ancient tool,' he replied.

'How do you know that? It looks genuine to me.'

'It has a wooden haft, for a start.'

'So what do you think they used back then – stainless steel?'

'No, they would have used materials exactly like this – hickory or oak, probably.'

'Well there you go . . .'

'But the point I'm making is that an original haft would have perished centuries ago. Archaeologists frequently turn up flint items, especially at burial sites – arrow tips, spear heads – but they rarely find more than a trace of the haft. So it's pretty clear that what we have here is a reproduction of a Neolithic tool, made by an expert. I'll ask Ned to examine it.'

'Whoa! Just hang on one damned minute. Are you seriously suggesting we take advice from a primary suspect?'

'Really, Shanti! As far as I know, Ned hasn't been anywhere near the stones today. All my instincts inform me that he is incapable of violence. He's a sad and gentle man. Besides, he must have trained thousands of people how to make tools like this. I remember his demonstrations on *Neolithic Neighbours*; I even made a few flint tools myself in my teens.'

'That makes you a suspect too.'

'As a matter of fact, I was thinking of teaching Paul next time you visit.'

'Look, it's nice that you're planning family handicraft weekends. But I prefer to be led by evidence rather than your instincts. Tull probably thought it was his lucky day when you drifted in out of the snow. In fact I bet he's halfway across the country by now, heading for the nearest airport.'

'I don't think he's a flight risk, Shant. He's lived here for decades.'

'Well, as soon as we return from our appointments, I have a few questions for Fred Flintstone. What time are we meeting him?'

'Ned doesn't really do clock time. We've agreed to meet at dusk.'

'Dusk? When the hell is dusk?'

'A little after twilight.'

'And when is . . .? Jeez, give me strength.'

'Let's at least wait until we get the lab results before we implicate him. In the meantime, I'm beginning to formulate a few theories.'

Shanti sighed. 'Let's hear them then.'

'Well, that hatchet is small, isn't it?'

'Small but lethal.'

'So you'd think it would take something more substantial to bring down a man of Finch's stature. And here's another thing I've been considering – Finch's beard was intact, wasn't it? Even if you could dispatch a large man with that hatchet, you would sever his beard in many places. Cut it to shreds, in fact. Now as far as I know, Dawn didn't discover any strands of beard. So how do you cut the throat of a bearded man without damaging his beard?'

'You're splitting hairs,' said Shanti.

'At the very least, it would be saturated with blood. And beard fibres would be embedded in the wound.'

'So the perp asks Finch to kindly raise his beard so that he can hack his throat?'

'My suspicion is that Finch was dead or incapacitated when he was raised on that trilithon. Then his beard was held aside while his throat was ceremoniously slashed.'

'But there was blood everywhere,' said Shanti.

'Those birds certainly made a mess,' agreed Caine. 'But in my opinion, there was minimal cast-off for a major injury. If the hatchet was the murder weapon, you'd have more arterial spray.'

'But why was it was placed by Dawn's van?'

'I suggest the offender is playing games. I suggest that the hatchet was deliberately planted where Dawn would find it, reinforcing my theory that they want to be noticed in the most public way possible – which is totally unlike Ned, who wants nothing more than a quiet life. It was put there, Shanti, in order to divert attention and frame someone else.'

'Of course, it's all a conspiracy against poor old Tull.'

There was a reflective pause, broken only by the distant clatter of cutlery and chatter from the kitchens.

'All right, Caine,' said Shanti. 'You're outstandingly irritating, but you are good at this stuff. I suppose that's why we work together.'

'That means a lot, Shanti.'

'Don't get too excited, I'm not inviting you for Christmas. In any case, none of this takes us any further forward. In fact, you've unleashed a whole avalanche of problems. Where was Finch killed? If he was already dead, why muck about with a flint axe? And still that crazy riddle – how did the perp raise him onto the triathlon?'

'I'm reminded of my favourite teaching—'

'If this is the one about embracing uncertainty, I may need an axe of my own. One thing seems certain – a ruthless, barbaric killer is terrifyingly close at hand.'

Chapter 16

The Dreaming Detective

As they stepped through the sliding doors, the DIs were hit simultaneously by an icy blast and the incoming bulk of Spalding and Dunster, befuddled by cold.

'Where are you two going?' asked Shanti

'Just finished duties, ma'am,' said Dunster. 'All right if we go home? Only we've got family coming and Mum needs me.'

'You must be joking.'

'Well, could we sit in the canteen? Just to get warmed up.'

'Right, listen and listen carefully. You've got twenty minutes to have a bite to eat, and not a second longer. The canteen's about to close anyway. After that, I want you, Spalding, to report to Sergeant Bennett, who is dealing with a new development at the stones. As for you, Dunster, I've got an important surveillance job for you.'

'Yes, ma'am.'

'See the exhibition centre over there? If you walk round the back, you'll find a group of huts – it's a sort of reconstruction of an early settlement.'

'I know it, ma'am.'

'Right, well, there's a man in there by the name of Professor Ned Tull. You can't miss him, he's a Neanderthal.'

'A Neolithic,' said Caine. 'Shanti, is this absolutely necessary?'

'While DI Caine and I are out, I want you to watch him like a hawk. This man is of major importance to our inquiries. You're to remain covert and keep a written log of his movements, do you understand? Don't engage unless absolutely necessary.'

'Is he violent, ma'am?'

'We don't know that, Dunster, but it's entirely possible. Be on your guard at all times.'

The clamouring hands of the journalists actually made the Saab rock as Shanti drove through the gates.

As she turned right onto the A303, it seemed that the gritting crew had also knocked off for Christmas, because a layer of snow had settled on the deserted surface. If it was bad here, what would it be like on those tiny rural lanes?

'Perhaps we should have borrowed a four-wheel drive,' said Caine.

'This car can handle anything,' she replied. 'She and I have been through tougher situations than this. Now, where's that turning?'

'A mile on the left. Would you like to hear about my dream?'

'Cops don't dream. It's a well-known fact.'

'Surely you dream sometimes?'

'I work. I sleep. I work again,' said Shanti, but as she spoke, a flickering image came to her of wheeling birds and the twin pools of frozen eyes.

Caine stretched himself in the passenger seat, as he was prone to do.

'Do you think insight comes in the form of symbols?'

'Did you just ask if insight comes in the form of symbols?'

'I'm convinced that my dream was meant to reveal something. It was so vivid, it was as if I was actually there.'

'Actually where, Caine?'

'Right here at Stonehenge. I remember an overwhelmingly ominous atmosphere, as if the sun was dying in the sky. And I don't know if it was the effect of sleeping in the roundhouse, or the solstice, or ...'

'Or the wind.'

'... or the fact that I've been fasting for my retreat – you know what it's like when your body is starved?'

'Not so much.'

'Everything seems heightened. Your vision and your inner vision too. Anyway, I saw these figures dancing among the trilithons.'

'Figures? What kind of figures?'

'You won't think I'm weird?'

'That ship has long sailed.'

'They were primeval figures, Shanti. With horns and strange headdresses. Half naked. Chanting. Covered in body paint. Both men and women.'

'Fur bikinis?'

'I was hiding out of sight, and to my horror, I realised they were preparing for a human sacrifice. As I watched, they led their victim from behind a monolith. He was taller than the others and I knew it was him – the Holly King. He was the sacrificial victim in my dream. Then – this is the creepy part, Shant – he turned his head very slowly, and spoke to me.'

'What did he say?'

'I couldn't hear the words above the wind and the chanting, but I could read his lips. He just said, "Help me!"'

'Dear Santa, please can I have an ejector seat?'

'But I was paralysed. Unable to move a muscle. I wanted to help with every fibre of my being, but I was incapable of doing a thing.'

'That part rings true.'

Caine settled back as if unburdened. After a while, he pointed out the entrance to the tiny lane they had taken to visit Quentin the previous day.

'So that was my dream,' he said. 'What do you think? There has to be a meaning there – the sacrifice of the Holly King and the overwhelming feeling of inertia. It will come to me, I know it will.'

Once again, Shanti had the sensation of driving through a subterranean burrow, but today a heavy fog created an unnatural sepia light, so that she had to drive with headlights and fog lamps on.

'You know what, I have a dream too.'

'But you just said—'

'I dream of working with someone normal. But it's wakey time now, DI Caine. Rise and shine. Your dreams and fantasies could not be more irrelevant. This case is about the brutal murder of an old man. You want to help Finch, don't you? Well, here's your opportunity. We need to identify his killer and bring him – or conceivably her – to justice.'

'Yes. Yes, you're right. You're always right. I must be mindful of the job in hand.'

'Good. In a few minutes we'll be passing Quentin's gaff, so keep your eyes peeled for suspicious activity.'

After ten minutes of bobsleigh driving, they approached the Old Vicarage. There were still no journalists, thank God, but it was only a matter of time. Shanti pulled up by the gateposts, each crowned with a snow-capped finial. Caine climbed out and examined the snow-covered ground. In less than a minute, he was back at her side.

'No one's been out today,' he reported, hauling on his seat belt. 'On foot or by car. The tracks are from yesterday – ours, of course, and Quentin's when he drove the nanny to the station. There's another set too – looks like a heavy SUV. Quentin's solicitor perhaps. And that's it, as far as I can tell. Shall we go on? We can easily be seen here.'

'Oh, I'm quite happy for Quinty to know we're keeping an eye on him,' she said, glaring up the driveway. At last she released the handbrake and the car lurched onwards, half sliding down the steep lane. Every now and then a tyre caught a rock hidden in the snow, forcing her to wrestle with the wheel.

'Tell me about Constanza,' she said.

'Well, according to Masako's notes, Finch took a kind of gap year shortly after his divorce from Tiggy. He attended an eco-logical convention in São Paulo, and that's where he met Constanza. She's an environmentalist too – originally from an indigenous family on her father's side. She was several years younger than Finch, but it's widely agreed that they adored each other . . . Could I just ask you to slow a little, Shanti? These lanes are treacherous and there are birds feeding . . .'

'Go on with the story, Caine.'

'That's it, really. Finch travelled back and forth to Brazil for a few months, but eventually they found they couldn't justify the air flights, so Constanza moved to the UK and settled into

Lovell Court. And that's where Sky was born.'

'OK, and what was all that stuff about hoodlums and squatters? I thought Finch lived alone with Constanza and Sky?'

'I thought so too— Whoa! Brake, Shanti! BRAKE!'

He seized the wheel so that the car lurched to the left, grazing the bank, before skidding to a halt.

'Jesus!' gasped Shanti. 'What the hell is that?'

Caught in the blur of the headlights, a huge animal loomed on the lane. The bedraggled creature had been walking unsteadily down the hill, with head hanging and tail between its legs like a starving wolf. Now it turned and gazed at them, trembling pathetically, with an expression of utter misery and dejection.

Before Shanti had even processed what had happened, Caine had thrown open the door and to her horror began walking slowly toward the beast, with one hand outstretched, talking softly all the while.

It was a dog. An oversized grey dog. As she watched in wonder, he spoke reassuringly to the creature, and a moment later guided it towards the open door.

'What the hell are you doing? There's no way that beast is coming in here.'

'This is Ganesh. One of Finch's dogs. Look, the name's on his collar.'

Once Caine had coaxed the animal into the footwell, it filled the space entirely with its shuddering body. And as he squeezed himself into the remaining space, Ganesh emitted a long, low bellow like a foghorn.

'Good grief!' said Shanti.

'Poor old boy,' said Caine. 'It's as if he's in mourning.'

'Don't be ridiculous. Animals don't mourn.'

'Of course they do. He's heartbroken, aren't you, poor old fellow? And frozen through. Do you have a towel, Shanti?'

'No I do not.'

Caine reached into the back. 'Could I use this old blanket, then? I'll wash it for you.'

'I'll hold you to that, Caine.'

As they continued their journey, the dog seemed to relax a little, even resting its nose against Caine's chest, gazing at him with doleful eyes as Caine massaged his ears.

'You were trying to find your way home, weren't you, boy?' he said. 'We'll take you there. You rest now, Ganesh.'

'I don't want to be rude,' said Shanti, 'but your friend stinks.'

'He's exhausted, Shant. And he can't stop shivering. Either he's frozen to the bone or something scared him badly – maybe both. In any case, Sky and Constanza will be pleased to see him . . . But where's your brother, Ganesh? Where's Albion?'

Enfolded in the blanket, the huge hound collapsed in a shuddering sleep against Caine's body.

At the bottom of the hill, Shanti reached an ancient cross-roads swathed in fog, with a wooden signpost and a bench half buried in snow. Here she swung right, driving more cautiously in order to navigate the milky gloom.

'Jeez,' she said suddenly. 'Look up there!'

In a brief clearing, they caught a glimpse of an ancient manor high on a hilltop, surrounded by a vast estate encircled by an endless wall.

'Lovell Court,' said Caine. 'It's magnificent. I suppose it's no wonder Quentin feels displaced.'

'But would he kill for it?' mused Shanti. 'That's what I'd like to know.'

High against the leaden sky, the house resembled a crumbling wedding cake, its craggy turrets and spires dusted with icing sugar. Strands of mist entwined the facade like silver ribbons.

With his arms around the sleeping hound, Caine recited a poem.

'*The stately homes of England, how beautiful they stand, to prove the upper classes have still the upper hand.*'

'I like that,' said Shanti. 'Is it one of yours?'

'Noël Coward.'

'But you remembered it, Caine. That's nearly as clever.'

'Why are you being nice to me, Shant? It doesn't feel right.'

'Being horrible is tiring. Besides ... I'm glad to have you here.'

'You are?'

'Ah, you may as well know ... I've got a bit of a thing about old houses. You know, like this one. When I was a kid, my mum used to watch these scary black and white movies. I wasn't supposed to look, but you know what kids are like ...'

'It's sad to think of you as a little girl, being scared like that.'

'Let's face it, this case is creepy as hell. I keep thinking about Finch's eyes, frozen and staring. And the killer is out there, Caine. Somewhere in the fog and the snow. If he's crazy enough to do that, he won't stop at anything.'

'Would you like a hug, Shant? We could pull over for a moment.'

'Would I what? Jesus, we're detectives on a murder inquiry.'

'I'm sorry. I went too far.'

'Damn right you did.'

Now they were following the shadow of the oppressive wall;

built, Shanti assumed, by a multitude of medieval menials under the orders of Quentin's forebears.

'Tell me about the hise . . .' she said. 'I mean the *house*.'

'Lovell Court is a calendar house.'

'Meaning?'

'Three hundred and sixty-five windows, fifty-two chimneys, twelve staircases, seven entrances . . .'

'And three hundred and sixty-five underpaid chambermaids to clean three hundred and sixty-five shitty toilets.'

'Imagine Quentin as an only child, wandering those silent corridors,' said Caine. 'It would be a strange place to grow up.'

'Yeah, he'd be great in one of Mum's films.'

They followed the wall for a quarter of a mile, until it opened into an impressive sandstone archway through which a long drive meandered like a silver river down the hillside from the distant house.

As they clattered over the cattle grid, Caine noticed rusting brackets where huge gates had once hung. Above their heads, a heraldic crest had been carved into the sandstone, featuring a dying bird impaled by an arrow.

'What's that about?' said Shanti.

'The motto of the Lovell-Finches, I suppose. *Ab ave cadir de caelo. Ave* is a bird, I think. You'd better ask Quentin.'

On their right, the broken gutters of a gatekeeper's lodge were festooned with icicles. Within leaded windows, the DIs saw ragged curtains and graffiti-covered walls.

'Everything looks half abandoned,' said Shanti. 'It gives you the willies.'

'Quentin's ancestors would definitely have kept it more manicured, but it has a certain charm, don't you think? It looks like we're entering the deer park now.'

'Don't tell me – it's three hundred and sixty-five acres.'

'More like three thousand six hundred and fifty.'

'Plenty of work for the hoi polloi then. But the place has gone to ruin, Caine. I suppose you can't get the staff these days.'

'According to Masako, Finch ran out of funds after the divorce. But I think it's more deliberate than that.'

'Deliberate ruin?'

'Rewilding, Shant.'

'Yeah, I do that in my garden. Won't let a lawnmower near the place. Paul and his mates need machetes to get to the trampoline.'

'When biodiversity is restored, all kinds of species return and everything finds a balance. It's very Buddhist.'

'Well it certainly raised Quentin's blood pressure, which is always a bonus.'

Beneath a frosty veil, the once formal estate had proliferated. Through misty flurries, the headlights picked out tangled forests of silver thorns and overgrown laurels, bowing beneath their snowy load.

'Like an illustration from "Sleeping Beauty",' said Shanti.

'Old Man Finch opened his gates and Mother Nature slipped inside.'

Through the ether, they caught glimpses of incongruous animals grazing side by side – herds of deer amongst long-horned cattle; and rooting amongst reeds on the marshy banks of a frozen lake, some unfamiliar beasts with steam rising from hot bodies.

'What the hell are those?'

'Wild boar!' said Caine. 'How wonderful.'

'They're dangerous, aren't they?'

'Well you wouldn't want a wrestling match.'

'Maybe he was creating a kind of safari park?' mused Shanti.

'I don't think captive animals were Finch's style. There are no internal fences, you see. The animals are free to roam.'

'Right. So what stops them straying onto the lanes?'

'The outer walls and the cattle grid, I suppose.'

'Lazy farming, then.'

'Wilding is about letting go. It's a celebration of the interconnectedness of all things. It's about the future, Shant.'

'Maybe the future is overrated. Did you ever think of that?'

A mile from the house, the lawns had mutated into scraggy waist-high tundra. Caine watched with delight as a ghostly barn owl sailed over the windscreen before swooping into the hollow of a blasted oak.

Shanti had her eyes fixed on the drive ahead, which was blocked by a rudimentary barrier – a brightly painted telegraph pole across battered oil drums. To one side, a group of eco-warriors stood guard near a brazier. In their heavy hand-made clothing, they appeared both ancient and futuristic.

'They look like your kind of people,' she said nervously.

As they approached, two of the group walked towards the car with hands raised – a stocky middle-aged woman with a mohawk and Celtic tattoos, and an older, skinny man with yellow-lensed spectacles.

Shanti lowered the window. 'We're police officers. We're here to see Constanza and Sky. They're expecting us.'

'You wanna leave that girl alone.'

The hostility was palpable. Caine leaned across and beamed.

'Hi. Look, we're here to help, we really are. We've found Ganesh, see ...'

The pair peered in at the bedraggled creature.

'Sky will be glad to see him,' acknowledged Mohawk Woman.

'How is Sky coping?' said Caine.

'How d'you think?' said the man. He had dreads stuffed into a knitted tam. 'All the Evolutionaries are in mourning.'

'Say that again,' said Shanti.

'In mourning for Finch. Every one of us.'

'No, you called yourself the Evo . . .?'

'Evolutionaries. It's the name of our tribe.'

'Could you explain that to me?'

'The clue's in the name,' said the woman, as if addressing a simpleton. 'Humans are either declining or evolving, right? The Evolutionaries are trying to evolve.'

'Although sometimes things conspire against you,' said the old man mournfully. 'What happened to Finch, woman?'

'We can't reveal too much at this juncture,' Shanti replied.

They both giggled. 'Juncture! What kind of word is that?'

'Is this a petrol vehicle?' asked Mohawk Woman.

'What do you think?' said Shanti. 'Coal?'

'See those trees? You can park there and walk to the house. It's not even a mile.'

'You are kidding . . .'

'You could borrow bikes,' the woman suggested.

'It's OK,' said Caine. 'We'd like a walk. The landscape is fantastic.'

When the barrier had been raised, Shanti accelerated irritably up the slope, parking the Saab in a row of vehicles buried in snow, like sheep.

'Did he call me woman?' she said, flipping the door locks and pulling on her hat.

'Don't take it personally, Shant. I must admit I'm rather enjoying this.'

'Wary of authority, I'd say.'

'I did wonder why they needed a guarded barrier,' said Caine, tugging the dog gently from the car.

'Everything about this place makes me nervous,' said Shanti. 'Right now, everyone I meet is a potential killer. Remember what Quentin said? This is where we'll find the hoodlums who murdered his father.'

Ganesh stood unsteadily on his spindly legs, but when they set off up the hill, he limped along at Caine's side.

'I can't get over the size of that beast,' said Shanti.

'He's as gentle as a lamb,' said Caine.

'He could eat a lamb without too much trouble.'

The drive was steeper here, and treacherous underfoot. A quarter of a mile from the big house, they came across a make-shift settlement with spires and turbines poking through the shrubbery.

On the verge, a hand-painted sign read:

SLOW KIDS

(and some fast ones too)

Through the fog, they heard peals of laughter coming from what looked like an adventure playground at the side of the drive, where a noisy rabble of children climbed and leapt and sledged.

'That's interesting,' said Caine.

'What are we looking at?'

'See what the kids are playing on?'

'Are they giant-sized letters?' said Shanti.

'I think that's exactly what they are. Remember Quentin telling us about an attempt to rename the family estate? I guess this is the name that made him so mad.'

As they drew closer, they could see that the children were indeed climbing on huge letters, constructed from reclaimed timber.

'E . . . V . . .' spelled Shanti. 'Jesus, Caine. Is this place called EVIL?' She felt the cold creep deeper.

'No,' said Caine. 'The third letter is an O. If Quentin's nihilistic tribe are the Evolutionaries . . .'

'. . . then this place is EVOL.'

A few of the kids ran to meet them. Like the older Evolutionaries, they wore customised clothes and random hairstyles. They could all do with a bath, Shanti thought, but they seemed healthy and happy enough.

'Ganesh! Ganesh!' they sang. 'Where did you find him?'

Caine grinned. 'He came home by himself, didn't you, boy?'

The dog stood taller than the kids, but he retreated warily behind Caine when they tried to hug him.

'What's wrong with Ganesh?' said a snot-nosed girl.

'He's had a long walk,' said Caine. 'He's tired now, aren't you, boy? Is Sky up at the big house?'

Without answering, they returned to their playmates, who were dive-bombing off the letters, with knees grasped to chests, emerging from a bank of snow white and wild with laughter. Shanti felt the ubiquitous pang of guilt as she thought of Paul.

Now they passed through the home-made hamlet, made up of domes, yurts, tree houses and space-age eco-homes, with solar panels gazing at the sky.

Half overgrown amongst the bushes lay a fleet of abandoned vehicles – buses, camper vans and lorries. There was even an old brown library van, with one axle propped on a log and the chassis hanging like the belly of a decrepit cow.

Along well-trodden paths, mournful Evolutionaries went about their business. A gaggle of teenagers comforted each other around a hammered fire bowl.

'What is this place?' Shanti asked. 'Some kind of steampunk Shangri-La? You know what? I'm actually beginning to sympathise with Quentin. There's a whole tribe living in the grounds of his ancestral home.'

'They seem harmless enough to me,' said Caine approvingly. 'I like the way everything is made out of recycled materials. It's incredibly creative.'

'Yeah, you should move right in,' said Shanti. 'There's an empty bender over there.'

'I can think of worse places to be,' said Caine with a grin.

Above the final stretch of the drive, the craggy flint face of Lovell Court emerged from the flurries. Three hundred and sixty-five leaded windows gazed down on them, and tattered hand-made flags waved from turrets.

Caine was about to ascend the twelve great steps when the mighty studded door opened and a small figure slipped outside – a girl of around fourteen years, with gleaming black hair and oversized eyes swollen with tears.

She saw the dog, and her eyes widened further. As she walked towards them, she seemed underdressed to Shanti. A loose sweatshirt hanging off one shoulder. Skinny jeans on skinny legs. It was then that she realised ... Sky's feet were bare in the snow.

Chapter 17

A Place Called Evol

'Ganesh,' whispered the girl. She wrapped her arms around the huge creature as if hugging some residue of her father. 'You found him. And ... Albion?'

'Not yet,' said Caine. 'But we're looking. We spotted this fellow wandering the lanes. It looks like he hasn't eaten in a while, and I reckon he's thirsty too.'

A sleepless night had seared rivulets under Sky's eyes, but she would not wipe away the tears. Rather, she glared defiantly at the DIs. And although this was a child only a few years older than her son, Shanti felt intimidated by her presence. There was something unworldly, almost alien about the slender girl.

'I'm Vincent Caine. This is my friend Shanti Joyce. We're here to help you, Sky, in any way we can. Our hearts go out to you.'

'They said you'd come,' she said. 'But I was expecting ... you know, uniforms.'

'None of that,' said Shanti, knowing that before long, the place would be crawling with officers.

'I'm sorry,' said the girl. 'I'm not at my best. I'll be OK ... really I will. I'm normally very strong. If Finch taught me anything, it is that sometimes battles are forced on us.'

'You mustn't apologise,' said Caine. 'Whatever you feel is OK.'

'Thank you, Mr Caine. You seem kind. And Shanti. I'll try to remember.'

'Don't you think you should put something on your feet?' said Shanti. 'Can I fetch you some shoes? It's freezing out here.'

'That's nice of you. But I always go barefoot. In fact ... in fact I started a campaign to go barefoot at school. It helps me feel connected with the earth, and right now I need it more than ever. People keep asking how I'm feeling, but the truth is, I'm not feeling anything at all. I'm totally numb. That's why I want to walk in the snow. I need to feel something, even if it's pain.'

Classic disassociation, thought Shanti.

A state of limbo, thought Caine. Like the solstice.

Ganesh was nuzzling at Sky's face, almost unbalancing her with his bulk.

'I'm afraid we'll need to ask you some questions,' said Shanti gently. 'And your mum too, if she's available.'

'It will help to actually do something,' Sky said. 'But I'm afraid you'll have more trouble with Constanza – her English isn't brilliant, especially when she's stressed. The women are caring for her, but it's like she's disappeared. Maybe seeing Ganesh will help.'

'Then we'll speak to you first if we may,' said Shanti. 'I don't know how much our officers told you last night?'

'Finch is dead.'

'I'm afraid that's correct. And did they tell you that we fear someone may have deliberately set out to harm him?'

'They told me. He was murdered . . . There, I've said it. Please, Shanti. Please, Mr Caine. I want you to catch that bastard.' Again the huge eyes overflowed with tears.

'With your help, we will,' said Shanti. 'Can you remember the last time you saw him?'

'I remember exactly. It was lunchtime on Monday in the gardener's kitchen. We had a little disagreement . . .' The words poured out like tears.

'A disagreement?' said Shanti.

'Look, maybe we should go inside?' said Caine. 'I think Ganesh needs feeding, then we can talk for as long as Sky feels able.'

When the girl stood upright, the dog was level with her shoulders.

'We can sit by the fire in the hall,' she said.

'Or maybe you could take us to the place you mentioned,' said Shanti. 'The gardener's kitchen.'

The pain was etched on Sky's face. 'If you want,' she said. 'We'll have to go round the side.'

Rather than returning through the front door, she led them to a semi-subterranean entrance at one side of the building. They went down a small flight of steps, thick with trampled snow, and at the threshold of a small doorway, the DIs scraped their boots before entering the labyrinth of Lovell Court.

They walked in single file along musty corridors lined with frayed carpets – the girl, the great dog, Caine, and Shanti at the rear. With a sense of incredulity, Shanti realised they were passing through what had once been the servants' quarters, where mysterious doors led to pantries, coal cellars and storage rooms stuffed with the paraphernalia of country life – boots, coats, shelves stacked with home-made preserves, and hanging from hooks, a vast array of dried herbs and medicinal plants.

'We're aware of a sizeable community living in the grounds of Lovell Court,' she said. 'Could you explain the set-up? What is their relationship to your family? Do some of them reside here in the house?'

'Everyone has their own home,' Sky told them. 'But people are free to come indoors if they want. Last night, for example, we all sat by the fire for hours and hours, trying to get our heads around what had happened. The Evolutionaries loved Finch.'

The mass of jet-black hair. The sunken cheeks. The wide imploring eyes.

'I realise this arrangement is normal for you,' said Shanti. 'But Caine and I may need a little help to understand how it works – the Evolutionaries and everything.'

'Sure,' said Sky. 'There are no secrets here. It's not a cult or anything.'

'Of course not,' said Caine. 'But Finch was an unusual man, wasn't he? To understand what happened to him, we need to form a picture of his lifestyle.'

'I'll try to help,' she said, almost inaudibly.

At the end of a passageway, a small door opened into the gardener's kitchen – a room of modest proportions as ancient as the house itself, but refurbished in the seventies or eighties with melamine cupboards and a raised breakfast counter. Colourful artworks in childlike or folk art style hung around the walls. Stone mullion windows looked onto a snowy kitchen garden, the windowsills crammed with pots of untidy plants.

In a corner of the uneven stone floor, an enormous pair of tattered dog beds emitted a musky odour. While Ganesh drank thirstily, Sky set about filling a huge bowl with dried food and scraps from a large battered fridge. Shanti watched as she worked. Her rough-skinned feet red with cold. Her quick intelligence. Her slow sorrow.

She placed the bowl on the floor and the dog lunged ravenously forward.

'Oh, what am I thinking! I should offer you tea or something. Look, there's fruit in the bowl – it's all from our greenhouses.'

She began frantically picking through grapes, discarding mouldy ones.

'No, no, you're fine,' said Shanti.

'Just a glass of water,' said Caine. 'I'll help myself if that's OK.'

As she took a seat at the raised counter, Shanti weighed up the forensic cost of carrying out an interview in what may have been the last room in which Finch had been seen alive. Ideally the room would have been sealed. The situation was far from ideal, but everything about this case seemed irregular.

'Any objection if I take notes?' she asked.

A sad smile flew to Sky's face. 'That's pretty funny. You still use notebooks . . . like the old movies.'

'Well, not necessarily. I can record on my phone if you don't mind.'

'Do whatever you like,' she said. 'I must admit I feel a little spaced . . .'

'Have you had breakfast, Sky?'

The girl admitted she hadn't, and with some persuasion poured herself a glass of almond milk and set down a bowl of dried fruit, before joining Shanti at the counter.

'Right, it's 11.38 a.m. on Wednesday the twenty-second of

December,' said Shanti. 'For the purposes of the tape, this is an interview with Sky Lovell-Finch in the gardener's kitchen at Lovell Court. Also present is DI Vincent Caine. Could we begin with a description of your father's movements over the last few days? As much detail as you can manage.'

Sky took a tiny sip of milk, leaving a fine white moustache on her upper lip, just like Paul. For a moment Shanti saw her for what she was – a frightened child in a fatherless world. Her maternal instincts cried out to cook her a square meal. Get some warm socks on those bare feet.

'He hasn't been around much,' Sky said. 'He was excited about a new project . . . something he was doing near Imber, up on the plains.'

Caine was standing on the other side of the counter, his hat almost grazing the dried herbs that hung in bunches from the ceiling.

'What project, Sky?' he asked gently.

'I didn't understand every detail. Finch was into ley lines and magnetic energy. It was a standing joke – he was always convinced that he was going to discover a sacred site to rival Stonehenge itself.'

'OK, we'll come back to that,' said Shanti. 'Now, you told us that the last time you saw your father was right here in the kitchen?'

'Yes. I'm sure of it. It was around midday, the day before yesterday.'

'Which was Monday. You said you had a disagreement?'

'It was nothing. Finch wanted us to join him to celebrate the solstice. Both the summer and the winter solstice were such a big deal for him. First he tried to persuade Constanza, but she's not good with the cold. Then he started on me. I told him it would be way too early and the weather was turning bad. He said I could bring some mates if I wanted, but you show me a teen who wants to get up before dawn. That's the thing about having an older father ...'

'What is, Sky?' asked Caine.

She stared at him wistfully.

'You see, Finch loves me ... loved me more than anything. But he treats me like another adult. He forgets that I'm ...' she dissolved into sobs, 'that I'm just a kid.'

Her body began to shudder violently, so that she almost slipped off the stool. To Shanti's consternation, Caine stepped around the counter and embraced the sobbing child. She had seen this before – this crossing of professional lines – and it made her more than a little uncomfortable.

Right now, there was a mumbled conversation taking place – too quiet for the recording, but she caught snippets of what was said, and none of it concurred with police procedure.

'He's free now,' Caine soothed. 'Finch is flying free.'

'Did you see him? Was it a terrible sight?'

'He was like a king. He was magnificent.'

'Thank you, Mr Caine,' Sky whispered. 'That helps. It really does. It sounds crazy, but I want to think of his blood replenishing the earth. Do you understand that?'

Shanti coughed loudly. 'Right, when you're ready ... Now, this exchange with your father took place at lunchtime?'

'Just before lunch. It was beginning to snow, but the big blizzard arrived later that night.'

'And there was nothing to suggest that he was worried about anything?'

'Nothing. He was a bit sulky because no one wanted to go

with him, but typical Finch, he couldn't leave without coming over and kissing me and Constanza.'

She touched her cheek lightly, as if she could still feel her father's lips.

'Then he left this room?' Shanti asked. 'Back the way we came?'

'Yes. With Ganesh and Albion too. And they were so happy to be going out.'

'And where did he go?' asked Shanti.

The conversation was punctuated by loud gulping and swallowing as Ganesh filled his belly.

'To his workshop, I guess. Maybe half an hour later, he appeared at that window right there. The snow was beginning to fall quite heavily. He was wearing the face paint and the holly wreath and he was ... Oh God, he was pushing his face against the glass and pulling silly faces to make us laugh.'

'So to be clear – Finch had gone to his workshop and returned dressed as the Holly King?'

'That's right. It didn't take much of an excuse for him to put on the outfit. Finch embraced paganism, so he wore it all the time around the solstice.'

'And after he came to the window, he set off down the drive with the dogs?' asked Shanti. 'There was definitely no one else with him?'

'No one.'

'Try to drink some of that milk,' Shanti said. The girl stared at the glass as if it had just appeared, and took another sip. 'Would you say your parents had a good relationship?'

Sky's face softened with benevolent memories. 'I've never seen a couple more in love. Constanza had a pet name for him

135

– she called him her magnificent beast, and that's exactly what he was. Dear, darling Finch. Big and gentle and so, so wise.'

Ganesh had chased the last scrap around the empty bowl. Now he loped towards one of the tattered beds and threw his hulking body down with a sigh.

'Look,' said the girl. 'That's so sad. Ganesh is lying in Albion's bed. I've never seen him do that before.'

They watched the dog for a moment, then Caine said:

'I'm still a little confused about timing. You told us that Finch and the dogs set off to walk to Salisbury Plain at around midday on Monday. But the solstice celebration wasn't until early on Tuesday morning. What did he do for the rest of that day? Where did he spend the night? Did he shelter somewhere from the storm?'

'I . . . I must admit, I have no idea. Maybe he intended to visit the dig near Imber, come home for a few hours' sleep, and then return very early for the ceremony. You need to understand that Evol is a pretty big community and the house is huge. We never monitor each other's movements. Sometimes I don't see Finch or Constanza for a day or more. It's quite normal. We bump into each other sooner or later. Until this happened, everyone was happily living their own creative lives.'

'So when did you begin to worry?'

'I guess it was around ten the following morning.'

'Yesterday? Solstice morning?'

'Yes. I slept badly because of the storm. So I got up late and had breakfast in here with Constanza. Looking back, I suppose Finch was already dead then, but we didn't know that. I keep thinking . . . Oh God!'

'What, Sky?'

'I keep thinking that if I had only gone with him to the ceremony, he would be alive now.'

'You mustn't blame yourself,' said Caine.

'But I do. I do.'

'Would you like to take a minute?' Shanti asked. The girl shook her head. 'Did you wonder where your father was at this stage?'

'I suppose I assumed he had stayed on after the ceremony. Dogs aren't allowed into the monument, so I wondered if he had left them at the visitor centre, or they'd become separated somehow. I was trying to reassure Constanza that he would walk through the door at any moment.'

'Your mother was anxious?' said Shanti.

'She told me she'd had a feeling of dread all night long. She kept talking about the weird solstice light.'

'But she didn't try to call him?'

'Finch never carried a phone. He didn't even own one, as far as I know. But I called some of the Evolutionaries and we were beginning to talk about sending a search party. It was at that point that someone arrived at the door . . . but it wasn't Finch.'

'It was our officers arriving to break the news.'

'Yes.'

'OK,' said Shanti. 'One last question for now, and I want you to think very hard before you answer. Was your father in conflict with anyone? Who would want to hurt him, Sky? That's what we desperately need to know.'

'I've been thinking about that, of course, and I know exactly what he would say.'

'Oh yes?'

'He'd say that anyone who speaks truth to power is bound to have enemies.'

'Could you give some examples?'

'Finch upset people. He was outspoken. I mean, it's no secret that he fell out with his own family. Then there were endless disputes with developers – he thought of the plains as sacred land. He spent years fighting the underpass on the A303 because he believed it would disturb the ancestors. Then there were the battles with English Heritage because he believed they had appropriated the stones and commercialised them. The list goes on and on. He was arrested several times, you know.'

'Yes, we're aware of that.'

'He thought of each arrest as a badge of honour. So yes, Finch had enemies.'

'OK, that's very helpful indeed. Right, it's 12.05. I'm ending the recording there. You mentioned your father's workshop . . .?'

'It's where he spends most of his time.'

'Has anyone been in since he went missing? Has anyone touched anything in there?'

'I don't think so. It was Finch's private space. Everyone respected that. I can take you if you want me to?'

'That would be useful,' said Shanti. 'But I'm going to insist on two things.'

'OK?'

'Firstly, I want to see you drink that milk, sweetheart. And secondly, you need to put on some more clothing. It's below freezing outside.'

Sky smiled weakly, drank half the milk and chewed a handful of fruit.

'Do you mind if I check on Constanza before we go? Maybe I'll take Ganesh, to see if that will help.'

When the girl had rallied the reluctant dog and left the

kitchen, Shanti turned to Caine.

'Jesus, that kid is . . .'

'She's extraordinary. But it's heartbreaking to see what she's going through.'

'The way she talks – I have to keep reminding myself she's only fourteen. But I'm worried about her well-being. Should we speak to social services?'

'I don't think so, Shanti. Don't forget she has a whole community around her. But you're right to be concerned.'

Shanti scrolled through her phone.

'Look at this – a message from Dawn. She seems to have recovered a little. She says we can expect the prelim pathology report on Finch by tonight. She doesn't want to jump the gun, but we should be prepared for a few surprises. What the hell does that mean?'

'I've no idea.'

'Well, so long as you don't tell me to embrace uncertainty, we're still friends. Oh, and here's a message from Benno. This is good – it seems we've been allowed a brief visit with Tiggy at the nursing home. Apparently she sleeps after lunch, so we'll need to be on our way reasonably soon. What do you think?'

'Let's take a look at Finch's workshop, then I think we should check in on Constanza. But before Sky returns, I just want to . . .'

He moved a few plant pots carefully from the windowsill and eased open a window, holding a glove in one hand to minimise contact with the iron latch. A freezing blast filled the room, and Shanti watched as Caine leaned outside, peering at the ground below.

'The tracks have almost disappeared,' he said as he re-emerged and fastened the latch. 'But the evidence bears out Sky's account. You can just about see a trampled area below the window where

Finch danced about. The top layer of snow has blown away in a few places, so you can even make out faint tracks from the dogs. Also ...' he scrutinised the window pane, 'you can actually see where he pushed his face against the glass. See – faint green smears here and here. Finally he and the dogs set off towards the drive, where their tracks merge with multiple footprints.'

'Very impressive,' said Shanti. 'Right, here comes Sky now. She likes you, Caine. See if you can ask her about Tiggy, and about Quentin too. Don't forget he's her half-brother, though it's hard to believe.'

Sky entered the kitchen without the dog, wearing an old green duffel coat and a woollen beanie, though her feet were still bare.

'Did you find your mother?' asked Shanti.

'Yes, she's on her own in the big hall. I'll take you to meet her later, but I'm afraid she's been self-medicating, so you won't get much sense from her today.'

'She what?'

'Oh, I don't mean anything illegal. I should have told you – Constanza is a herbalist. From the earliest age, she taught me to forage from the land. To know which plants heal and which plants kill. Really, she's incredibly skilful. Most people don't know the difference between one tree and another. Constanza used to say that our ancestors could read the landscape like a menu in a restaurant, but now, for the first time in history, humans have become plant blind.'

'That's very true,' said Caine. 'You say she's has been self-medicating?'

'Yes, she's heavily sedated. Probably a tincture of CBD oil, camomile, lavender, mugwort and hops. Anyway, she seemed pleased to see Ganesh, so I left them to rest together by the fire.'

Chapter 18

The Heartbroken Herbalist

The wunderkind winced as her feet touched the snow. She stood for a long time gazing up at the milky sun.

'Mr Caine,' she whispered. 'Is this the end of days?'

'It's the solstice,' he replied. 'And you've just lost your father.'

They set off slowly along the front of the building, the fragile girl with the DIs on either side.

'Ask me questions,' she said. 'Lots of them.'

'All right,' said Caine. 'Shanti and I went to the Old Vicarage yesterday. We met your half-brother and his family. But he didn't seem very cooperative. Tell us about Quentin, Sky?'

'Quentin is one of the Unevolved.'

'That's a curious word,' said Shanti.

'Maybe that's not fair,' she said. 'To tell you the truth, I've never met him.'

'But he lives less than five miles away.'

'I suppose he does,' said Sky. 'Although I don't think he's there very often. I see him on TV from time to time, and I don't imagine we'd have much in common. Finch and Quentin fell out before I was born. Their differences seemed irreconcilable. My father's views would be anathema to someone like Quentin.'

'Can you be specific?' said Shanti.

'Almost everything really. You know about Quentin's politics, right? Well, my father believed in super-taxes for the super-rich. Huge penalties for polluters. He believed it was time for young people and women to have their say.'

'Amen to that,' said Shanti.

'Throughout history, our decisions have been made by narcissistic grey men ... like Quentin, I suppose. And what has it brought us? Poverty, warfare, oppression, the depletion of biodiversity. They haven't done a very good job, have they? Finch used to say that "young people must unite and tell old fools like me that time is up".'

'And your mother shares these views?' said Shanti.

'Constanza's from Brazil. You know what's happening there. She thinks of the rainforest as the lungs of the world.'

To their right, the flint walls rose dizzyingly overhead; to their left, the ghostly landscape rolled down to misty wetlands where a steaming herd of longhorns grazed.

'If this wilding project is an example, then your father taught you well,' said Caine.

'The wilding project is just the smallest of beginnings,' said Sky, almost choking with passion. 'We have to do this *everywhere*, don't you see that? Otherwise the earth will die. Finch dreamed of forests within cities. "It's a minute to midnight" – that's what he used to say.'

They turned the corner towards the back of the house, where a doorway in a high wall opened onto walled gardens and ornate courtyards, once geometrically formal but now returned to silvery nature. Enclosed by walls and espaliered trees, a series of ponds seemed frozen in time, with grotesque fountains hanging with icy stalactites.

Finch's workshop was a substantial coach house at the far end, surrounded by discarded machine parts protruding through the snow.

Almost instinctively, Shanti gave Caine time to do his thing – analysing the scene. Reading the hieroglyphics on the ground, like letters on the pages of a book.

When they had hauled open the rickety door, Shanti asked Sky to wait as she entered the cave-like interior. She wanted a chance to check the place over, in case there was anything dreadful in there – the child had suffered enough.

She found the light switches, and a huge untidy space came into view, crammed with timber, racks of tools, and cluttered workbenches with hefty vices. There was a dreadful chill in there – colder than outdoors if that was possible – and the air was thick with the aroma of oil and wood and paint.

The only troubling thing she could see was an untidy bundle of clothes on an old swivel chair. After a few minutes, she asked Caine to let the girl inside.

'Nothing to worry about,' she said. 'Can you shed any light on these clothes?'

Sky padded across the cobbled floor and stared in dismay.

'They're Finch's. He must have changed right here. Look, that's his face paint.'

On a bench lay a hand mirror and a muddle of theatrical greasepaint.

'Right. Please be very careful not to touch anything,' said Shanti. 'Our forensics team will want to look this over.'

143

Sky said nothing. Just watched mournfully as the DIs made a tour of the workshop, Shanti taking many photos on her phone.

Several metal detectors stood propped against a wall, like the one they had observed in Masako's photo. A large pair of mechanical devices like huge flies rested on pallets on the floor, with robotic legs and gleaming rotor blades.

'Drones,' said Shanti quietly.

'Unusually large ones,' said Caine.

'Big enough to raise a man?' mused Shanti.

She took photos of the machines from every angle, then called to the girl, 'Could you join us for a moment, Sky? I'd like you to talk us through some of this equipment.'

Sky drifted over, submerged in gloomy thoughts.

'Oh yes,' she said. 'A few of the young ones are into drone technology. It's not really my thing, but Finch always encouraged them.'

Caine had roamed to the back of the workshop, where he discovered two customised vehicles in the shadows – a double-seated snowmobile and a quad bike, both with unusual apparatus attached.

'And what about these?' he asked.

'Magnetometers,' Sky told him. 'Finch loved them. He taught me to drive them when I was a kid.'

'And what would you use them for?' asked Shanti.

'The device on the back detects deep-lying geological anomalies. My father used to ride all over the plains, searching for artefacts or subterranean structures.' She smiled wanly. 'It used to get him into trouble when he strayed onto army land. He was fixated with Arthurian and pagan legends, and he truly believed there were undiscovered temples and necropolises out there.'

She blinked away a tear. 'It breaks my heart that we used to tease him about it. If only I had shown more interest in his work . . .'

'None of this is your fault,' Shanti assured her. 'But I'm wondering why your father chose to walk to the stones on Monday? Surely the snowmobile would have been perfect?'

'The dogs couldn't keep up with it, and anyway the snow had barely begun to settle when he left. Sometimes he cycled to the plains, but in any case, he loved to walk.'

After ten minutes of 'look don't touch', they returned to the door, where Sky showed them a large key hanging on a nail and on Shanti's insistence, the workshop was secured.

Emerging into the half-light, they returned to the steps at the front of the house, where Caine took a moment to confer with Shanti.

'Could I make a suggestion? Constanza sounds pretty overwrought, right?'

'Self-medicated,' said Shanti.

'So perhaps she would find it easier to talk to just one of us.'

'Me, you mean. And where are you off to, Caine?'

'We haven't got long, so I thought I'd have a chat with some of the Evolutionaries. You never know what you might learn. Shall we meet at the car in, say, an hour?'

'Forty-five minutes max, if we're going to see Tiggy and interview Tull this evening.'

Caine spoke a few reassuring words to Sky. Then, giving her a gentle hug, he set off down the drive in the direction of the place known as Evol.

'He's kind,' said the girl as they watched him go. 'You're lucky to work with him.'

145

Shanti followed her up the wide steps and through the huge front door, reproached all the while by the voice of her inner child reminding her that she had no business in a great house like this.

As they walked along a wide corridor, she glanced at the framed portraits on either side – rows of gloomy Lovell-Finches, some with the regal benevolence of Finch, some with the angular arrogance of Quentin, but none resembling this black-haired spirit of the rainforest.

At the end of the corridor, Sky opened a leather-bound door, and Shanti was astonished to find herself in a hall of cavernous proportions, with great rugs laid on flagstone floors and ornate wooden panels around towering sandstone walls. A spindly Christmas tree decorated with hand-made toys stood rooted in a tub. Overhead, cobweb-draped chandeliers cascaded with glassy tears. A semicircle of battered chairs and settees had been arranged around a blazing hearth.

Constanza stared hypnotically into the flames, almost subsumed in an oversized armchair. She was a handsome woman in her late thirties, with jet-black hair like her daughter, and a string of turquoise beads around her neck. At her feet, the huge dog twitched jerkily in sleep.

'Will she talk to me?' asked Shanti quietly.

'Let me try. Like I say, she tends to forget her English when she's overwhelmed, but I can translate for you.'

As the girl knelt at her mother's side, Constanza smiled at her. She seemed dozy and unnaturally calm.

A brief conversation transpired: '*Querida Mamãe, esta senhora gostaria de falar com você. Você pode confiar nela, eu prometon . . .*'

'She says she'll try to help,' said Sky. 'But she seems confused about what's going on.'

Shanti asked various questions, which Sky translated. Constanza smiled constantly as she replied, placing her hands reassuringly around her daughter's tear-stained cheeks. After a while, Sky squeezed her mother's hand, kissed her forehead and returned to Shanti's side.

'It's awful. She says not to worry. She says he will return very soon. I couldn't understand what she meant . . . then I realised she's talking about Albion. She thinks all the fuss is about the dog. She says that now that Ganesh is home, Albion will be sure to follow.'

'That's very distressing for you,' said Shanti. 'I suppose it's her way of coping. She'll come to terms with the situation in her own time, but in the meantime, there's no point in pressing her. She has plenty of friends, doesn't she?'

'Oh yes. She says the women have been looking after her night and day, but she had to send them away because they kept talking about Finch as if he's the one who's missing! She assured me that he is resting upstairs. She says that when we have slept, everything will be as it was before.'

From the armchair, Constanza spoke sharply to her daughter.

Sky looked at Shanti in dismay. 'She wants us to keep our voices down. She says we will wake him.'

They crept quietly from the great hall, past the framed Lovell-Finches to the front door, where Shanti reassured Sky they would do everything in their power to bring some closure for her and Constanza.

'Here's my card. That's my personal number on there, so don't hesitate to call if you need support.'

'Will you talk to Quentin again?'

'Yes, we'll definitely be doing that. But right now, we have an appointment with Tiggy Antrobus-Lovell-Finch. That's Finch's first wife, right?'

'I guess so.'

'You're saying you haven't met her either?'

'I did meet her once, a few years ago. I cycled to the nursing home with a school friend – just out of interest really. My friend said I should try to make peace with that side of my family. It was all a bit weird . . .'

They were standing outside the front door now, looking down the steps and across the misty valley.

'In what way?' said Shanti.

'We were shown up to her room and there was this funny little lady who stared at me in a very creepy way. She seemed vacant, like there was no one home. And yet I sensed something . . .'

'Like what?'

'Hatred, I think. I never told Finch that I had been.'

'OK, that's interesting. I need to get going now, but I always say this to everyone – is there anything else you can think of? Anything at all, no matter how trivial, that might help our investigation?'

Snowflakes melted on Sky's cheeks. Like kisses, Shanti thought. Or tears.

'I don't know if this is any help,' she said eventually. 'But Finch kept a journal.'

'A journal?'

'He was old-school, you know. He didn't like computers, but I always remember him writing at his desk. A kind of log of his archaeological work, I think.'

'You're right. That could be significant. Where might we find this journal?'

'Upstairs in his study probably. I can look for it if you want?'

'You do that, Sky. I'm particularly interested in the entries for the last couple of weeks.'

Chapter 19

The Epiphany

'She's very intense, isn't she?' said Shanti, reversing out of the parking space beneath the trees. 'I think I'd prefer my child to be a little dim. Besides, her philosophy is spectacularly naïve – the world run by children . . . forests within cities . . .'

'I couldn't find one single thing I disagreed with,' said Caine.

'That's because you have the brain of a fourteen-year-old.'

'Maybe you'd rather people like Quentin were in charge?'

'Fair point. I'd rather Ganesh was in charge than that douche-nozzle.'

She half slid the car towards the barrier, where the retro-futuristic guards warmed their hands around the brazier.

'Look at this place,' said Caine. 'The animals. The sense of community. Hey, Shanti, you know the big letters the kids were playing on?'

'They spelled EVOL, you told me.'

'Ah, but did you look at them as you walked *away* from the house?'

'What are you blathering on about, Caine?'

'In reverse they spell LOVE. That's beautiful, isn't it?'

'Oh for God's sake. It's not 1963.'

As the barrier was raised, Caine and the eco-guards exchanged waves and warm smiles.

'Seems you made some friends,' said Shanti as they trundled past the gatekeeper's lodge. 'But did you learn anything of interest?'

'I did,' said Caine. 'I learned about Finch's epiphany. And it's quite a tale.'

'Are you going to tell me or keep it to yourself?'

'Of course I'll tell you, but let's make sure we're heading the right way. Did Benno send directions for the nursing home?'

On top of the cattle grid, Shanti stopped and checked her phone.

'Er ... OK, according to Benno, Tiggy Antrobus-Lovell-Finch resides at a very upmarket nursing home about thirty miles east of here. That's what? Forty-five minutes in this weather. And check this out, Caine – the place caters exclusively for former stars of stage and screen. This should be enter-taining.'

They passed beneath the ancient archway and turned left onto the deserted road, driving parallel to the perimeter wall of the Lovell Court estate.

'You were about to tell me a story,' said Shanti. 'About Finch's epiphany.'

'It's all about the Battle of the Beanfield,' he said.

Shanti's mind hit replay, whirling backwards to a conversa-tion in the Land Rover as they drove to view the body. It seemed like years ago, but it was only yesterday. Benno's father had come home very shaken . . . not the finest hour in British policing history, he had said.

'According to Silas, the story of the Battle of the Beanfield is the key to understanding Finch,' said Caine.

'Who's Silas? Not the one who called me woman?'

'He's actually a very sweet old man. You'll never guess where he lives?'

'A tree house? No, wait – a telephone kiosk.'

'A library van, Shant. Silas lives in a converted library van. It's very cool indeed.'

'Er, why?'

'Back in the day, he was a librarian in the Handsworth district of Birmingham. But it's important to put this in context. We're talking about the Thatcher years – the poll tax riots, the miners' strikes . . .'

'I was a baby. You can't blame me.'

'Me too, said Caine. 'But I learnt a lot from Silas.'

'And you were sitting in his library van while he was telling you this?'

'He was incredibly hospitable. We drank tea by his woodburner, surrounded by shelves of books. For some reason, Silas felt able to trust me. He claims he has an ability to read people . . . like books, you see!'

The lane merged into a wider road, and Shanti was relieved to see that the snow had been recently cleared. Following the directions on her phone, she settled into the journey as Caine continued the story.

'It was a tough time for his generation. Most of the council houses were sold off. Rents were unaffordable, and when his library closed, Silas took to the road.'

'You're telling me he stole the library van?'

'I don't know about that. Maybe. Anyway, he joined a group of travellers – there were thousands of them across the UK, and the authorities began to think of them as a major problem and a threat to society, whereas in reality most of them were simply young families trying to survive.'

'I don't understand what this has to do with Finch?'

'A few times a year, the travellers headed off to the festivals, and the best of them all ...'

'...was the Stonehenge Free Festival.'

'You've got it. Silas and his friends headed off for the summer solstice in a convoy of buses and vans. Back then you were free to camp on Salisbury Plain for months at a time. It sounds amazing actually – like an ancient fayre, with communal kitchens, free bands and free love.'

'As opposed to overpriced love.'

'But in 1985 it all came to a horrible end. The government banned the festival. They set up roadblocks and pretty soon there were pitched battles with the police. It was horrible, Shanti. And inevitably the stones became a kind of Holy Grail. Like a symbol of the division in society. Maybe you've heard the phrase "Avenge the Henge"?'

'I have now.'

'Finch and his good lady Tiggy Antrobus-Lovell-Finch were in residence at Lovell Court. The estate was farmed in a very commercial way in those days, and they were leading the life of the privileged aristocracy with their teenage son, who was home from boarding school.'

'Quentin.'

'Meanwhile, in his library van, Silas was amongst a convoy of about a hundred and forty vehicles that were attempting to reach Stonehenge. Following orders from above, the local police had prepared an ambush ...'

'Good grief. Benno's father.'

'Perhaps. Anyway, it was an exceptionally hot summer and things escalated rapidly. The police forced the convoy off the main road onto country lanes. The travellers had nowhere to go, so someone opened a gate and they drove onto farmland – a bean field, in fact ...'

'... which belonged to Hector Lovell-Finch.'

'Call it serendipity or call it karma, but Silas and his friends ended up on the Lovell Court estate. They set up camp in the field, with all the children playing, and that evening, the twelfth earl drove down in his Land Rover to meet them. According to Silas, he was all smiles and benevolence. As I said, Silas has the ability to read people, and he described Finch as a big man with a big heart. Although they inhabited different worlds, there was an immediate connection between the Tory squire and the nomadic librarian. Finch realised that these were simply poor families down on their luck and he wanted to help. But at his side was his teenage son, and Silas says he'll never forget the hatred in Quentin's eyes when he saw the travellers on the family land.'

'But Finch let them stay?'

'He did better than that. He brought down trailer loads of provisions. Set up portable toilets and running water. He understood that most of the travellers were peaceful folk who presented no threat.'

'Most of them?'

'Silas admitted that there were a few anarchists and trouble-makers who were eventually asked to leave.'

Caine paused to rummage in the paper carrier bags that Benno had ordered from the kitchens. He handed Shanti a BLT.

'Good old Benno,' said Shanti. 'Jesus, Caine, what have you got there?'

'It's delicious. Bean sandwich.'

'I don't care what it's been, what is it now?'

'That's really very funny, Shanti.'

'So this was Finch's conversion?'

'The epiphany took place the following day. Before first light, around a hundred officers came creeping through the trees, with dogs and batons. All the travellers were asleep, including Silas in his library van. He was woken by glass crashing on his bed, police officers yelling and children screaming. He believes the officers used paramilitary techniques imported from Northern Ireland.'

'Good grief. The bad old days of policing.'

'Silas claims he saw pregnant women hauled from their beds. He was dragged outside by his dreads and beaten unconscious.'

'Can he verify this, Caine?'

Caine poured tea from a flask and handed it to Shanti.

'I'll tell you something, Shant. When he invited me into his van, I noticed that several windows were boarded up, or repaired with polythene and tape.'

'But this happened in 1985 – you're telling me he never replaced the glass?'

'He says he's waiting for the police to repair his home.'

'Nice weekend job for you, Caine.'

'Silas ended up in hospital, in a coma for twelve hours. And more than five hundred travellers were detained. I googled it – this was the biggest mass arrest since the war. But here's the thing – Finch witnessed it all. He was horrified about what had taken place on his land. He called the press to bear witness, and he released a statement to say that the travellers were guests on his estate and the only trespassers were the authorities. He put up his own money for legal aid, and even testified in court. Many years later, the authorities were forced to pay damages, and a few senior officers lost their jobs—'

'Wait. Hold on there. This could be significant, couldn't it? I mean, Finch was clearly making enemies as far back as the 1980s.'

'We should definitely register that,' agreed Caine. 'Dawn suggested specialised knowledge, didn't she?'

'On the other hand, those cops would be old now,' said Shanti, handing back the cup and taking the wheel with both hands. 'And there was no DNA awareness until a few years later.'

'The Colin Pitchfork case, 1988,' said Caine. 'Anyway, that was Finch's epiphany. He visited the hospital every day, and when Silas had recovered a little, Finch personally drove him to Lovell Court, where many of his friends were still sheltering. Silas was incredibly touched to find that his library van had been towed up to the house. He told me that Finch had washed away the blood with his own hands. He had even replaced the books that had been thrown across the floor – in alphabetical order, according to Silas. From A for Angelou to Z for Zephaniah.'

'Very touching.'

'You know, I honestly think Finch was some kind of saint. He provided sanctuary to anyone who needed it. That's an extra-ordinary act of generosity.'

'Or maybe he was just bored with Tiggy. Presumably she wasn't pleased about this?'

'According to Silas, that was when the arguments began. To

be fair, I suppose it was hard for Tiggy. Her career was in the doldrums, her husband was questioning everything they had ever known and her home was filled with strangers. But Finch was on a crusade. He had seen this great injustice, which he thought of as state-sponsored ethnic cleansing.'

'That's a bit strong.'

'The travellers started receiving anonymous threats – they were told that the minute they stepped off the estate, they would be brutally punished.'

'Jeez. So they never left?'

'Exactly. Finch invited them to stay for as long as they wanted. They built the village and that was the beginning of the whole Evolutionary thing.'

'And the people who live there now are the original travellers?'

'Finch had the tricky task of evicting a few thugs and anarchists who didn't get the peaceful spirit. But apart from that, Evol grew organically over the years. Some of the older ones passed away. Others sold out to the man, as Silas put it – meaning they got jobs, I suppose. New arrivals came. Other people had children. It's beautiful really, Shanti. All those families working together to set up the wilding project, educating themselves about green politics, with Finch as the old Holly King. I think they found true happiness.'

'Except for Tiggy.'

'In the spring of 1986, Tiggy walked out of that big front door taking young Quentin with her. Finch was so exhausted by the tension that he went travelling . . .'

'. . . and ended up in Brazil.'

'He called it a late gap year. Don't forget that he had studied anthropology at Cambridge and had always dreamed of visiting

Brazil. He met Constanza at a conference in São Paulo and it was love at first sight.'

'Masako said they struggled with the hypocrisy of international flights.'

'But one day young Constanza walked up the drive of Lovell Court with a big suitcase. There was a romantic green marriage, and a few years later . . .'

'. . . along came Sky.'

'Could you stop for a moment?' said Caine as they entered a small village. 'The shop is open.'

'Run out of cigarettes?' said Shanti.

Caine hurried inside and she watched as he chatted amiably with the girl behind the counter. It seemed like a long time before he emerged, loaded with paper bags and an elaborate bouquet of red roses and pine cones dusted with silvery snow.

'For Tiggy,' he told her.

'That's very sweet, Caine.'

'Oh, and this is for you. I thought you needed cheering up.'

It was a miniature Christmas tree with a tiny reindeer on either side, which Caine set on the dashboard.

'It's Christmas, Shant. There's a little something for your mum and Paul too. I'll put them on the back seat. The lady told me we're only ten minutes from the nursing home. I must admit, I'm looking forward to meeting Tiggy Antrobus-Lovell-Finch. She's an intriguing character.'

'I need to make a confession,' said Shanti. 'I haven't read the Solstice Files – promise you won't tell Masako. I was so tired last night.'

Caine smiled and switched on the minuscule lights of the tree.

'In brief, Tiggy Antrobus was a teen debutante who was feted for her beauty. She hung out with people like Ken Russell and Antony Armstrong-Jones, and she even modelled for Biba. According to Masako, she also had small parts in several not very memorable films.'

'Try me. I bet Mum watched them.'

'Her most successful appearance was in an Anglo-German production called *Naked Vampire Women*. I watched a little last night. It all seems rather innocent.'

'I'm sure you researched it carefully.'

'At first she embraced life as the lady of the manor at Lovell Court – there were endless society balls and so on – but clearly she and Finch began to grow in different directions, and the divorce hit her very hard.'

'That's when she had the stroke?'

'When Finch heard, he was mortified and blamed himself for everything. Then the lawyers began buzzing like flies. Poor old Finch just threw up his hands and more or less let them take everything.'

'Except Lovell Court, of course, which was a bit more than I got after *my* divorce.'

'Yes, but imagine the upkeep . . .'

'There's no upkeep. The place has gone to rack and ruin.'

'Anyway, Finch became responsible for Quentin's school fees, and the divorce settlement and crippling nursing care for Tiggy cleaned him out completely.'

'A tragic story,' said Shanti. 'Looks like we've arrived. We're about to see where all that money went. Thanks for the Christmas tree, Caine. It's quite sweet actually.'

Chapter 20

The Once-a-Star Rest Home

Caine turned the highly polished brass door handle and they entered the opulent interior of the Once-a-Star Rest Home.

It was hot in there. Absurdly hot. Shanti felt her body being hauled from Arctic to oven.

The reception area was like the foyer of grand country hotel – all plush carpets and polished mahogany. A young man in a short-sleeved shirt with a bow tie stood smiling behind a wide desk. He wore a large name badge declaring: *Hello, my name is . . . JAMAL.*

'Welcome to Once-a-Star,' he said. 'How may I help?'

'Hi, Jamal,' said Caine. 'We're here to see Lady Antrobus-Lovell-Finch.'

He checked a screen.

'Ah yes, Matron has made a note. If you'll follow me, I'll take you through.'

'Sorry, but could we leave some of these clothes here?' asked Shanti. 'It's very warm.'

'No problem,' he said. 'The staff get used to it.'

Caine rested the bouquet on the counter and they began to peel off layers, handing them to Jamal, who hung them carefully on hangers in a closet behind the desk.

As they followed him along the heavily carpeted lobby, Shanti analysed the collective odour of the place: air freshener – Febreze, perhaps; the cloying stench of orchids from a vast bouquet on a plinth; disinfectant certainly, and urine too; over-cooked cabbage and undercooked mince; and the scent of damp dog from an overfed Labrador who slept near a tangle of walking frames and folded wheelchairs.

They passed an immaculately uniformed maid, who offered a deferential smile as she polished the balustrades of a mighty staircase. The background sounds were as complex as the smells: piped show tunes; the distant moan of vacuum cleaners; the swish of washing machines and the clatter of plates.

Jamal ushered them into a huge communal drawing room, populated by thirty or more venerable residents. Signed photos of smiling thespians in their heyday hung from the flocked walls. Shanti thought she recognised a few faces from Mum's movies, but she couldn't be sure.

Some slumbered in armchairs. Some played patience on padded trays. Others sat entranced by a bellowing television on which a black-and-white movie played.

Near an elaborate Christmas tree, a veteran pianist in a tuxedo tinkled the ivories, while a frail couple pirouetted languidly.

For every three or four residents, there was a uniformed member of staff – nurses, masseuses giving shoulder rubs, art therapists, and a solemn man like a valet or butler serving sherry from a tray.

An extraordinarily agile white-faced nonagenarian per-
formed strange slow movements in and out of the armchairs,
and it took Shanti a moment to realise that she was witnessing
a mime artist from a bygone age.

'Could you point out Tiggy?' asked Caine. 'We've never met
before.'

'Oh, Tiggy never sits with the other guests,' said Jamal. 'She
has her own apartment on the third floor.'

At the far end of the drawing room, they entered a lobby,
where Jamal pushed a button to call a lift.

'When you reach the third floor, turn right and you'll find
the apartment at the far end,' he told them as the doors parted.

'Thanks for your help,' said Caine.

'You're welcome,' Jamal replied. 'Although I'm afraid you're
wasting your time.'

More show tunes played in the elevator, where Shanti gazed
at her many reflections in the infinity mirrors of the walls. She
was so overheated that her shirt clung to her body.

'Jeez, look at the state of me,' she said.

'You look amazing,' said the million manifestations of Caine
with his countless bouquets. 'As you always do.'

At the end of the landing, the door was opened by a surly
matron.

'DIs Joyce and Caine to see Lady Antrobus,' said Shanti.

The woman looked them up and down as if excreting a
lemon.

'You don't look like police officers. Do you have some
identification?'

Shanti patted her pockets. 'I'm afraid I've left everything in
the lobby, but I assure you that's who we are.'

'Lady Antrobus will give you five minutes. Any longer will distress her. Please talk distinctly without shouting. I'll take those flowers – she's extremely allergic.'

They followed Matron's bulging white uniform into the extensive apartment, with its strangely retro colour theme of purple, moss green and orange. Shanti noticed a lavishly equipped kitchen. To the left, a gleaming bathroom with an array of rails and hoists. To the right, a splendid bedroom, with a huge poster of *Naked Vampire Women* above an adjustable bed.

They entered the central living space, which featured a sunken seating area, accessible by a ramp. At the far end, a set of French windows opened onto a snow-piled balcony, high above the grounds.

She was sitting in an olive-coloured recliner chair on a raised dais with her back to them, staring at the misty world below. On either side of the chair, a set of stands supported an array of drips, monitors and ventilators, each with a trailing spaghetti of tubes.

'Your visitors are here, madam,' said Matron loudly. 'I'm going to rotate the chair.'

She pushed a button and the chair revolved. Shanti lurched in alarm – the diminutive person who confronted them appeared at first to be a teenage girl. It took a long, confusing moment to unscramble the paradoxical phenomenon. Although Tiggy Antrobus-Lovell-Finch was a fragile lady in her late seventies, she chose, for reasons best known to herself, to dress like a seventeen-year-old actress of the 1960s: a psychedelic paisley blouse; mummified legs in a miniskirt; a smear of tangerine lipstick; eyelashes like tarantulas, and a flowing blonde wig.

The expression on her heavily plastered face was exactly as Quentin had described. Flummoxed. Befuddled. Discombobulated.

When Shanti had steadied herself, she said, 'Lady Antrobus
. . . I wonder if we might ask a few questions?'

Tiggy stared with vacant spidery eyes.

'You can ask as many questions as you like,' said Matron
sharply, 'but you won't get a response.'

It was Caine's turn to try.

'Tiggy,' he said softly, kneeling at her side, 'my name's
Vincent. I wanted to tell you how much I enjoyed *Naked Vampire
Women*.'

There was the faintest flutter of awareness.

'Naked . . .' said the old-young lady. 'Vamp . . .'

'Quentin tells me you'll be spending Christmas with him
and Petronella?' he said, taking the dappled claw of her hand.

'Quent . . .' she said.

'They have a new baby. Your granddaughter, Velveteen.'

'Velv . . .'

'The reason we're here,' said Caine, 'is to talk about Finch.'

At the mention of the name, there was a sudden cacophony
of bleeps and buzzers, and the corners of Tiggy's tangerine lips
turned downwards.

'Madam would like you to leave now,' said Matron, hurrying
forward.

'What? Hang on,' said Shanti. 'We've only just arrived. We've
driven miles, you know.'

'Can't you see?' she replied severely. 'Her blood pressure is
rising. You need to go.'

'Damn that matron,' said Shanti, as the Once-a-Star Rest Home
receded in the wing mirrors of the Saab. 'You were just establish-
ing a rapport.'

'I don't know about that,' said Caine. 'I think Tiggy was heavily medicated. It's sad to see anyone in that state, especially someone who was famed for her eloquence.'

'And her naked bloodsucking,' said Shanti.

'It was weird, wasn't it?' he said, setting the satnav for Stonehenge, and switching on the lights of the mini tree. 'It's as if she's trapped in the 1960s.'

'Suspended at the height of her fame,' agreed Shanti. 'But one way or another, we've just wasted an hour and a half of our precious time. Do you think we're actually getting anywhere, Caine? I mean, are we any closer to discovering who killed Finch?'

'You know the way these things work,' he replied calmly. 'The patient gathering of intel. The sifting of clues. The synthesis of elements, and then . . .'

'And then what?'

'And then it suddenly tumbles into place.'

'That tumbling needs to happen right now,' she said as she accelerated past a van abandoned in a snowdrift. 'You know what Mum told me? Paul has written me a letter.'

'He's a very sweet boy.'

'It's a letter of complaint.'

'Oh Shanti. I wish I could help.'

'You know how to help. Look at all that whiteness, Caine. There's a killer out there. We need to bring him in before something else happens . . . something utterly unspeakable.'

Chapter 21

DNA Don't Lie

'It's not up to the usual standards,' said Benno, arranging McDonald's bags on a table in the incident room. 'But it's the best I could get. Cheeseburgers, fries ... and doughnuts if you fancy one.'

'Jammy ones?' said Shanti.

'Yes, boss.'

With a shudder, Caine took a cardboard cup of tea and shuffled his chair away from the meaty aroma.

'Right. Fifteen-minute debrief,' said Shanti, peeling the lid from her coffee. 'Then Caine and I have an appointment with another POI – Professor Ned Tull. Dunster, you've been monitoring him. What have you got to report?'

The young constable laid down his burger, wiped his fingers and opened his notebook. 'Stakeout commenced at 09.14 hours when target emerges from dwelling and utilises visitor centre toilet facilities. 09.32, target travels approximately two miles to densely wooded area – he's on foot but pulling a wooden sledge.

PC Dunster continues observation for a further fifty-five minutes, employing binoculars and stealth. Grid references are available.'

'Cut to the chase, Dunster. What was he doing there?'

'Collecting firewood, ma'am. 10.27, target returns to dwelling at rear of visitor centre, where he proceeds to light a small bonfire. 10.55 to 12.30, target sits by fire, carving wooden toys.'

'Wooden toys? What are you talking about?'

'For his grandchildren,' said Caine. 'Look, I'm sure I mentioned that the professor will be spending Christmas with his family – Yule, as he calls it. And I suppose he's making presents. I bet they're beautiful.'

He took a spoonful from a tiny jar of Henge Hives Honey – *Beehive yourself at Christmas*, said the slogan.

'Hang on,' said Shanti. 'Are you saying he intends to leave the area?'

'As I mentioned, Ned has been invited to spend the holiday with his family.'

'His family? Why doesn't he *live* with his family?'

'I did explain this, Shanti. Around the time *Neolithic Neighbours* came to an end, there was some kind of tragic incident with their son. Ned's wife and teenage daughter moved out of the roundhouse to an apartment in Amesbury. The daughter is grown up now, with children of her own.'

'And where is the Professor at the moment?'

'Over in the museum area,' said Dunster.

'Unmonitored?'

'Shanti, this is absurd,' said Caine. 'I can tell you exactly what he's doing there – he's curating an exhibition of Neolithic figurines ready for reopening in the New Year. That's where I arranged to meet him. Isn't this a waste of police resources?'

'May I have permission to knock off now?' said Dunster.

'What's that? Oh, yes. On your way, Dunster,' said Shanti.

'Thank you,' he said. 'Merry Christmas, ma'am. Merry Christmas everyone.'

'Yeah. Right. Merry . . . you know . . .'

Dunster headed rapidly for the door, where he almost collided with Masako, who was entering at speed.

'If that girl says "so". . .' muttered Shanti.

'So,' said Masako, waving a sheaf of papers. 'Here's the prelim pathology report, hot off the press.'

She handed the document to Shanti, who scanned it rapidly.

'It looks like Dawn was correct. The throat injury was indeed caused by that axe – they found additional fragments of flint embedded in the wound. But it's doubtful that's what killed him.'

She handed the report to her colleague.

'I hate to say I told you so,' said Caine. 'But the pathologist is confirming my theory that the wound may have been ceremonial or ritualistic in nature.'

'But if the axe didn't kill him, what did?' asked Benno.

'It says that a full toxicology report will be forthcoming,' said Caine. 'I guess we'll have to wait.'

'But in the meantime,' said Masako dramatically, 'there's been another key development. I had a video call with the guys at the lab. As you know, they've been running tests on Finch's clothing and the hatchet Dawn Knightley discovered.'

'They found DNA?' asked Shanti hopefully

'So, the clothing was saturated with snow, meaning DNA results were confused. But the hatchet was a gold mine! The lab examined the finger marks, and they discovered a single DNA profile. They submitted their results to the national DNA database, which generated a clear match.'

'Don't keep us in suspense,' said Shanti.

'The DNA on the hatchet is a perfect match for Professor Ned Tull, as are the fingerprints, which have an unusually greasy and sooty quality. The chances of that DNA coming from someone else are a billion to one.'

Shanti leapt to her feet.

'Bingo!' she shouted. 'Suddenly everything tumbles into place, isn't that what you said, Caine? But on this occasion, your instincts were badly mistaken.'

'Hold on, Shanti . . .'

'The good news for us is that this case could be wrapped up by the end of the day. The bad news for Tull is he could be trading a little round room for a little square room.'

'I agree, this doesn't look good for Ned,' said Caine. 'But it's not enough to—'

'Not enough? First rule of policing – DNA don't lie.'

'But we've just established that the hatchet didn't deal the fatal blow. Besides, we have to ask ourselves *why*. Why on earth would Ned want to kill Finch?'

'That's what we're about to find out,' said Shanti, hauling on her jacket. 'That's the exact question we're going to pose to Professor Tull. Why did he murder Hector Lovell-Finch? Why did he place him on that trilothing?'

She checked her bag for pepper spray and handcuffs.

'Will you require backup, boss?' asked Benno.

'I think we've got a handle on this,' she said. 'A greasy wooden handle with Tull's fingerprints all over it.'

Chapter 22

The Tragic Tale of Talin Tull

They stood side by side in the dark centre of Stonehenge as the millennia swirled around; their faces illuminated by dreamily tumbling snowflakes.

'Where the hell are we?' said Shanti.

'We're in the Mesolithic period. Around 9000 BC. It's the winter solstice and we're watching the construction of Stonehenge. You can see that it started as a simple wooden circle, much like the one at Woodhenge—'

'I mean where are we really, Caine?'

'Oh, I see. They call this the Stonehenge Experience. Isn't it great? It's a panoramic diorama in CGI. In a minute we'll begin to travel through the seasons.'

'For Christ's sake, will you stop wittering? Now listen, I've just had a thought. Why were Tull's fingerprints and DNA on the national database in the first place?'

'I have no idea.'

'There can only be one reason – he's a career criminal.'

'Ah, I don't think so, Shant. I'll admit it's odd, but I'm sure there's an innocent explanation.'

'Well, where is he then? Where is your innocent friend? I thought you arranged to meet him here.'

'He's probably in one of the next rooms setting up his exhibit. You wait, there are some fantastic displays through there.'

'Oh are there? Perhaps there's a question-and-answer sheet we can fill in on the way.'

'I—'

'Don't answer that, Caine. Just assume everything I say to you is sarcastic and we'll save a lot of time.'

They crept stealthily through the shadowy museum, where illuminated cabinets glowed. All around were bones, bowls, skulls, skeletons and life-sized figures of hirsute people with protruding brows.

'Looks at these waxworks, Shanti. He's a Neanderthal, I think. It's incredibly skilful how they bring our ancestors to life. Now we're moving into the Neolithic era.'

'Skilful? They're ridiculously over the top. Look at this one – the hairy face, the manky furs. I swear I've seen him drinking lighter fluid outside Camden Tube station.'

'Ah, this is Professor Tull, Shanti. I thought we'd find you here, Ned. How are you?'

He was deeply immersed in the task of arranging figurines on a glass shelf within a cabinet. Slowly and carefully he closed the cabinet door and nodded sadly at the DIs.

'Ned,' said Caine, 'I'd like you to meet my colleague and best friend, Shanti Joyce.'

Tull removed a white glove and reached out a grimy hand, which Shanti ignored.

'Professor Tull,' she said, 'I need you to come with us to answer some vital questions. On record, if you don't mind.'

'Of course,' said Tull. 'I'll be with you as soon as I've locked the cabinet.'

They sat beneath a high wall decorated with famous quotations about Stonehenge. Shanti and Caine on folding chairs, Tull, with his grey plaited beard, hide trousers and hand-stitched boots, on a small bench. Above his head were the words: *'What is Stonehenge? It is the roofless past.' Siegfried Sassoon, soldier and poet, 1928.*

Having cautioned the professor and recorded the particulars of the interview, Shanti began. 'It is my understanding that you knew the deceased?'

'As I explained to Vincent, Finch attended a few of my ancient craft workshops, and we sometimes waved at each other on the plains. I used to see him driving around on his magnetometer. Although we inhabited different worlds, we had shared passions. I respected him.'

'And his son, Quentin Lovell-Finch – do you know him?'

'I know who he is, but we've never met.'

'Where were you at dawn yesterday, Tuesday the twenty-first of December?'

'Waking up in the roundhouse, I suppose.'

'You suppose? You have no alibi?'

'I live alone. I wake at first light.'

'I'd like to inspect your hands, if I may?'

He looked at her quizzically, then reached out both arms, showing first the backs of his hands, then the palms.

'For the record,' said Shanti, 'the professor is compliant. His hands and nails are uncommonly sooty and greasy.'

'Or perhaps yours are uncommonly clean,' he said.

'Professor Tull, have you ever had a run-in with the law?' continued Shanti. 'Specifically, have you ever been asked to supply fingerprints or DNA swabs?'

'Yes. Both those things.'

'Right. And why was that?'

A silence fell in the museum, as deep as time itself. Caine saw a tear build in the corner of Tull's eye.

'You want to know the story?' he asked.

'If it will help to clarify your position,' said Shanti.

'I suppose there's no harm in telling. You keep these things locked away like exhibits in glass cases, but they do no good in there. Where to start . . .'

'Why don't you begin with *Neolithic Neighbours?*' urged Caine gently.

A faint smile passed over the craggy landscape of Tull's face.

'The 1980s and '90s were the happiest time of my life. That's when we constructed the Neolithic village, my time-team colleagues and I. It was a unique experiment, using nothing but contemporaneous tools and materials. Imagine it! The kids running in and out of the roundhouses without a care in the world. The whole place bustling with activity – dogs, chickens, pigs and a small tribe of like-minded friends. What I remember when I look back is the smiles – the smiles on all our faces. And when a TV company approached us, I discovered I had another gift – not just as an archaeologist and craftsman, I found I was a storyteller too. The camera was my audience.'

'You captivated a generation,' said Caine. 'I learned more from *Neolithic Neighbours* than from any history lesson at school.'

'It's kind of you to say so.'

'Nothing but the truth, Ned.'

'Over the years, Pamela and I watched our son and daughter grow into young warriors – so healthy and wild and free. It was like a run of good fortune that would never end.' As he spoke, Tull's face twisted into a mask of despair. 'And then one fateful August morning, it all came to a bitter end. My lad, Talin, had just turned eighteen. He had developed a bit of a thing for a Dutch archaeology student who was doing her work experience with us. All very innocent, although Pamela and I weren't especially keen – we knew she would have to leave and they'd both be heartbroken. But you can't stop them at that age. Love conquers all. Talin and the girl used to sneak off together, foraging on the plains. And then one day . . . they never returned.'

A haunted look lingered in his eyes.

'We searched for hours. The whole village. Eventually the police arrived. We were all questioned by Wiltshire Constabulary, including me, Pamela and our daughter, Aylin. Every member of the group willingly supplied DNA and fingerprints.

'So now you know. After five weeks, your lot – the police – concluded that Talin and the girl were consenting adults who had willingly absconded together. The Dutch police got involved too, but nothing was ever found. With no sign of the young lovers and an absence of bodies, the case was eventually dropped.'

'I'm so sorry,' said Caine.

'I never accepted it,' said Tull forcefully. 'I wasn't satisfied with that conclusion. My boy would never have run off like that. But what *was* the answer? The lad was gone. I spent day after day walking the plains. In a week, my hair and beard turned white. I went a little mad, I expect. I convinced myself that they had been swallowed up by the stones. That each of those mega-liths contained some poor lost soul.'

Caine's eyes were drawn to another quotation above Tull's head: *To all those questions beginning "Why?" there is but one answer: We do not know and probably never shall.*

'And that's the thing with bad luck,' continued Tull. 'Once it starts, it never ends. The production company were determined to keep the story out of the press, so *Neolithic Neighbours* was quietly cancelled. Even worse, the incident generated so much ill will within the group that the community fell apart. Not long afterwards, Pamela and Aylin left too. And who can blame them?

'But I couldn't leave. I had built that place. The stones were my life. I convinced English Heritage that I could provide ancient craft workshops and continue my research. I had to stay, see? My lad's still out there. How can I leave?'

He placed his shaggy head in his sooty hands and wept.

In a moment, Caine had scuttled across to the bench to comfort the wretched man, who sobbed and shuddered, wiping his nose on the fur of his sleeve.

'I am deeply sorry for your loss,' said Shanti at last. 'I have a son of my own, so I can empathise a little.'

'Thank you. How old is your boy?'

'He's eight.'

'Tell me about him.'

'Well, maybe another time, Professor. I don't want to give you false hope, but it strikes me that if we can solve the murder of Hector Lovell-Finch, it may shed some light on your son's dis-appearance. We might be prepared to reopen Talin's case in the hope of bringing some closure.'

'Thank you,' said Tull, with almost pathetic gratitude. 'I know in my heart that Talin is dead, but if I could only lay him to rest, I could begin to move on. And if I can help to solve Finch's murder, I will be only too glad to help. He was a good man.'

'I'm pleased to hear that, Professor. So, could I ask you to look carefully at this image?'

She changed places with Caine, taking a seat on the little bench, where she became aware of Tull's musky animal odour.

The professor took the phone in his hands, blinking at the harsh light of the screen.

'It's a facsimile of a Neolithic axe hammer,' he said.

'Did you make this implement, Professor?'

'It's possible. The blade has been bound with hide, which is something I do. On the other hand, there's an antler ring on the shoulder of the haft, which is a nice touch but not really my style.' He returned the phone to Shanti, who noticed greasy fingerprints on the screen. 'In general, it's an attractive tool, but not quite up to my standards. There's blood on the blade, did you notice that?'

'We are aware of it.'

With a look of horrified realisation, Tull said, 'Oh! You're not telling me that's Finch's blood?'

Shanti ignored the question. 'I'm wondering why this instrument should carry your fingerprints and DNA on the handle, Professor?'

After a while, Tull said, 'English Heritage provide me with a storage unit at the back of the visitor centre. You can look for yourself. It's the last door in the row. There's a combination lock that I set to the date Talin went missing, so I'll never forget the number. You'll find a large shelf unit in there stacked with plastic boxes. And almost every one of those boxes is packed with replicas of prehistoric implements, including hand axes similar to the one you just showed me. As I keep telling you, I've taught hundreds of ancient craft workshops to countless visitors over the years, including Finch himself. Sometimes people take the implements home with them, and sometimes I store them in those boxes, which presumably means – although I've never thought about it up till now – that every one of them must carry my fingerprints and DNA.'

'Right. OK, thank you. I can assure you that we will explore all avenues. Who else has access to the storage unit?'

'Only the security team at GoodGuys, and English Heritage, who are effectively my landlord.'

'I would ask you to stay out of that storage unit until we give you permission. I understand you intend to spend Christmas with your family?'

'Aylin will collect me tomorrow. Is that a problem?'

'For the time being you are at liberty to go where you please. However, I would ask you to leave contact details with our team.'

As Shanti concluded the interview and Tull shuffled into the dark museum, Caine noticed another quotation on the wall: *Pile of Stone-henge! So proud to hint yet keep thy secrets ...' William Wordsworth, 1794.*

'Poor old Ned,' said Caine as they emerged into the premature night. 'To lose your son in that baffling way. It's unthinkable.'

'He was good,' said Shanti. 'He's either the most proficient liar I've ever met, or—'

'Or my instincts were right?'

'Damn you, Caine. I'm still not excluding him. He was chewing gum, did you notice that? That's not very prehistoric, is it?'

'The gum is interesting. I remember him chewing gum on *Neolithic Neighbours*. He used to say that our ancestors chewed birch tar – the same sticky resin they used to adhere axe or arrow heads. Of course, they didn't have the sugar craving that we do now ...'

'Nobody in their right mind goes around dressed like that. The man's a fool.'

'A wise fool, Shanti.'

'I want that storage unit checked over millimetre by millimetre.'

'Of course you do. Because an intruder may have crept inside to steal one of those hatchets.'

The night was astonishingly clear. The snowflakes were slow and sparse, but so large you could almost make out their intricate geometry.

Far across the plains, the mysterious stones glowed iridescent. Caine exhaled loudly, and the flaps of his hat fell backwards as he gazed at the cosmic colander of the night.

'It's so romantic,' he said. 'Just you and me floating in the universe.'

'Don't be a snowflake, Caine.'

'We're all snowflakes, Shanti.'

'You see, you say these random things, but what does that even mean?'

'It means that each of us is unique and perfect, but our lives are ephemeral.'

'I suppose that's almost clever.'

'Don't tell me you never think about that night by the bay. Or the time we shared my tent at Glastonbury ...'

'See those stones over there, Caine? They're ancient history, right? Just like any relationship that might exist in your fevered imagination.'

'I understand why you do this, Shant. You need to separate work from love.'

'Love? Who said anything about love? Right, it's like Siberia out here. I'm heading back to the Stonehenge Tavern for a long soak and an early night.'

A flicker of a memory of a party. An invitation to an officers' ball.

'Of course,' said Caine. 'I'll walk you to the car. Would it help to have a quick review of Operation Solstice? We could draw up a list of our protagonists.'

'Fine. But don't stand too close – you're very hairy and rather pungent. Right, I'll start … First we have the deceased, Lord Hector Lovell-Finch.'

'The Holly King.'

'Then we have his usurped son, Quentin Lovell-Finch.'

'The Politician.'

'Why are you doing that, Caine?'

'Doing what?'

'Using those weird terms – the Holly King, The Politician? This isn't *Game of Thrones*.'

'I think it was that dream. Everyone seems like a Jungian archetype.'

'You're a very odd cop, Caine. Did anyone ever tell you that?'

'You've mentioned it before.'

'Next we have the daughter of the deceased, Sky Lovell-Finch.'

'The Young Hero, or the Warrior Princess. Which do you prefer?'

'Then Finch's widow, Constanza.'

'The Herbalist.'

'Also your friend Silas.'

'The Old Librarian . . . wonderful man.'

'I suppose we should include Tiggy Antrobus-Lovell-Finch. Quentin described her as flummoxed, befuddled and discombobulated.'

'Should we call her the Deposed Diva?'

'Call her what you like. And last – and in many ways least – your shaggy pal Professor Ned Tull, also known as the Accused.'

'The Wise Fool. It's so tragic, Shanti. I'd love to help him find the truth about his son.'

A tiny part of her cried for her own lost son, but she quickly admonished herself. Paul was alive and well. She'd see him very soon for too many sweets and too much Christmas TV.

She pointed the key at the car, but there was only a dull clunk. She tried again, but the locking system was frozen. Damn it! How she longed to be home. She did not want to be here on these haunted plains, trying to solve some impossible crime.

Very gently, Caine took the fob from her numb fingers. He turned it over in his hand and slid out a traditional-style key that was concealed inside. This he slid into the lock, and with one firm twist, the door was open.

Damn him. Damn Caine. Why was he always so composed?

'Sleep tight, Shanti,' he said. 'Tomorrow everything will tumble into place.'

'Here,' she said, tossing over the blanket he had used to dry the prodigal hound. 'You'll find a washing machine in the shower block.'

Chapter 23

You Sentient Beings

As she soaked in a chin-deep bath, a few degrees below boiling, Shanti sipped another glass of champagne.

The muffled sound of swooning sax and thumping bass drifted through the floorboards, as the Flirty Fusiliers tuned up in the lounge bar below.

When she emerged, she squeezed herself into a blood-red satin dress and a murderous pair of red stilettos. As she dried her hair, she viewed herself in the full-length mirror of the wardrobe. The zip at the back was liable to burst and take out a man's eye, but holy moly, she didn't look too damned shabby.

In fact, she fully deserved another glass of that Moët. It was Christmas, after all.

She looked again at the handwritten note she had discovered propped against the ice bucket on the table in her room. The inscription was strangely childlike, shaky and replete with exclamation marks.

enjoy the bubbly!! cu on the dance floor at 10!
troy x
ps got a helluva finch fable for u!!!

All these items – the dress, the shoes, the hairdryer, the make-up – she'd kept hidden from Caine's prying eyes in a plastic carrier bag concealed beneath a battering ram in the boot of the Saab.

Not that Caine would even register the shit-hot dress if she wore it to a murder scene. If he were scandalised by anything, it would be the reckless employment of a single-use carrier bag.

But now Caine was snoring in a sooty shack with his hirsute hut-mate. And she was off to the ball with the oh-so-dashing Major Troy McAble. All right, don't judge me, she told her reprimanding reflection – it's all part of a highly strategic police operation. McAble might not be the brightest bulb on the Christmas tree, but there was a chance he could be massaged for valuable intel about Hector Lovell-Finch.

And besides, a few slow dances at the Everkill Officers' Ball wasn't a crime. Think of it as compensation for the hardships she'd had to endure in the chilly wind with Caine.

Hilariously, the journos failed to recognise her as she tottered downstairs and squeezed through the public bar. A few eyed her salaciously, but most were too drunk to care.

A couple of squaddies at the door were enforcing a much-appreciated no-paps policy. All she had to do was flash a smile and the gold-trimmed invite, and she was inside the lounge bar, which had been transformed into a glittering winter wonderland. A mirror ball rotated on the ceiling, sending a galaxy of shooting stars into the seductive shadows. On the stage, a five-piece band in tartan tuxes and Santa hats played sultry Christmas medleys, with much brushing percussion and doo-wop vocal harmony.

Troy, close-cropped and immaculate in tuxedo and bow tie, was holding court at the very epicentre of the room, laughing uproariously with a cohort of back-slapping comrades in identical attire.

As Shanti walked across the dance floor, his conversation faltered and ceased. He turned to her as if he had suddenly noticed something utterly captivating. And the captivating thing, she realised with a complicated shudder, was Shanti Joyce . . .

Returning to the roundhouse, Caine shared a brief meal with Ned at the fireside, but the old man was too tired to sit up and talk. His daughter was coming to collect him in the morning, and already the thought of the lights and the children's electronic gizmos was bringing on an early migraine.

Caine left him to rest, but it was too cold to sit outside. The truth was that this distressing case was making him restless and uncentred. It came to him that he had not meditated for two days.

Nodding at a couple of the GoodGuys security team out on patrol, he stepped into the warmth of the visitor centre. To his relief, he found the incident room unoccupied and almost dark. Having located a quiet corner, he made himself comfortable, cross-legged on the floor. After a few minutes of slow breathing, his eyes closed and he began to dive inwards, aware of accumulated tension like a ball of elastic bands.

Long ago in Thailand, his master, Tu, had taught him that the way to release 'that which no longer serves you', was to simply sit with it. Do not judge. Do not fight. Just be the watcher, as thoughts diminished like clouds in a clear sky.

There had been a wonderful occasion when old man Tu had chosen him out of all the novices to receive a gift – a beautiful book of Buddhist texts. But before he handed it over, he had read aloud a particular text by the sage Cheng-Li, encouraging his students to learn it by heart: *You sentient beings who seek deliverance, why do you not let go? When sad, let go of the cause of sadness. When covetous or lustful, let go of the object of desire . . .*

How profound and simple the advice had seemed to the young Caine. But now he could not let go. What a cruel trick the universe had played. Of the billions of sentient beings on this planet, he was destined to work with the one who fixated him most.

'Billy No-Mates' she had called him. And as ever, she had put her finger firmly on the button of truth. Caine pretended that Christmas meant nothing to him, but the very opposite was true. These traditional holidays highlighted the fractured nature of his own family. The only person who would remember him on Christmas Day would be his elusive half-sister, Misty, who was currently travelling in India, Thailand or Indonesia with one or more of her many friends. And the worst thing about Christmas was that it forced Caine to remember painful things, long buried, about his father . . . and yes, his brother too.

When sad, let go of the cause of sadness . . .

He was not cut out to be a DI. He had never learned the trick of disassociating from the pain of others. He was a cop who felt too much for his own good.

His mind was made up. As soon as this case was over, he would truly let go of everything – police work, his family and, most painfully, Shanti too. After all, we can only lose what we cling to.

Now he longed for the seclusion of his cabin. He was better off alone.

But first there was the case in hand. When he had gazed at the extraordinary face of the Holly King, he had been moved to the core of his being, and he had vowed to Finch, to Sky, to Constanza, to Ned, to Shanti that he would seek justice in this convoluted case.

As he tumbled further into meditation, he felt the subtle and familiar process of his subconscious doing what it did best – slowly and intuitively piecing together the elements of the puzzle. It was almost as if he were following clues like footsteps through a swirling blizzard. All he had to do was push steadfastly forward, one step at a time, using his inner wisdom as his guide. Up ahead, he could make out blurry forms in the ether. The murderer was there, he was sure of it, carrying out unspeakable deeds. One of the shadowy figures turned towards him, and here, at the deepest point of his meditation, Caine sensed he was about to look on the face of the killer . . .

Affectionately squeezing the shoulder of the officer at his side, Troy McAble excused himself from his comrades. Caressing his moustache and grinning radiantly, he aimed himself at Shanti like a missile towards its target.

'Well hello, Goddess Shantala,' he intoned, lifting her hand and touching it to his furry lip.

She felt that conflict again – flattered, yet vomity in her mouth. And all the while, Troy gawped at her in wonder, as if Woman was a New Thing. Which perhaps it was.

'You look absolutely ... Dammit! What's the adjective I'm searching for?'

'Shrink-wrapped? Well basted?'

'No. No, that's not it at all. Look, would you hang on for just one second?' He turned and beckoned to the Santa-topped lead guitarist, who bent down from the stage. Troy whispered into his ear; the musician nodded, and immediately the Flirty Fusiliers launched into a cheeky cheek-to-cheek version of the James Blunt classic.

'There we are,' Troy told her. 'That's the word I was searching for – *You're beautiful. You're beautiful, it's true . . . I saw your face in a crowded place . . .*'

In all the world, in all the history of musicology, Shanti loathed that song more than any other. It was the song her ex had played the first time they met. 'Your song', he had called it, just like every douchebag man called it. He'd played it at their wedding too, and it was the first song she deleted from her playlist when she finally escaped with Paul.

More and more people swarmed into the large, low-ceilinged room. There were women too, but the night belonged to Troy and his brave brethren, who gave the appearance of men who had seen it all and lived to tell the tale. Cool. Confident. In command. Arrogant men who had cracked this amusing thing called life.

As they orbited the dance floor, Troy told her that the event was in a good cause – every year the officers raised a tidy sum for charity. Fundraising was something the officers of Everkill garrison were famous for. At midnight, there would be a grand raffle, and he very much hoped that as his guest, Shantala would join him on the stage to draw the winning tickets. The prizes were out of this world!

186

As the band launched into 'Driving Home for Christmas', Troy loosened his bow tie and handed his jacket to a passing minion – 'Don't crumple it, man!' – to reveal a tight-fitting dress shirt and a torso as toned as a tank turret.

He had taken dancing lessons during a tour of Afghanistan, he explained. You needed something to take your mind off the hell and the sand. Now, in the lounge bar of the Stonehenge Tavern, he began to shimmy and gyrate, glancing approvingly at the artistic movements of his own gleaming shoes.

And as they swayed, they were waited on. Numerous lower-ranking soldiers materialised with hors d'oeuvres and a sickly-sweet cocktail called a Howitzer – guaranteed to blow your head off, in the most pleasant way possible!

'Shouldn't really,' said Troy, downing one glass after another. 'Doesn't mix with the meds. But if you can't let your hair down at Crimbo . . .'

'Meds?' enquired Shanti above the music

'Nothing really. Prozac. Seroxat. Zoloft. Effexor. Helps with the heebie-jeebies. Most of the lads have a touch of the old PTSD. Back in the day, no one talked about it, but now the therapists encourage us to bare our souls.'

'I'm sorry to hear that.'

'Not a problem. But that's why we prefer our own band tonight. No sudden bangs. Otherwise you'd have every man jack in the room diving for cover or kicking out the windows. You keep looking around, Shantala – is there something you want?'

What Shanti wanted was not to be here. The place was horribly oppressive. She had already drunk too much, and McAble was dancing way too close. His gym-ripped body seemed fake and vain, like the man himself. But amidst the blur, she remembered her job.

'I'd like to know about Finch,' she yelled.

'You'd like a little pinch?'

'About Finch.'

'Don't you people ever take time off? Even the Great War paused for Crimbo.'

'Your note said you had a story about him?'

'More of a ruse to entice you, because I knew you'd love it when you got here.'

'A helluva Finch fable, you said.'

'Did I write that? That's rather good, isn't it? But we don't want to talk about that old peacenik . . . Mmm, this one's a classic . . . "When a Man Loves a Woman" . . .'

'All right, Major,' said Shanti, suddenly exasperated and exhausted. 'Let's call it a night. I'll be in touch in the morning.'

'Hey, you're no fun. Very well, I'll tell you the story. I'll tell you how I hunted down Finch in a jeep and pinned him to the ground . . . It was an absolute hoot!'

All the clues had led him here. In the swirling depths of his meditation, the killer turned towards him. 'Show me your face,' said Caine.

But at that instant, his reverie was disturbed. A remote part of his mind became aware that someone had entered the incident room and was walking quietly towards him. Now he sensed that they were standing silently, watching his meditation.

It took a supreme effort to haul himself upwards into consciousness.

'I'm so sorry,' she said. 'I didn't mean to disturb you.'

With eyes half closed, he smiled gently. Masako was not to blame.

'It's fine,' he said 'You're working late. How can I help?'

Her arms were piled with files and a laptop, her young face glowing with enthusiasm.

'Is it OK to talk?' She pulled up a chair to face Caine, who remained cross-legged on the floor.

'Of course. I was taking a moment to—'

'So, the toxicology report came through. It's not for me to judge, but I'd say this is a game-changer.'

When Caine's vision came into focus, he saw that she was handing him an official-looking document, which somehow he could not take. It seemed to epitomise the incompatibility of his dual lives.

'Could you paraphrase it for me, Masako?'

'Sure. The results show that Finch suffered respiratory collapse caused by the ingestion of a substance called ... erm, *Conium maculatum*. Does that mean anything to you?'

He hauled himself to his feet and took a chair opposite the girl.

'Hemlock,' he said. '*Conium maculatum* is hemlock. I can't think how I know this, but hemlock is a deadly poison, which grows profusely in this part of the world.'

'That's impressive,' exclaimed Masako. 'If I can't google something, I'm lost.'

'My brain has a tendency to store useless information.'

'But it's obviously not useless!' She beamed at him as if he were an idol.

'Listen, it's very late, Masako. I'm sure you need to get some sleep.'

'You too,' she said. 'You look tired.'

'I'm a little restless at the moment. But you're right – this is an important development. I'm going to call Shanti straight away. Thank you, Masako, your work has been invaluable.'

'No need to thank me. It's the most exciting thing I've ever done.' She rose to her feet, gathering her files and laptop.

'Sleep well,' said Caine.

She turned and looked at him shyly.

'So, I hope you won't take this the wrong way, but I think you're pretty awesome, DI Caine.'

He felt astonished. Tongue-tied.

When she had gone, he attempted to resume the meditation, but it was not there. Instead, his head churned. He called Shanti's phone, but there was no answer. He called again. Left a voice-mail. Sent a text . . .

'Look at my hands!' hollered McAble above the relentless rhythms and whooping dancers. 'No shaking, see. Must be the Howitzers!'

'Listen, Troy,' yelled Shanti. 'This is absolutely crucial . . . I need you to tell me everything you know about Finch.'

'You're certainly persistent,' shouted McAble. 'Obsessive almost. But I can barely hear myself think.'

Taking his steely arm, Shanti steered him towards the windows at far end of the lounge bar, where it was a little less deafening.

'I've got a feeling you know more than you're letting on,' she said.

'All right, I'll tell all,' he said, swaying from side to side with his hands on her shoulders. 'But you'll need to dance closer – tinnitus, remember.'

Her instinct was to shove him firmly away, but this wasn't about her. It was about Finch.

'Picture the scene,' said McAble melodramatically. 'It's the passing-out parade. Two hundred cadets lined up on the parade ground in front of the general and his wife. All the families enjoying the sunshine. Military band in full swing. The chaplain delivers a sermon. Local press are there too. Cadets going through their paces. Sergeant major yelling commands. Plenty of arm-swinging. Eyes right! Wonderful stuff! And then suddenly . . .'

'Suddenly?'

'Suddenly a sodding great green man comes wobbling across the parade ground on a bicycle. He pedals directly between the sergeant major and the cadets and he's holding a massive great placard. Band stops playing. You can hear a pin drop as Finch trundles right in front of the sergeant major and clear as a bell says a single word: "FASCIST!" When we've gathered our senses, a few soldiers give chase, but Finch gives them the slip and takes off on his bike. Guess where I am?'

'I have no idea.'

'Only sitting at the wheel of a jeep, with half a dozen soldiers on board. We set off in hot pursuit – in and out of the Nissen huts. Just like the hunt after a fox . . . Taroooh!' He imitated a hunting horn.

He was staggeringly drunk, Shanti realised. And leaning on her so heavily, she was almost propping up his brawny body.

'It takes nearly ten minutes to flush him out,' he slurred into her ear. 'Then we manage to chase him onto the plains. I'm driving the jeep alongside the bike. Four men leap out and we finally bring him to ground. Nearly died laughing.'

'When was this?' she said, backing away as far as she was able.

'A few months ago. End of summer. I put Finch under arrest and the parade was concluded without further ado. Unfortunately, it made headline news in all the local papers, which was rather humiliating for Everkill. Finch gets away with a fifty-quid fine for trespass. Bloody funny, though! We've still got the placard in the mess. Sort of souvenir.'

'What does it say?'

'What does who say?'

'The placard. What's written on it?'

'Oh, right. Well, on one side it says AVENGE THE HENGE! and on the other it says SAVE THE SUNRISE!'

'What does save the sunrise mean?'

'Oh, Finch was terribly worked up about a building he claimed blocked the solstice sunrise. It was all a bit of a lark. Some of the lads were provoking him, but he didn't see the funny side. Too bloody intense, these tree-huggers.'

'It sounds like you hated him.'

'Me? Hate him? Not me. I get along with everyone, Shantala. But a few people I know would have strung him up by his shaggy beard.'

'Which people, Troy?'

'What do you want? A bloody list?'

'Do you know anything about an excavation that Finch was carrying out on the plains?'

'You'll have to come a little closer. You keep drifting away . . . Look, I spend a lot of time riding out there, so I often saw Finch hurtling about on that bloody stupid quad bike, which terrified the horses. And now you mention it, I did catch him digging a sodding great hole, which is absolute insanity on restricted land.'

'Why so?'

'Ordnance! The place is littered with it.'

'When did you last see him there?'

'Oh, I don't know. Quite recently.'

'When? Weeks ago? Months?'

'A few days back. Before the weather turned bad. He was furious with me – Finch was always furious with someone.'

'Why was he furious?'

'I suppose it was the stag . . . All right, hands up. I was doing a little shooting. I took down a big fellow. Finch didn't like that at all. Anti-hunting brigade, of course. But I reminded him he was the one in the wrong, digging up military land – you can go to prison for that, you know.'

'Right. It's imperative that I hear more. But this isn't the place.'

'I agree. You have a room, don't you? We could finish that champagne . . .'

'Jesus Christ,' she said sharply. 'I'm tired, Troy. I'm trying to solve a murder. I'm trying to be a mum. Can't you understand that?'

'Ooh, I like it when you're all severe.'

She steadied herself. 'I could come to the barracks tomorrow morning to take a statement. I wouldn't mind viewing the building you were talking about. And I definitely need to see the excavation site you mentioned.'

He had his hands on her waist now, and she was reminded of sweaty school discos with boys who suffered from what was flippantly known as wandering hand trouble, or WHT, which was, in retrospect, the fiddly fingertip of misogynistic entitlement. In every way, Major Troy McAble struck her as an over-inflated public schoolboy.

'By a stroke of luck, my Christmas leave begins at noon,' he burbled. 'I was planning to go riding. Do you like horses, Shantala? Bit of a pash. I'm chair of the Royal Everkill Saddle Club.'

'Bit of a class thing maybe. You either ride them or you bet on them.'

'And which do you do, Shantala?

'Neither. The last time I went near a horse was at Kentish Town City Farm when I was sixteen.'

'That recently?' he said. She felt his moustache nuzzle her ear, like a persistent hedgehog. A hedgehog that smelled of Hai Karate aftershave.

She needed to leave. This very minute.

'Shall we say ten thirty?' she said. 'Whereabouts do I go?'

'Centre East Block. First floor,' he replied like a dejected child. 'There's a rather phallic field gun parked outside.'

Something impelled her to look over Troy's beefy shoulder. Outside in the darkness, a face peered in through the black window – a wild face, with tortured eyes ... Caine!

She shoved McAble aside. 'I have to go.'

'Don't desert me, Goddess. Who will draw the raffle? Who will hand out the prizes?'

Chapter 24

Clonehenge

He was sitting on the miniature version of the same trilithon on which the body had been found.

'What the hell are you doing?' asked Shanti. 'You didn't walk, did you?'

His eyes were moist in the moonlight.

'I'm sorry,' he said. 'You go back in. It's right that you should enjoy yourself.'

She hobbled around the henge to confront him, her heels spearing the snow with every step.

'What? Wait . . . You don't think McAble and I . . .?'

Caine turned his face away, as if it was too painful to look at her. 'You were kissing him, Shant.'

'Jesus! I absolutely was not kissing anyone. If you want to know the truth, I was five seconds away from pepper-spraying him.'

Caine was doing something weird – unbuttoning his great-coat, which he wrapped carefully around her shoulders.

'It's freezing,' he said quietly. 'You're hardly wearing anything.'

The coat did not smell of Hai Karate. It smelt of woodsmoke. It smelt of Caine.

'Listen to me,' she said. 'I understand how that must have looked, but I assure you it was entirely professional. Troy has tinnitus and I was gathering vital intel. In any case, what business is it of yours? I am a free, absolutely independent woman and I will do exactly what I please, when I please.'

'You're quite right, Shanti. I'm sorry.'

'Damn right, Caine. Even if I wanted to have passionate sex with Troy McAble – which I absolutely do not – on the raffle table, with the whole battalion watching, that would not be your issue.'

'*When sad, let go of the cause of sadness. When covetous or lustful, let go of the object of desire . . .*'

'What? What did you say? You're delirious. What are you even doing here?'

'I suppose he's everything I'm not.'

'Who is?'

'That man,' said Caine disdainfully. 'The soldier with the dickie bow and the ludicrous moustache.'

'Well that's not very Buddhist, is it? And I mean, look at the state of you. You look more like Ned Tull every day. Maybe you should ask Troy for a few grooming tips.'

'*Troy!* You keep calling him Troy . . .'

Caine was backing away from her, dressed incongruously in a hemp shirt, black jeans and the flying hat. His man bag hanging from one shoulder.

'What are you even doing here?' she asked again. 'Did Tull kick you out? Did you two have a tiff?'

'I came to tell you about a development in the case. The toxicology report came through.'

'Well why didn't you call me? You know, *push push, ring ring*. You do know how to use a phone, even if you pretend not to.'

'Check your call log, Shant . . .'

There were seven missed calls from Caine, and two from Mum.

Suppressing the annoyed, drunk part of her consciousness, she engaged the DI part.

'Jesus. Right, well you'd better fill me in. That report was clearly important enough for you to hike across the country in sub-zero temperatures and gawp . . . or should I say spy on me through a window.'

'Finch was poisoned.'

'Poisoned? With what?'

'*Conium maculatum*, commonly known as hemlock.'

'And what the hell is hemlock?'

'Hemlock is a herbaceous flowering plant, which grows profusely in these parts. It's carried in the waterways, so you often find it beside streams and ditches. It's closely related to celery and carrots, so you need to know what you're looking for.'

'Finch died of carrots?'

'Hemlock contains a deadly poison called coniine, which has a horrific effect on the nervous system. The victim develops muscular paralysis, which means they can feel and think perfectly clearly, but they are unable to move. The plant has purple splotches on the stems that are known as Socrates' blood. You remember Socrates?'

'The footballer?'

'The Greek philosopher. He was forced to drink hemlock. As

197

I remember, they made him walk around until his legs went numb. He said a lot of wise things. Then he died in agony.'

'And I suppose you remember those wise things?'

'I probably do. Do you want me to—'

'No. I really, really don't. Wait a minute, though . . . I've just remembered something . . .'

'Yes?'

'Something Sky said. *For the first time in history, humans have become plant blind.* I recorded the whole conversation.'

'I remembered that too. She said the ancient ones could read the landscape like a menu in a restaurant. The phrase struck me as astonishing for a fourteen-year-old.'

'And she mentioned that it was Constanza who had taught her to forage from the earliest age . . .'

'. . . to know which plants heal and which plants kill.'

'But come on,' said Shanti. 'You don't think . . .? Not Sky, surely?'

'Never. Not in a million years.'

'Constanza, then?'

'Constanza adored Finch. You spoke to her. She was grief-stricken, wasn't she?'

'Was she, Caine? As I recall, she was in total denial. Is that how you'd react if someone you loved had been brutally murdered?'

'I don't know. I'd prefer not to imagine.' He looked at her and shuddered. 'But it makes you wonder what poor Finch went through in those final hours.'

'You mean he might have been conscious but paralysed when his throat was cut?'

'Perhaps we'll never know.'

'Right,' she said. 'There's plenty to digest there. Let's sleep on it. Jump in the car and I'll drive you back to your hovel.'

'I'm fine, Shanti. I really don't want you to worry about me. Besides, I think you may have had a few drinks ...'

'What? Oh, yes, I suppose I have.'

She received a mental memo of an upcoming appointment with tomorrow's hangover. *Hello*, it said. *Can't wait to be with you.*

'Besides, it's good to walk when you're trying to figure things out,' said Caine gloomily.

She handed back his coat. 'Won't you be lonely, Caine?'

'I'm used to being alone. And you're absolutely right – I have no right to be here, and no right to harass you with my feelings.'

He turned towards the plains. *When covetous or lustful, let go of the object of desire . . .*

'Come back. You're being childish.'

He offered a weak smile.

She gazed at his unshaven face, and for the first time on this case, she realised something she had known all along but didn't want to acknowledge because it just made everything so damned complicated. Caine was annoying, that was certainly true. He wasn't even handsome in the way that Troy was handsome. But there was something about him that she simply could not ignore. Her son, Paul, adored him, and she knew why. The man was authentic. He was a real person. With real emotions. When he was sad, he cried. When he was happy – which was, to be fair, most of the time – he smiled. And when he cared for you, he simply could not hide his feelings away.

'I'll see you at breakfast, Shant. And can I say something unprofessional?'

'Add it to the list. You've already said so many unprofessional things tonight.'

'That dress is absolutely stunning. You look extraordinary. Like a ruby in the snow.'

'Yeah. Don't overdo it.'

'I'm going to help you resolve this case, then there are things I need to sort out. You know . . . family stuff. On the way over, I had a song stuck in my head. I just can't shift it.'

'If it's "You're Beautiful", I really don't need to know.'

'"Father and Son", by Cat Stevens.'

'Good night, Caine.'

'Good night, Shanti.'

He walked to a stile, half hidden within a white-capped hedge. As he climbed towards the footpath beyond, she saw his profile against the moon – the tall man with hair and coat tails flying.

'Oh, wait. I nearly forgot . . .' He came rushing back to her side, pulling open the flap of his bag.

'What is it?'

'I washed your blanket. Although tumble dryers make me a little uncomfortable.'

He handed it over, dried and neatly folded.

She almost cried into it as she walked back to the inn.

Chapter 25

How the Ancients Raised Great Weights

The corvids were restless. They watched as he passed the timeless arena.

There was Dawn's tower, tall and ominous beneath the monocular moon. There was the cordon with the police tape still fluttering.

As he walked, Caine admonished himself sharply. Jealousy was the most base of vices, but it had ripped his heart to see Shanti dancing with that man.

Stonehenge at night reminded him of another tragic love story – the climactic scene from *Tess of the d'Urbervilles*, in which Tess sleeps on a stone, as Angel Clare holds her hand one last time, before she is hauled away to meet a horrible Hardyesque end.

Although the area was no longer forensically sealed, Benno had put six uniforms on watch tonight, alert for the brazen fugitive who had placed the weapon on Dawn's van. Caine saw two pairs patrolling the perimeter, while another pair drank tea in a van. He raised a hand in greeting as he passed. Was it his imagination, or did they laugh at him?

As he stepped onto the moonlit avenue that led to the visitor centre, he reflected that Shanti had been right to rebuke him – she was indeed a free and independent woman, not something for him to possess.

She was right about so many things; like his unquestioning tendency to trust his instincts. Take Ned, for example – could it be that Caine's automatic conviction of the professor's innocence was based on something as naïve as the fact that he had idolised the man in his teens? As he walked, a sense of doubt began to stir. Was it possible that Tull was not what he seemed? A horrible image came to him of the wild man hacking at his throat with a flint blade as he slept.

And then, with a cold rush of anxiety, Caine realised why it was that he knew so much about those obscure substances – coniine and hemlock. There had been a particular episode of *Neolithic Neighbours* in which a younger, more confident Ned Tull had talked about the ancient art of foraging. Teenage Caine had been intensely interested and had assiduously noted Tull's warnings about a range of dodgy plants, of which hemlock was the most notorious.

As he marched briskly up the moonlit road, he began to question everything about his own intuition and judgement. Earlier that evening, for example, he had shared another of Tull's home-cooked meals. Imagine how it would look in court if Tull was found to be complicit in this crime! DI Vincent Caine, the cop who had slept in a roundhouse with a prime suspect! He would never live it down. Perhaps he was fatally naïve. Perhaps that was why other cops laughed at him.

Ned's soup had been good. Knowing that Caine was a vegetarian, he had used pulses, herbs and fresh winter vegetables, served piping hot in an earthenware bowl. But was it possible that he had slipped something else into his guest's food? Was that a slight ache Caine felt in his belly as he approached the soft lights of the visitor centre? Or the first tremor of paralysis creeping through his limbs?

As he crunched across the snowy courtyard at the back of the centre, he found a row of storage units near a white-topped parade of wheelie bins. Each door was fitted with a push-button combination lock, and Caine remembered that the unit at the far end belonged to Tull.

The code was unforgettable to Tull, being the date that his son had gone missing. But what on earth was that date? Tull's son had been eighteen when he disappeared – the same age as Caine at that time. So that would have been 2007. He and his Dutch girlfriend had gone missing at prime foraging time – say early August.

Caine tapped in the numbers 010807.

He tried 020807.

030807.

At 040807, the lock clicked open.

His fingers located the light switch on the concrete wall inside, and he imagined how Tull would hate the banks of fluorescent tubes that crackled reluctantly into life. In the harsh glare, he found himself in a freezing-cold high-ceilinged room like a small warehouse. The interior was divided into corridors by rows of industrial shelving. On the shelves sat numerous transparent storage tubs. Two of them were packed with dozens of faded books – it was Tull's autobiography, *Caught Knapping*, once a bestseller but now long forgotten.

In other tubs, Caine discovered prehistoric artefacts of many kinds, including intricately patterned pots, folded furs and animal skins, bone and antler tools, and, he noticed with a shudder, ancient bones and skulls.

In another set of plastic boxes, he found dozens of knapped flint tools, including hand-made hatchets very similar to the instrument that had opened the throat of the Holly King.

Finally, in the shadows at the back of the lock-up, he was confronted by something that turned his confidence inside out like a flayed rabbit on a rail. It was a huge object, rising almost to the ceiling. Constructed from hewn tree trunks and woven ropes, it was in effect, a reproduction of a Neolithic crane. The device would be capable of lifting a full-sized sarsen weighing many tons. It was also capable, he realised, of raising the body of a large man onto a seven-metre-high lintel.

As he trawled his pockets for his phone in order to take pictures, he became aware of a soft noise behind him – the padding of hide boots on the concrete floor. When he turned, he was met by the extraordinary sight of Professor Tull dressed in nothing but hand-stitched boots and a goatskin loincloth, brandishing a raised flint hatchet. His eyes blinked furiously in the fluorescent light as he approached.

'We need to talk, Ned,' said Caine softly. 'Put down the hatchet.'

It was as if the old man was waking from a dream. He looked at the weapon as though noticing it for the first time. Very gently, Caine took the instrument from his hand and laid it on a shelf.

'I thought you were an intruder,' said Tull. 'Someone come to steal my belongings and finger me for things I've never done.'

'You look cold,' said Caine. 'Let's go back to the roundhouse. I'd like to ask a few questions, if you don't mind?'

As if counting a rosary, the sinewy man toyed with the beads in his plaited beard.

'If you want. I wasn't sleeping anyway. Too many thoughts.'

'What was troubling you, Ned?'

'What do you think? The dead man on the stones. The thought of spending Yule with Pamela and the children . . . And Talin. I never forget Talin.'

Caine laid his hand on Ned's bony back and guided him out of the storage unit and across the crusty snow to the round-house. Ducking inside the low door, he felt grateful for the wall of warmth within.

'I hope this doesn't sound rude, Ned, but did you kill Finch?'

The professor seemed dismayed. 'Oh not you too. I thought we were friends.'

'I'll be straight with you,' said Caine. 'There are many things I don't understand about this case. Tell me about the lifting device at the back of the storeroom. It's huge, Ned, and beauti-fully made.'

'Thank you. It's hewn with antler axes from oak trunks. Ropes and pulleys, all contemporaneous materials.'

'But what's it for?'

'I would have thought that was obvious – it's a hoist for rais-ing heavy weights.'

'Like the body of a large man?'

'Oh, I see . . . I see where this is going. You think I used my machine to lift poor Finch onto the trilithon. Listen, I built that device to understand how a sarsen lintel could be raised using ancient technology. That bad boy can lift in excess of thirty-five tons. I've carried out the experiment dozens of times using teams of squaddies from the barracks.'

'But surely you understand my dilemma?' said Caine. 'A murderer might have used a similar device to raise the body of poor Lovell-Finch.'

'To be honest, I'm disappointed in you, Vincent. I thought you were one of the more astute members of your profession. Did you notice tracks in the snow from the rollers? Of course you didn't. Has my device been used since last summer? Of course it hasn't. You're sounding a little desperate, if I may say so.'

'There's another question, too ...'

'Oh yes?'

'You're a proficient forager, right?'

'I know a thing or two,' Tull said as he went about his regular routine of preparing tea, using pinches of herbs and dried plants.

'So could you tell me which toxic plants you might find on the plains?'

'You can take your pick around here.' He poured steaming water into bowls. 'There's mistletoe, for a start. And plenty of very stimulating mushrooms. Then you have deadly nightshade, digitalis, giant hogweed, hemlock—'

'OK, stop there. Would you ever have reason to administer these substances yourself?' Caine accepted a steaming cup from the professor.

'Why on earth would I do that? I would never administer anything dangerous. Of course, many of these plants have medicinal properties, but they have to be handled with extreme caution – in minute quantities normally.'

'Who else knows about pharmacology around here?' said Caine. 'The Druids?'

'Don't talk to me about that lot. Listen, Vincent – can I tell you something in the kindest possible way?'

Caine stirred in a little wild honey and sipped the tea cautiously.

'Of course.'

'I've been watching you lot go about your investigation. You're really struggling, aren't you?'

'We're at an early stage, Ned. We have to follow every lead.'

'But if only you had asked for my help from the start, you could have solved the case by now. I know Stonehenge better than anyone.'

'You're saying you know who killed Finch?'

'I'm not saying that, but I'm saying that your thinking is all wrong. In my opinion, you and your friend are making a fundamental error in your search for the killer. Do you want to hear more? Are you ready to listen now?'

'Of course I am, Ned. I'm fascinated to hear what you have to say.'

'All right, I'll help you. The only thing I ask is that you let me lie down while we talk. It's late. I'm cold and tired. And in a few hours, I will forced into the twenty-first century.'

Ned Tull walked to his bed and laid himself wearily beneath the furs.

Late into the night, into the small hours of the morning, Caine hung on the words of his old mentor.

Chapter 26

Dogsbody

Shanti's nerves were raw.

As Benno enjoyed a doughnut in the incident room, it was as if every grain of sugar offended her eyes and every sound was magnified.

The day had begun badly. After repeatedly hitting the snooze button, she had staggered to one of the little tables that had been hurriedly set out in the lounge bar, where the stage and glitter ball were a sickly reminder of the night before.

Declining the 'Full Stonehenge' in favour of sweet black coffee, she threw an equally black but decidedly less sweet glare at a fat pap who had asked to share her table.

She recalled something that Touchy-Feely Troy had warbled in her ear: 'I'll let you in on a little secret – if you stick to the best champagne, you get no hangover at all. Trust me, Shantala, you'll skip out of bed like a filly.'

The lightning bolt wedged behind each eyelid negated the theory.

And if she felt woozy, what state would McAble be in? He had downed four glasses for every one of hers, and she had fled before the night was done.

If it weren't for the cascade of leads that the major had disgorged throughout the evening, she would happily cancel their appointment. But in spite of everything – her perpetual failure at motherhood, the looming burden of Christmas, her car-crash love life – she felt a sense of determined anticipation. As Caine had pointed out, these convoluted cases had a way of coalescing rapidly. Today was the day. She felt it in her bones. It bloody well better be, because tomorrow was Christmas Eve, and Paul was on the verge of forgetting he ever had a mother.

Her irritability was heightened by Benno's intern, Masako, who sat poised and slender at his side, glued to her laptop, as if she'd just returned from a spa.

Beyond the vast windows of the canteen, the morning was bright with flurries of snow. She could see Caine up at the gates, saying his farewells to Tull – even helping the wild man to load hand-crafted gifts into his daughter's electric Peugeot. Caine would not like their morning schedule at all.

After a while, she cautiously tested her voice. 'Is it my imagination, or are there fewer paps this morning?'

'Yeah, I thought that,' said Benno, shovelling sugar into his coffee like he had shares in Tate & Lyle. 'Less than half, by my reckoning.'

'Why is that, Benno?'

'I suppose everyone's entitled to time off,' he said. 'Can I say something, boss?'

'I'd rather you didn't.'

'We all admire your tenacity. I mean that. But you need a

break, just like everyone else. In my judgement, there'd be no harm in suspending the case for a few days.'

'I suggest you keep your judgement to yourself, especially as it was you who invited me on board this psychopathic panto-mime. And in case you're forgetting, our killer hasn't gone into retirement, Benno. Trust me, he's waiting for his moment to strike again. To be honest, I'm not entirely sure why you turned up this morning. You're giving an excellent impression of a man preparing for a game of Scrabble and a nap.'

Benno was long-suffering. Renowned for his patience with even the most provocative detainees.

'Dawn has asked me to oversee the dismantling of the tower. Oh, and I think you'll need to formally release the scene of crime when you have time.'

'Whoa, just wait one damned minute. Why do we need to take the tower down? How do we know there isn't more evidence?'

'Dawn's satisfied she has everything.'

'Yes, but what's the harm in simply leaving the cordon in place until after Christmas?' She looked at Benno questioningly. 'Ah, this is about resources, isn't it? We haven't got the uniforms to guard the scene. Maybe the cost of scaffold hire is a factor too.'

'It will be more cost-effective to outsource to GoodGuys, that's true. But in my judgement . . . sorry, I mean the sooner we get that tower down, the better. It's liable to blow away at any moment, and I wouldn't want the paperwork if those stones get damaged.'

'Yeah. Yeah, I see what you mean. Destruction of ancient artefacts isn't a good look.'

'But you can rest assured that we'll carry out a full and final search once the tents and stepping plates have been removed.'

'OK, Benno. You and Dawn know what you're doing.'

'Thanks, boss, and if you're not going to eat that dough-nut ...'

She shoved it in his direction.

Up at the gates, Caine was shaking hands warmly with Tull, which irritated her further.

'Little job for you, Masako,' she said. 'Unless you're planning to desert me like Benno.'

'I'm here as long as I'm needed,' the young woman replied, as keen as freshly knapped flint.

'I'd like you to check out a historic MISPER case. Circa 2007. A young man named Talin Tull and his Dutch girlfriend disappeared from here, and it was never resolved.'

With thumbs blazing, Masako tapped notes into her phone.

'I'd be happy to do that, DI Joyce. Presumably Talin is related to Professor Tull?'

'His son, yes. The long-lost brother of that lady up there.'

She pointed to Aylin Tull, who appeared as normal as any mum on a school run. Around thirty, with small glasses and hair in a tidy knot. Her children were hopping around the Peugeot in excitement, clearly delighted to greet their unconventional grandfather, who climbed anxiously into the passenger seat.

As the car headed out of the gates, Caine gave Tull a final wave. Oh no, he would not like what she had planned at all.

She watched him walking towards the sliding doors. The unfair thing about Caine was that although he looked as rough as she felt, the straggly hair and four-day beard with the faintest fleck of grey actually suited him.

'Excuse me, everyone.' Shanti turned to see a burly woman in GoodGuys uniform holding up a large set of keys. 'I do apologise, but we're closing the canteen now.'

'Closing?' repeated Shanti.

'That's correct. English Heritage have asked us to lock up the visitor centre for Christmas.'

'But . . . but this is our incident room . . .'

'I do understand. I'm just following orders.'

'Do you know about this, Benno?'

'I do, boss.' He turned to the guard. 'Could you give us another ten minutes, just to wind up?'

She nodded and walked the length of the canteen, where she stood by the doors, jiggling her keys like a jailer.

'This is ridiculous,' said Shanti.

'To be fair,' said Benno, 'English Heritage have been incredibly helpful. You realise they haven't even charged for refreshments for the entire team?'

'I get that. But we need a base.'

'Yeah. They've agreed to let us in if there are any major developments between now and Christmas. But this is what everyone is telling you, boss – we need to wind up now and reconvene after the holiday.' He rose to his feet, brushing sugar from his uniform.

'Forget it,' said Shanti. 'I don't care if I'm the last person on site – I will not rest until that perp is under arrest.'

'I'm still here,' said Caine, arriving at her side.

'And don't forget, I'm less than half an hour away,' said Benno. 'So you can call me night or day. Oh, and I put something nice in the Secret Santa back at the nick.'

'Yeah. Yeah, right, Benno,' said Shanti wistfully. 'All the best to the family.'

As the big man and the slight girl left the building, the morning sun lit up the room and the world outside. There was an optimism out there that was at odds with the way she felt.

'It's going to be a beautiful morning,' said Caine, far too loudly.

'I see no evidence for that. I can't believe it, Caine. Benno has deserted me. Even your man Tull – who remains, let's face it, our number one suspect – is entitled to time with his family.'

'Like I say, I'm with you to the end.'

'Do stop saying that. Now listen, we've got a busy morning. I thought we'd start by turning over Tull's lock-up.'

'I checked it over last night.'

'Right, well his hut, then. Is it locked?'

'No. There's no lock. As a matter of fact, Ned has kindly allowed me to stay on in the roundhouse for as long as I need. But you won't find anything, Shanti, I guarantee it.'

As Shanti stood up, it was as if her migraine had been hovering a few feet above her head, and she slipped into it as easily as her woollen hat.

'I must admit, I had a few misgivings about Ned last night,' said Caine as he helped her with her jacket, even retrieving her bag from under the table.

'Ah ha,' said Shanti.

'But I can tell you that I've totally eliminated him from our inquiries.'

'That's very reassuring,' she said sarcastically. They walked towards the sliding doors, where Caine smiled and Shanti scowled at the security guard.

'Why the rethink about Tull?' asked Shanti, fumbling for her sunglasses as they stepped into the dazzling morning.

'It's a bit complicated to explain right now . . .'

'Thank God for that.'

'. . . but I can tell you that we sat up most of the night while he shared his theory about the case. It made me rethink everything. Oh, by the way, he left a present for Paul.'

'He did what?'

'He remembered that you had a son, so he made an extra Yule present for him. That's the kind of man he is.'

'Right. You understand it's a major breach of protocol to accept gifts from a POI?'

'He's a good man, Shanti. Unusual, yes. But he's not hiding anything.'

'We shall see,' said Shanti as they headed towards the back of the exhibition area, where more GoodGuys personnel in heavy coats and balaclavas were checking and double-checking the locks on doors.

'I want to say that I'm sorry about last night,' said Caine quietly. 'I know my behaviour on this case has been . . .'

'Has been what?'

'Unskilful. Mindless. I hope you had fun.'

'Forget it.'

'Only . . .'

'Only what, Caine?'

'Do you honestly think it suits him?'

'That what suits who?'

'The moustache? You don't think it's a bit . . .?'

They entered the Neolithic hamlet where Tull's roundhouse alone stood snow-free. As Caine pushed open the tiny door, Shanti followed him into the shadowy interior, where a fire glowed on the pummelled chalk floor.

'Jesus,' she said. 'It's very . . .'

'Neolithic,' said Caine.

'Well it's bloody dark.'

'Your eyes will adjust. Shall I make tea?'

'Forget the tea. We won't be long. As everyone keeps reminding me, this is our last day, and I think it's going to be a big one.'

Caine squatted to rekindle the fire, while Shanti used the torch on her phone to scan the domed interior, casting the rough-hewn furniture and primitive utensils into dramatic relief.

'Isn't it wonderful?' said Caine. 'That's my bed, and the professor sleeps— Oh! What is that on Ned's bed?'

She swung the torch towards the woven cot at the back of the roundhouse. There was a body lying there, half hidden beneath a pile of furs, with its legs projecting into the room.

Shanti felt her senses reel. This was her worst nightmare. The thing she dreaded most. In a fleeting moment it all came back to her – the botched case in Camden. And now it was happening again. She had allowed it to happen on her watch.

Caine seized the phone from her hand and shone the beam onto the large figure, which lay motionless on its back. In a second, he had taken control, easing back the furs to reveal the victim's face. Shanti could hardly bear to look.

'It's a dog,' he said quietly.

'A dog?'

'Must be poor Albion.'

Shanti felt relief. Then shame at her relief. Then confusion.

'But why? Why would someone kill a dog, for Christ's sake?'

Caine was kneeling. Searching for a pulse.

'I've got something. Wait . . . wait . . . He's alive, Shant . . . Hold the phone while I check his airways.'

She saw Caine's hands busy in the torchlight, prising jaws apart, using a bone ladle to shift the lolling tongue.

'He's breathing. It's faint, but he's still alive.'

Shanti needed to leave. She needed to inhale some of that sweet chilled air.

'I'll call Benno,' she said. 'He's down at the tower. We'll need, what? An ambulance?'

'A vet. As soon as possible. He's absolutely rigid. Paralysed. You don't think . . .?'

'What, Caine?'

'Hemlock. The same plant that was used to incapacitate his master. I think poor Albion has been drugged.'

He stood up and came to her side.

'Listen to me,' he said earnestly. 'Whether Albion recovers or not, you have to tell Benno that we need samples taken from the animal's gut, to be sent for analysis. Right now. Today.'

She staggered outside and let the air freeze her thumping head. As she attempted to call Benno, she felt overwhelmed. Faint almost. As if she hadn't eaten, which of course she had not.

But it was more than hunger. More than the after-effects of alcohol. What Shanti felt was stone-cold dread.

Someone was sending another sinister warning.

Chapter 27

A Buddhist in a Barracks

'You know what terrifies me?'

'Tell me, Shant.'

'He's watching us as we work. I can almost feel his presence.'

'That's what Dawn said.'

'Dawn is a rational woman, but I think she was right. This latest episode with the dog – it happened in a very short window of time, right? That means he must be incredibly close at hand. Doesn't that terrify you? Because it scares the crap out of me.'

Caine said nothing. She could almost hear the cogs of his brain whirling within the flying hat.

As she nudged the Saab through the dawn chorus of journos, she realised that what she and Benno had suspected was correct – there were half the number of paps today. And that just didn't make sense. The case was exploding in every direction, so why were the media losing interest?

Pulling down the sun visor, she swung east onto the A303, where snowploughs had excreted a dirty coil along the verge.

'Run through it again,' she said.

'There's not much to say. I was with Ned every minute. He never left my sight. We had breakfast together – tea and porridge – then I helped him carry his belongings to the car park. I waited there by his side until Aylin arrived to collect him. It's physically impossible for him to be involved.'

'But who else had access to his hut?' demanded Shanti, with quiet desperation. 'I mean, the entire site is like a ghost town now.'

'Yeah, but I was chatting to some of the GoodGuys team last night and they were telling me how difficult it is to secure the site properly. There's hundreds of acres of wilderness out there, so anyone who knows the area could just slip in off the plains, from almost any direction.'

'But you can't just rock up with a giant-sized comatose dog without being noticed. You'd need, what? A cart or something ... a wheelbarrow at least.'

'Let's think it through rationally ...'

'Oh, I'm all for rationality.'

'Albion was rather emaciated, did you notice that? Just like Ganesh. So he would probably follow anyone who had food. Which means it would be easy to entice him into the roundhouse and spike his food with hemlock. In a short time, he starts to feel unwell and lies down on Ned's bed. Job done.'

'What job, Caine? What is this sick individual trying to achieve?'

'To scare us off. To create more drama. To frame Ned.'

'Here we go again. Poor old Tull is a sacrificial lamb.'

'Well, yes. If anything, this latest incident reinforces the theory that someone is trying to set him up. You don't honestly believe he's still a suspect, do you?'

'I most certainly do. In my mind everyone is a suspect until proven innocent, and that includes you. Look, you've been in this game as long as me, so tell me who commits the vast majority of murders.'

'Relatives. Or people who knew the victim well. Are we going the right way, Shanti?'

She ignored his question. 'Precisely. So at the top of my list are Quentin and, I suppose, Constanza, who certainly has a few questions to answer.'

'About foraging, you mean?'

'But I cannot exclude Tull, even if he makes hand-crafted Christmas presents for children.'

'I think he'd call it Yule. But go on, tell me what your suspicions are based on.'

'Oh boy, where to start? Right. Number one: Tull was an associate of the deceased. Two: his greasy fingerprints and DNA were all over that weapon. Three: as he keeps boasting, he is a master knapper. He literally collects axes. Four: the man has extensive knowledge of toxic herbs. Five: he has history, Caine. And I don't mean Neolithic history. I mean that he was previously questioned about the disappearance of his son and another individual . . . and by the way, I've asked Masako to reopen that file. Six: he has unique access to the scene of crime. Seven: he lives in a hut in his very own spectrum.'

'That last one isn't a proper reason.'

'It's good enough for me. The more unusual the crime, the more we need to hold on to tried and tested principles.'

'But Dawn's first impression was that the perp was DNA-aware. She said that the whole crime scene had been wiped. The job was done by a pro, she told us. And that doesn't fit Ned's profile in any way.'

'Jeez, maybe you're right – Tull is like Stig of the Dump.'

Over the hedgerows they caught glimpses across the shining plains, where the monument stood spectacularly illuminated in the morning sun. The tower was down now, and the scaffolders were struggling to load their truck, as the winds made sails of the awnings.

'The good news is that the vet thinks Albion will make a full recovery,' said Caine. 'That will be a huge consolation to Sky and Constanza. I definitely want to talk to them again today . . . Where are we heading, Shanti? Surely Lovell Court is back that way?'

'Didn't I mention it? We're going to have a word with Troy McAble.'

'You didn't tell me that.'

'Yeah, we've got an appointment at the barracks in fifteen minutes, so we need to step on it.'

'Ah, Shanti, I think I'll pass on this. I didn't sleep very well last night. In fact I don't think I slept at all. I need a shave and a shower.'

'Yeah, what is that perfume you're wearing? Eau de Goat by Dior?'

'I can't face it, Shant.'

'Face what?'

'The whole . . . you know, military thing. Everyone will stare at me.'

She tossed a packet into his lap.

'What's this?'

'Baby wipes. Give yourself a tidy-up. You've let yourself go.'

They swung left off the main road, past the mini-henge at

the Stonehenge Tavern, where Caine had wept on a pint-sized sarsen.

'Just drop me anywhere along here,' he said.

'You're being very silly.'

'It's fine. I can walk to Lovell Court from here.'

'I've put the child locks on.'

'I don't want to be difficult, but I simply don't belong in a place like Everkill. Yeovil HQ is bad enough, but an army base!'

'Right. Listen. It's spectacularly simple – you and I are senior police officers, heading up a major investigation. You get that, don't you? Now, our current line of inquiry happens to take us inside a military establishment, which makes you a little edgy on account of your peacenik tendencies. But this is not about feelings, Caine, it's about safeguarding the community and bringing justice to the bereaved family. If I didn't think it was worthwhile, I wouldn't waste our last morning.'

'*Where no self is, there can be no sorrow, no desire . . .*'

'What? What did you say? Listen, I know you find McAble rather obnoxious, but trust me, he's not my type either.'

'That incessant talking, Shanti . . .'

'Mansplaining, it's called.'

'. . . I think he's some kind of narcissist.'

'You may well be right. But that's really not relevant. We need to follow this up because Troy knew the victim. He was very drunk last night, but he told me an extraordinary story about how Finch was arrested for disrupting a parade, and that was only the most recent episode in a long history of conflict with the army. Also – and this may be critical – McAble knows where Finch was digging . . . his excavation, I mean. He found him there just a few days ago, trespassing on MoD land.'

'This is Salisbury Plain, Shanti. It doesn't belong to the army. We're talking about the ancient lands of the Druids.'

'Yeah. You see, some jobs are becoming obsolete in the modern age, Druid being one of them. Also, some DIs are less essential than they used to be.'

'It's funny you should say that. You may as well know, I've arrived at a decision. This will be my last case. It's time to hand in my badge.'

'Here we go – welcome to the daily Caine crisis of confidence. Massage ego thoroughly to restore normal service.'

They had entered a wide and shabby high street – a military metropolis, where off-duty soldiers hung out in eateries named Battle Burgers and Kombat Kebab, hung with dismal Union Jack bunting. They saw slush-covered sports grounds, red-brick gyms, gaudy primary schools and identikit housing estates. On snowy building sites, vast cranes like wading birds stood dormant beside half-completed dormitory blocks, which Shanti supposed would eventually accommodate hundreds of teenage recruits.

As they drove alongside fences topped with razor wire, Caine stared dolefully at dreary hangars and Nissen huts on snow-coated asphalt, and his heart slumped into his boots.

'This must be the place,' said Shanti as they approached a sentry box by a barrier. 'Centre East Block.'

Even the signs seemed to bark orders:

ALL MUNITIONS MUST BE DECLARED AND HANDED TO GUARD ROOM
PRIOR TO ENTERING EVERKILL BARRACKS

'Anything to declare, Caine?' asked Shanti.

'Only a yearning for world peace and an infinite sorrow for war.'

A heavily tattooed guard scrutinised their ID and gestured with his sub-machine gun towards a large two-storey office complex.

They passed beneath the raised barrier and entered a parking area, where freshly scrubbed squaddies were being collected by their families for the holidays. Shanti orbited a small roundabout on which a Second World War field gun stood half submerged in snow, so that only the phallus of its barrel thrust into the dazzling sky.

As she unfastened her seat belt, she glared at Caine, who remained slumped in his seat. 'Jesus. It's worse than taking Paul to school.'

'The thing is, I didn't get a chance to meditate this morning, so I feel a bit uncentred. Maybe I should wait in the car. I don't want to let you down.'

'Listen, I *need you*, Caine. Is that what you want me to say? Even if you are wetter than an otter's pocket. Now take some deep breaths and let's do this.'

Buildings have faces, Caine often thought, and the snow-capped shoebox that housed Troy McAble's office carried the hollow-eyed face of woe.

An unnaturally immaculate female officer led them along a corridor to an open-plan office, which was sparsely and efficiently adorned with bargain-basement decorations. A dozen fresh-faced soldiers worked purposefully at computers as Caine followed reticently, hat in hand like a peasant in a cathedral.

At the far end they could see McAble behind a large desk within a glass-walled office. He looked pale and weary, dressed in fatigues and a skin-tight T-shirt.

Their chaperone tapped at the door, and McAble's gloomy expression morphed into enthusiastic smiles as he saw Shanti. He bounded towards her with exaggerated enthusiasm.

'*I saw your face in a crowded place* . . .' he hummed. 'Good morning, Shantala. Twice in twenty-four hours. Troy is a lucky boy. Although one thing makes me sad . . .'

'Oh yes?'

'You're not wearing that knockout red dress.'

'Strictly business, Major.'

Carefully selecting the most comfortable chair, he ushered her to sit. It was a full minute before he noticed Caine's unkempt form at the door. His chiselled features seemed to fall. 'Hello . . . are you delivering something?'

'This is my partner, DI Caine,' said Shanti. 'We work very closely together.'

'Ah ha, I see,' said McAble, exaggeratedly tapping his nose. 'Undercover chap, is he? Embed yourself with the activists and all that . . . very ingenious. Right, you'll find a chair over there somewhere . . .' He waved vaguely towards a stack of green tubular chairs with slack canvas seats.

As his face swivelled back to Shanti, his moustache parted like the curtains in a theatre to display a row of pearly teeth like dazzling ballerinas.

'Coffee, or something stiffer? It is Crimbo after all.'

'I would have thought you had more than enough last night. We're on a very tight schedule, Major.'

'Troy, please. As I said, I'm just starting my leave, so I'm entirely at your disposal.'

'We'd like to ask a few questions about your association with Hector Lovell-Finch.'

Caine managed to wrangle one of the chairs from the pile. He placed it beside Shanti, where he sat forlornly.

'I'm particularly interested in the locations you mentioned,' she continued. 'You saw Hector Lovell-Finch working at an excavation site just a few days ago. Where was that?'

'Up Imber way. Well off the beaten track.'

Caine's sense of invisibility was so acute, it was as if his spirit was levitating through the snow-covered roof, like a bird ascending over the sunlit plains. He had to haul himself back in order to follow the conversation.

'Would you have any objection to me recording our interview?' asked Shanti.

'Crikey. Let me think about that . . . Erm, no, I'm afraid you can't do that. MoD premises, you see. Damned rules about everything, I'm sure you understand.'

She fumbled for a notebook. 'I'll take notes then. Could you tell us a little about Everkill?'

'Of course. My pet subject . . .'

He handed them each a brochure from the desk, and before she could object, he had launched into one of his incessant monologues. She decided to let it run.

'You may not know this, but Everkill has been earmarked as part of a super-garrison,' he bragged. 'So if all goes to plan, we should see a substantially larger military presence in coming years. I'm sure you noticed the building work as you arrived – our target is to house upwards of four thousand personnel, along with three thousand family members. We have a new canteen, which feeds over twelve hundred personnel, three times a day . . . and you should see the menu, Shantala – not just ham and spuds like when I joined up . . .'

As McAble's voice drifted in and out of focus, Caine heard phrases like 'action plan' and 'mission objective'. He thought longingly of his cosy cabin, perched on the Undercliff, far from men he did not understand. The room in which they sat was the antithesis of that homely interior. Instead of soft treetops with silvery glimpses of sea, the harsh rectangles of Troy's windows looked over a frigid parade ground where a faceless sergeant barked at his troops. Whereas Caine's room contained poetry books, the wood-burning stove and his zafu cushion by the shrine, this lino-floored workspace was dominated by khaki-coloured filing cabinets, flags in glass cases, and a vast, horrific acrylic painting in photorealist style, showing Troy and several muscular comrades grinning atop a tank in some far-flung war zone. On the sandy ground, a cluster of street children gazed up reverently at the suntanned gods.

'... to date, we've spent in excess of a billion pounds on the Salisbury Plain site alone, but the way we see it, our people risk everything, and in return we have a duty to ensure they have the best possible quality of life ...'

What was it about his accent? Something about that public school cadence wasn't quite authentic.

'... if there's time, I'd love to show you round the RESC – that's the Royal Everkill Saddle Club. I'm the chairman, did I mention that? The club boasts a full suite of showjumping facilities, indoor and outdoor schools and, of course, direct access to mile after mile of the finest hacking in the country ...'

Caine's spirit abhorred every detail of this place, from the MAKE WAR, NOT LOVE mug on the desk to the immense set of stag antlers mounted on an oak shield. Then his eye settled on a photograph in an aluminium frame, almost hidden on a high shelf. There was something familiar about it.

In an instant, he awoke.

'Could I interrupt?' he said.

'It looks like you just have,' retorted McAble.

'I'd like to ask about that photograph up there.'

'Which photograph?'

Caine rose to his feet, walked across the office and lifted it down.

McAble seethed. Here was a man who was not used to being cut off.

'What the hell has that got to do with anything?' he snapped, snatching the photo from Caine's hand. 'It's from my school-days. I haven't looked at it in years.'

'Let's look at it now,' said Caine. 'I'm guessing that's you – slightly hidden in the back row, with the red hair.'

'The good-looking one? Yes, that's me.'

'And who is *that*, Major? Your very self-assured classmate in the front row, with the glasses?'

'I've no idea. This picture must be twenty years old.'

'I'd say that young man was unusually distinctive. Surely you wouldn't have forgotten Quentin Lovell-Finch? He went on to do quite well for himself.'

McAble flushed crimson. 'Yes. Come to think of it, Quentin Lovell-Finch and I did cross paths briefly at school, but we were anything but friends.'

'It's one of those coincidences. I spotted the exact same photograph at the Old Vicarage.'

'The where?'

'Quentin's country retreat, not far from here. Did you say you hadn't met since your schooldays?'

'The odd reunion, perhaps. Look, Detective ... what's your name?'

'Caine. Vincent Caine.'

'Right, well there's something I should explain. I'm not particularly proud of this, but I was a scholarship boy. I came from a very different background from the other boys, and they never let me forget it.'

'You were bullied?'

'There was a rhyme: *Troy, Troy, scholarship boy!* You know what schoolboys are like.' McAble's hands quivered as he held the frame. 'Quentin and I inhabited different worlds.'

'You're from a working-class Glasgow family.'

'I ... How did you know that?'

'Just a guess. I'm very fond of Glasgow, actually. But you must have been academically talented?'

'Anything but. I'm left-handed and a little dyslexic, if you want to know the truth.'

'Then how ...?'

McAble indicated a glass cabinet brimming with silver cups and rosettes.

'Sport. Equestrian stuff mostly – dressage, polo and show-jumping ... Which reminds me, I promised Shantala we'd ride out to Finch's excavation. Better get along.'

'Hang on,' said Shanti in alarm. 'Who said anything about riding?'

'We had a conversation last night. Don't tell me you've forgotten. You told me you learnt to ride at sixteen. It's going to be beautiful day, and I thought—'

'You can think again,' said Shanti.

'But the horses are saddled and raring to go. It's a marvellous ride, especially in the snow.'

'I'm sure you've got a jeep or something.'

'That really wouldn't work,' McAble explained. 'Finch's excavation is at the end of a narrow bridleway. You'd never get a vehicle along there. I only came across the place because I was on horseback.'

'And how did Finch get there?'

'On that quad bike thingy with the gadget on the back.'

'This is madness,' said Shanti.

'I've asked for one of our most docile trekking ponies,' he told her. 'But of course, if you're frightened ...'

'I'm not frightened of a pony, Major McAble.'

'That's settled then. It's about thirty minutes' steady trot.'

Caine pulled on his hat, as if galvanised by the prospect of getting outside.

'I'm up for it,' he said. 'I haven't ridden since I was in Thailand, but I'll get the hang of it quickly, I'm sure. It'll be fun.'

'Ah, slight problem there,' said McAble. 'Don't want to disappoint you, but the groom has only prepared two horses. Shantala omitted to mention that anyone else would be joining us.'

There was a long pause.

'I see,' said Caine. 'Well, I suppose I'll have a wander about until you get back.'

McAble stared at him as if he were mad. 'I'm afraid it doesn't work like that. We can't have people roaming about like a theme park. That's what got Old Man Finch into so much trouble.'

'I'll remind you that we're pursuing a murder inquiry,' said Shanti. 'I don't think we'll have much trouble obtaining permission.'

'I don't want to argue with you, but I'm afraid police have no jurisdiction on MoD property. Everything is classified, you see.'

'So how is my colleague supposed to get back?' Shanti demanded. 'We arrived together in a single vehicle.'

'Leave it with me,' said McAble. 'I'll be back in five minutes.'

As soon as he had left the office, Caine and Shanti entered into a whispered conversation.

'I can't leave you with that man,' said Caine.

'I'm a big girl. I can handle it.'

'He's manipulative, Shanti. There something almost predatory about the way he looks at you. Why don't we apply for a warrant and come back?'

'Come back? After Christmas, you mean? I need to look at that excavation today. And I want Major McAble to answer a few questions. That photo was a good spot, Caine. The fact that he went to school with Quentin is mighty curious. God knows what it means, but I detect a scent ... Stop looking so worried – I've got this.'

McAble returned with two large military police officers in red berets, who waited silently outside the glass partition. Caine gave Shanti a long, anxious look, then stepped outside. As he was shepherded briskly through the office, a dozen eyes glanced up from computer screens.

'What an extraordinary chap,' said Troy. 'Why the hell was he looking at school photos? Is there something wrong with him?'

'There's nothing wrong with DI Caine,' said Shanti. 'He's a first-class detective, I assure you.'

'I'll take your word for it. Not sure if I'd want him at my side in a tight hole. Anyway, Shantala, this is all rather fortuitous.'

'And why might that be?'

'Because I've got you all to myself. Don't tell me there wasn't a tiny frisson last night.'

The smell of his Hai Karate aftershave made her tender stomach heave.

'Major McAble, let me make this perfectly clear. I am here for one reason only . . .'

'Why don't you tell me all about it?'

'. . . which is to solve a uniquely unpleasant homicide. Time is very much against me, so if you don't mind, we'll get down to those questions.'

'I've never met a woman who asked so many. All right, you win. I'll gather a few things and you can ask me on the way to the stables. Fancy a snifter en route?'

Chapter 28

Mindful at Last

'Right. Here's the visitor centre.'

'Thanks for the ride,' said Caine.

'We'll wait here in case you accidentally stray. Merry Christmas, buddy.'

'Right. Thanks. Same to you.'

Caine stepped down from the military police Land Rover and headed across the slushy carriageway towards the gates. The measureless relief of escaping those barracks almost compensated for the shame of abandoning Shanti.

She could handle it. Shanti could handle anything. And Caine had urgent things to see to. But first he needed to sort himself out.

Even the newshounds at the gates did not unsettle him as he grinned politely and jostled through the throng. Everyone had a job to do.

Having borrowed a key from the GoodGuys crew, he let himself into the shower block, where he showered and washed his hair. As he scraped off his beard in front of a steamy mirror, he pictured Tull in Pamela's modern apartment, surrounded by noisy video games and flickering TVs.

Once he was dressed in clean clothes, he found a secluded corner, where he meditated briefly, emerging fifteen minutes later, restored and reinvigorated.

The snowy tunnel that meandered towards Lovell Court was illuminated in the most agreeable way. As he fell into a steady gait, Caine was glad of his strong boots on the slippery ground, and he found a length of hazel, which he stripped with his pocket knife into an excellent walking stick. It struck him that in former times these ancient lanes must have been streams, or riverbeds. The high banks and twisting roots were a metropolis for wildlife, whose tracks were everywhere.

Wasn't it Tu who had taught him the art of walking meditation? Place your awareness in your contact with the earth. Be mindful of every step. Dear old Tu. There was a wise elder – the antithesis of McAble in every way. *First, do no harm*, he always said.

As Caine walked, he felt that finally the oppressive bardo of the solstice was lifting. He breathed deeply, and for the first time in days, he felt steady. He had let himself go. Thrown by the solstice. Thrown by the crime. Thrown by desire. He had allowed himself to be swept along on a tide of emotion and desire.

The sound of a fast-approaching vehicle wrenched him from his reverie. In an instant, he flattened himself against the bank as a car came hurtling down the hill – a maroon Derby Bentley.

It is extraordinary how much information the mind can assimilate in a fleeting glimpse. Although his attention had been focused on his own safety, an image had burned into Caine's retina of the driver and his passenger, who were involved in some kind of altercation. In his mind's eye, he saw the large head of the driver, in a trilby, spectacles and a camel-hair coat; and his passenger, a teenage girl in a floppy hat, who was positively shrieking at him.

He had seen that vehicle before. A highly polished classic car beneath a tarpaulin at the Old Vicarage. The extended occiput and owlish glasses belonged to Quentin Lovell-Finch. But who was the belligerent passenger? Quentin's children were not teenagers.

As he considered this, he heard a clamour of voices around the bend. He increased his pace until he saw what he was already beginning to suspect – a dense crowd of highly animated journalists filled the lane outside the Old Vicarage. The story had broken. Word was out. And of course, this accounted for the decrease in numbers outside the visitor centre. The identity of the deceased was known, and so was the identity of his infamous son, the notoriously right-wing MP Quentin Lovell-Finch.

As he approached, Caine saw four police officers, who had the unenviable task of keeping the journalists at bay. With much hooting, Quentin was attempting to enter his driveway, leaning half out of the window to remonstrate with the reporters.

'How do you feel about the tragic death of your father?'

'Do you have no concept of privacy? The family will deliver a statement through the appropriate channels.'

'When will that be, sir?'

'Whenever we deem appropriate. Now step aside.'

'What kind of man was your father?'

'Constable, would you kindly arrest these persons for trespass?'

After much tussling, the unhappy uniforms managed to clear a path, and the car disappeared up the drive.

Caine squeezed his way through the crowd. He spoke quietly to one of the constables, showing his warrant card discreetly, then slipped into the driveway.

Pulling himself tight against the snowy laurels, he crept towards the house. Up ahead, he could hear raised voices and the sound of slamming car doors. There was no mistaking the reedy, superior tones of Quentin Lovell-Finch. But the second voice was unfamiliar – loud, imperious and petulant.

Peering through the foliage, Caine spotted the Derby Bentley parked near the porch. The lanky parliamentarian was attempting to haul his young companion up the short flight of steps. Young? Although she was dressed in a miniskirt, fur coat and floppy purple hat over abundant blonde curls, Caine was disconcerted to see a heavily painted skeletal face, with spidery eyelashes and a gash of tangerine lipstick.

'For God's sake,' snapped Tiggy Antrobus-Lovell-Finch. 'If you'd told me we'd have half of Fleet Street iteside, I'd never have come. Get me inside the hise, pronto. It's absolute brass monkeys out here.'

'Well, if you would only take my arm, Mummy . . .'

'And how do you suppose I manage when you're not about? When I'm stuck in that godforsaken sanatorium, with those despicable old farts?'

'You told me you were happy at Once-a-Star.'

'Happy? I've forgotten the meaning of the word. I merely count the days until the reinstatement.'

'The great day may come sooner than we dared hope, Mummy.'

The wreath-laden door opened, and Caine spied the fretful form of Petronella Lovell-Finch; large and pale, with the new baby in her arms.

'Merry Christmas, Tiggy,' she said nervously. 'I'm so glad you could join us. Come and meet your granddaughter, Velveteen Valeria Lovell-Finch.'

'You look like a large grub,' Tiggy told the infant. 'I daresay you plan to keep me awake all night.'

With many protestations, the young-old matriarch was ushered through the door, which closed firmly behind her.

All the way to Lovell Court, Caine processed what he had seen. Family squabbles were common at Christmas, that was true. But why had Quentin described his mother as flummoxed, befuddled and discombobulated? The description had been borne out by their unproductive visit to the Once-a-Star Rest Home, and yet as she'd cursed and struggled up those steps, Tiggy had appeared – to use one of Quentin's Latin terms – entirely *compos mentis*.

Caine pictured the Lego in Shanti's car, and in his mind, it was as if another brick of the case had clicked firmly into place.

Treading carefully across the cattle grid, beneath the heraldic archway of the Lovell-Finch estate, he paused for a moment to absorb the silence of the place, broken only by the flap and fluster of a gold and green pheasant perched on the boundary wall.

Caine liked it here. He liked the wild white foliage and the tumbling oceans of grass. He liked the biodiversity, which sang and swooped and rustled all around. As he headed up the satin ribbon of the drive, he felt easier in his soul.

Shanti had observed that he had plenty in common with the people of Lovell Court; or Evol as it was now. The gentle raggle-taggle Evolutionaries. The feral children. And Sky, that extraordinary savant, whose wisdom exceeded her years.

Among the frosty trees, he caught glimpses of foraging deer in quiet companionship with shaggy cattle. His spirit responded to this fenceless savannah style of farming. Without borders, the animals were free to roam.

Without borders? As he approached the ever-burning brazier, he realised that there was an inconsistency here. Finch had shunned fences and boundaries, so why would he insist on the phalanx of Evolutionary guards who waited by the barricade? What were the Evolutionaries defending? Who were they keeping at bay?

'Hello, Silas. It's me again, Vincent Caine.'

Silas peered at him through his yellow-lensed spectacles.

'Where's your car? Where's your woman?'

'It's a beautiful day, so I decided to walk. Shanti had other business. I've come to speak to Sky and Constanza.'

Silas turned to his companions. 'Let this one through. I'll walk him to the house.'

They set off up the drive, past the noisy kids sledging on the slope by the giant wooden letters – EVOL, or LOVE, depending on your perspective.

'I wanted to ask about the barricade,' said Caine. 'At first I wondered if it was a self-isolation thing. Then I wondered if it might serve another purpose. I mean, Finch had enemies, didn't he, Silas? You told me about the people he upset over the years. All the way back to the Battle of the Beanfield.'

'You'd better save those questions for Sky.'

'Help me out, Silas. What's the barricade for? To keep people in? Or to keep people out?'

'Talk to Sky, man. Talk to Sky.'

They had reached Evol village, where the placid inhabitants wandered amongst the tepees, domes and tree houses. Silas seemed tired. As if he too had been up all night. He nodded at Caine, then turned towards his home – the ancient library van with the smashed windows still waiting to be repaired.

At the foot of the steps, Caine was met by the huge trembling form of Ganesh, come to guide him into Lovell Court.

Chapter 29

Deep and Crisp and Even

'I knew you'd be a natural, Shantala.'

McAble had been right. The grey trekking pony was docile and easy to handle, unlike the major's stallion, Rufus, which was huge and black, and jittery as its rider.

Shanti recalled those Saturday-morning sessions at the City Farm, with a gentle, stinky nag named Scooby. She had loved to trot in and out of the oil drums . . . But this? This was like a scene from one of Mum's over-the-top movies, for which the director would have been quite rightly panned for the clichéd backdrop – the sweeping snow-covered plains, beneath a cloudless sky. And the distant edifice of Stonehenge, illuminated by shafts of sunlight, looking positively artificial.

They travelled at a steady trot, with hooves piercing the crusty snow. Half a mile from the barracks, they entered a bridle path, bordered on either side by hedges and a fence – as McAble had said, just wide enough for two horses, but too narrow for a large vehicle.

'To be clear, you are taking me to the last place you saw Finch?' said Shanti, struggling to trot at his side. 'The excavation, I mean?'

'Yes, it's near a place called Imber ... Isn't this wonderful? You took a little persuasion, but I knew you'd enjoy it when you got here.'

'You don't have a family, do you, Major?'

'Not a soul to call my own. I don't know why, but I seem to frighten women away. Perhaps they think they can't match me.'

'Right, well as I mentioned last night, I'm a single mum. And for some reason, single mums tend to feel guilty most of the time. Multiply that by ten at birthdays and Christmas.'

'Children are clearly a terrible burden. I suppose I'm lucky that my free time is my own.'

'Surprisingly, I adore my son, and I wish I was home with him right now.'

She faintly remembered that she had mentioned her parenting dilemma to Caine, and although she couldn't remember his precise words, she imagined he had been a little more empathetic.

As he rode, Troy reached into the pocket of his camouflage jacket and pulled out a leather hip flask. He unscrewed the lid and offered it to her.

'This'll blow away the cobwebs,' he said. 'It's made by a local company and they claim the recipe has been unchanged for thousands of years. It's ridiculously good.'

The horrified expression on her face told him all he needed to know.

'Tell me about the building at Everkill,' she said. 'The one that upset Finch so much. What was the story there?'

'The queen of questions,' he said, slapping the neck of his

mount. 'I'm afraid she isn't here for our looks, Rufus.'

'What did it say on that placard, Major? SAVE THE SUNRISE ... wasn't that it? AVENGE THE HENGE.'

McAble took a long swallow from the flask and shuddered in delight. Again she noticed his unsteady fingers as he fumbled to replace the lid.

'I can see I'll have no peace till I tell you. Finch got wind of plans for a new building at Everkill – it was only a storage facility, but it was on the skyline, and he claimed it would obstruct the sunrise at the summer solstice. I must admit it was pretty amusing to see him getting so irate. He told us that the first rays hit Stonehenge in a very precise way – "an astral calendar" was the phrase he used. He said it would be a desecration to interfere with that.'

'It sounds like you were taunting him.'

'Ah, not at all. We had a few frank exchanges over the years, but I'll even admit to a grudging respect for the man. He could have done anything with that heritage, so you couldn't doubt his sincerity, naïve as it was.'

'But not everyone felt the same?'

'Some of the lads ... No, I shouldn't say it.'

'You agreed to answer my questions.'

'You need to understand that people who have risked their lives in Iraq or Afghanistan don't take too kindly to some hairy aristocrat pontificating about the immorality of war, and telling them they have no right to carry out manoeuvres on the plains. I suppose Finch-baiting became a kind of sport for them. But as I told your scruffy colleague, I was the victim of bullying at school, so I won't tolerate it in others. In the end, Finch and I reached a compromise.'

'What sort of compromise?'

'I swore that we would leave a gap in the buildings so the sunrise would be unaffected.'

'So what was the problem?'

'Ah, well, the night before the solstice, a few of the lads had a tipple of this stuff . . .' He pulled out the flask and took another long gulp. 'In defiance of my orders, they thought it would be amusing to throw up a prefab building overnight. As soon as I found out, I gave instructions to have it removed, but by then, Finch was incandescent with rage. Hence the spectacle at the passing-out parade.'

They had reached the end of the bridle path, and the horses tiptoed across the panoramic plain. The area was clearly used for military exercises, as Shanti could see scar-like ruts beneath the snow, which could only have been created by tanks or heavy artillery.

To her alarm, she spotted several large signs:

MILITARY FIRING RANGE KEEP OUT

Danger of unexploded ordnance!

No civilian access beyond this point

'Jeez,' she said. 'Is this safe?'

'It's what I warned you about,' he said calmly. 'That's why Finch was such a damned fool to play his games here. And I'll tell you another thing – it's an absolute nuisance when they discover something; you know, ancient tombs and all that. It means that construction and training exercises come to a complete standstill, for years possibly, while the excavation takes place. Chaps like Finch are clever – they know how to exploit the historical significance status to thwart our work at Everkill, which is in the national interest as any damned fool can see ... You need to stick close here, Shantala. I know exactly where we're going. Up there – near the summit.'

'These men who liked to taunt Finch – where can I find them?'

'The thing is, Shantala, they're no longer with us.'

'You mean they died?'

'Not dead, no. They got honourable discharges. Booted out of the military.'

'Who ...? I mean, why were they discharged?'

'Those boys were a little unstable. They'd experienced some horrific things in Helmand, and sadly, they'd lost it a bit. We were all offered counselling, but for their own reasons, they declined. Some of them had anger management issues, and you can't have that in service. It's all about discipline, you understand.'

'And where are they now?'

McAble fired an angry glance at her. 'Look, could you stop asking so many damned questions? You haven't let up since we met. I was really looking forward to spending time with you, and now you're spoiling everything. I wish you could understand that these people are unpredictable.'

'I can take care of myself.'

'I don't doubt it. You're a tough cookie, Shantala, but in the end, you're only a civilian police officer. You've become obsessed with the life of one man, but the people I'm talking about have been to hell and back.' He took another guzzle from the flask and moved forward. 'In any case, I'm actually not feeling very well today. I told you I was on medication, and the doctors strongly advise me not to drink.'

'Then perhaps—'

'Now, you said you wanted to see where I last saw Finch. Look down there ...'

They stood on the summit of a ridge above a valley. Below them lay a sprawling village, with an old church and snowy roof-tops. There was something static about the place – frozen by frost, and frozen in time. Not a vehicle on the roads. Not an animal in the white fields. Not a person on the pavements. Nothing moved except a family of magpies amongst the skeletal trees.

'What is this place?' Shanti asked.

'That's Imber.'

'And what's so special about Imber?'

'It's a ghost village, Shantala. Strictly out of bounds to civil-ians. The place was commandeered by the military for the national good in 1943 and it's been used ever since for training purposes. The original villagers were offered alternative housing, but many fell into depression and a few even committed suicide, so we're told. Some of their descendants hold resentment to the present day. I'll tell you what, Shantala, I've visited war zones all over the world, but you'll find every bit as much conflict and resentment in the Wiltshire countryside.'

And then Shanti heard something that made her skin crawl – distant buzzing, like a hive of angry bees or the sound of engines. At the far end of the main street, something moved. A convoy of motorbikes, ridden by men in hoods and robes.

Chapter 30

Diary of a Dead Man

The girl was sitting behind her father's cluttered desk, in a turquoise study filled with books and sunlight.

'You hear that, Ganesh?' she told the dog affectionately. 'Mr Caine has found your brother. That's right, Albion is coming home.'

It was as if the animal understood. His tail swayed and he pushed his nose against her hands.

Caine scanned the room, taking in numerous anthropological artefacts: framed mandalas; images of the sun and moon, alongside deities like Christ, Brahma and what Shanti would call his pal, the Buddha.

On the wall above a chaotic bookshelf, someone had painted a phrase in gold calligraphy:

We do not inherit the earth from our ancestors, we borrow it from our children.

'I love that,' he said.

'It was Finch's favourite quote,' Sky replied.

Caine took a seat on the other side of the desk. 'You found the diary?' he said.

She lifted a large volume from the drawer and cleared a space on the surface of the desk, black eyes glistening as she turned the pages.

'I was up half the night reading it,' she said. 'He recorded everything. All the successes. All the dreams. All the conflicts.'

'Your father was a man of powerful convictions,' said Caine. 'And like those prophets up there, he inevitably made enemies along the way. Did you find references to his recent project – the dig on the plains?'

'Yes, it's here in the final pages . . .' She turned the journal to show her father's dense handwriting, accompanied by diagrams, sketches and maps. 'These are the coordinates, if that helps. Finch's writing is difficult to read, but he says: *Exciting day! The magnetometer draws me to a specific location near Imber, four miles north-west of the Stones. The army have placed warning signs, but I will not be deterred . . .*'

'Go on,' said Caine. 'What else does he say?'

'He thinks he has discovered what he has always searched for – a sacred site to rival Stonehenge. With increasing excitement, he begins to dig, sometimes working all night. On the third morning, he begins to unearth flint tools and even fragments of bone. Now he thinks the site must be a Neolithic tomb . . . And that's it. That's where the journal ends.'

She rotated the book again, so that Caine could see that the remaining half of the journal remained as white as the virgin plains. As white as an unfinished story.

In an armchair beside the great fireplace, Constanza seemed

more lucid today, though her English was faltering. Speaking in Portuguese, Sky conveyed the news that Albion had been found. Caine saw Constanza's face light up. She spoke rapidly to Sky, who answered, '*Não, Mãe, não!*'

'She still believes Finch will return,' the girl told him.

'Maybe we shouldn't force it,' he said. 'She'll come to an understanding in her own time. Do you think she will answer some questions?'

'Yes, she's happy to help.'

'Constanza has an interest in herbal medicine. Would she be able to identify hemlock?'

The lack of a shared language was strangely helpful. It meant that Caine could study and read Constanza's face as the words were translated. It was hard to believe that the grieving mother and daughter felt anything but love for the man they had lost.

'Constanza says she had to relearn her botanic skills when she came to England,' Sky told him. 'She taught Finch the art of foraging and she says that he never came home without handfuls of mushrooms, herbs or berries. But of course, the first thing she taught him was how to identify toxic plants – this is a universal law of foraging. So yes, she could certainly identify hemlock.'

'OK,' said Caine. 'Now I'm afraid I need to ask your mother some harder questions.'

'*Questões mais difíceis . . .*' Constanza nodded resolutely.

'When Constanza and Finch first met, did he mention problems with some of the travellers?'

Constanza paused, as if reluctant to revisit an oppressive memory. When she did speak, her words were hesitant and anxious, and the effect on Sky was like a dark cloud passing across her face.

'My mother says she doesn't want to upset me, but maybe I am old enough to understand things they kept from me ...'

Sky went back and forth to her mother, checking details and asking her to repeat phrases until she was clear. Then she gave her attention to Caine.

'OK. I guess I already knew some of this. There were always rumours and stories amongst my friends in Evol. Constanza tells me that a small number of the original travellers were trouble-makers – aggressive anarchists, she calls them – who liked to settle arguments with fists or knives. They never accepted the peaceful spirit of Evol. Finch opened his heart and his home, but they stole and abused his hospitality. In the end, my father had no choice – he told them to leave, which didn't go down well. There were a couple of occasions when they even attacked him. Although he was a pacifist, Finch was a big man, and exceptionally brave.'

'And where are these people now?'

She spoke with her mother again.

'Some went back where they came from. But a few remain in the area.'

'This explains the barrier across the drive?'

Constanza spoke rapid staccato Portuguese punctuated with English phrases. Caine caught the familiar term: *Battle of the Beanfield*.

'She's saying that back then, your colleagues were not so helpful – they harboured resentment from the Battle of the Beanfield. So Finch and the Evolutionaries had to learn to look after themselves. They set up their own security detail, and since that time, Lovell Court has been defended day and night.'

'I need to know who these people are – these disaffected travellers.'

Another intense discussion, with Sky seeming more anxious by the minute.

'This is weird,' she said. 'Constanza tells me that these guys merged with a local gang ... a gang that still operates in this area. It grew bigger over the years, and Finch told her that it even formed a pact with some of the renegade cops who were dismissed for excessive use of force at the Battle of the Beanfield.'

The expression of dread on Constanza's face needed no translation.

'My mother says most of them are not so young now, but they're very scary. They drive around on motorbikes, and some wear leathers, but also they dress like—'

'Like Druids?' said Caine.

'Exactly. I think I've seen these people, Mr Caine. They wear robes and hoods. Constanza describes them as the closest thing to the KKK in Wiltshire.'

'This is vital information,' said Caine. 'Please ask your mother if they have a base. I mean somewhere they congregate.'

Sky put the question, while Caine waited impatiently for the answer.

'OK. This is creepy. There's a place out on the plains, near Finch's excavation, which is strictly out of bounds to civilians. It's a village that was taken over during the war and has been used ever since for urban warfare practice. A ghost village, essentially.'

'Imber?'

'That's right. Finch had the idea that these guys hang out in the empty buildings and drive their bikes around the streets.'

Constanza spoke earnestly to Sky.

'I didn't know this ... My mother says that back in the day,

Imber was part of the Lovell-Finch estate. In the 1930s and '40's, Finch's grandfather was ... I suppose you would call him the squire of the village. Although it was a compulsory eviction order from the government, many of the residents held him responsible for the loss of their homes.'

Constanza was agitated now, sitting upright, staring intently into the flames. Caine caught the words *soldados do exército*. Each time Sky tried to translate, however, her mother cut her off with more fretful details. Eventually the girl said:

'This is only speculation, but my mother has the idea that some of this mob are ex-soldiers, who were dismissed from the army.'

Caine felt his anxiety levels rise. 'So they might have access to military locations?'

Constanza spoke one final phrase to her daughter before sighing and settling back with arms folded, as if she had exhausted her testimony. The last two words were in English. And they had a chilling resonance.

'My mother says that these bad people – these *caras maus* – have a name around here. People call them the Psyche Squad.'

Chapter 31

The Dark Lord of Death

'The Psyche Squad,' said Troy McAble.

'What kind of a name is that?' said Shanti.

'Bit of a joke, I suppose. But somehow it stuck. Look, Shantala, you're a lovely girl—'

'I'm a woman, Major McAble.'

'You certainly are. The thing is, I really don't want you getting out of your depth. That's why I was reluctant to mention any of this. Some things are best left alone . . . Christ! This stuff's got a kick like a mule!'

'I'm going to ask you to stop drinking, Major.'

'A little late for that.' He tipped the flask so that the last golden drops tumbled into his mouth. 'But look – no shakes, see!' He held out one arm, which seemed to waver over the church spire below.

'I need you to show me the excavation site. Immediately, please. And after that, I'm going to leave.'

'I used to love soldiering, Shantala. But the PTSD and the

medication have created all kinds of problems. My relationships have all failed. And between you and me, I've run up some pretty hefty gambling debts. It's lovely to have someone to talk to, actually . . .' There were tears streaming from his bloodshot eyes.

'What is that stuff you've been drinking, Major?'

'Henge Hives Mead. Made by Druids, you know. They say the recipe hasn't changed in a thousand years. *Guaranteed to give you a buzz* is the slogan. That's rather clever, don't you think? I doubt they get many complaints.'

'Who are those people down there? You told me the village was a restricted zone.'

'Questions, questions, questions . . . Here's a question for you, DI Shantala-Whatever-Your-Name-Is . . . *Voulez-vous couchez avec moi sis wah?*'

He was slurring his words, unsteady in the saddle, a wild expression on his handsome face.

'You know what?' said Shanti. 'I'm going to call it a day now. You told me this area was inaccessible to vehicles, but that's clearly not true. I'm going to send over a team this afternoon to examine Lovell-Finch's excavation. And don't tell me it's restricted land, Major, because this is a murder inquiry.'

Seizing the reins, she turned the pony and headed back in the direction they had come.

'STOP!' roared McAble, flopping back into his seat. 'I ORDER YOU TO STOP!'

Shanti heard his voice echo for miles around.

'You absolutely cannot go off alone. You've seen the signs, haven't you? Even if you're prepared to risk your own life, I will not risk the lives of these horses. Now wait for me there, Shantala. Do you hear? Do not move to the left or right. That's an order!'

Shanti reached for her phone and pulled up Caine's number. The instrument was dead in her hands.

'What's wrong with my phone, Major?'

He imitated her voice in a spiteful whining snarl. '*What's wrong with my phone, Major?* There's nothing wrong with your phone, Detective Inspector. We don't have a signal at Imber. We don't have electricity either ... or running water. This is about survival, Shantala. Every man jack for himself. And now I'd like to introduce you to some of my friends ...'

From the woods and forest they came.

Swarming like bees.

On motorbikes.

In sidecars.

And olive jeeps.

The men in robes.

The Druids.

At Lovell Court, Caine's serenity was long gone as he desperately fumbled with his phone. Again and again he dialled Shanti's number, but all he got was her calm, funny voice on the answerphone.

Next he tried Benno. But the call went unanswered, until eventually it was picked up by the sergeant's wife. It was most unlike Benno to leave his phone in his uniform, she told him. Mind you, he'd been in such a rush to meet the train and collect their daughter and son-in-law, with the grandchildren. She assured Caine that he wouldn't be more than an hour, and she'd be sure to pass on his message the minute he returned. In the meantime, she wished him a very peaceful Christmas. She was sure he'd be glad to put his feet up.

There was a time for contemplation. There was a time for action ...

'Sky, I need to get to Imber immediately. Is there any way you can drive me there?'

'I'm fourteen, Mr Caine. Do you think I have a car?'

'Of course. I keep forgetting. Perhaps one of the Evolutionaries ...'

'I've got a better idea,' she said. 'Follow me.'

In boots, greatcoat and hat, Caine followed the girl in her scruffy green duffel coat and woollen beanie, her feet bare on the ground as they sprinted along the front of the great house. It was not yet four o'clock, but the rolling wilderness of the estate was bathed in the blood of the setting sun.

'I know I'm not supposed to go in here,' said Sky. 'But it's the best way.'

She found the key, unlocked Finch's workshop and hurried inside. Within minutes, they were accelerating down the drive, with Caine clinging to the back of the speeding snowmobile.

As they approached the barrier, Sky yelled a warning to the Evolutionary guards, who hauled it up so they could pass through. As they rattled over the cattle grid, Caine hollered into her ear:

'You wouldn't like me to drive, Sky?'

'Don't worry, Mr Caine. Finch taught me well. Here, you might need these ...' She reached backwards and handed him a pair of goggles.

'How long?'

'Twenty minutes, maybe. Not much more. We can cut cross-country.'

In the snowy burrow of the lanes, Sky switched on the

headlights and Caine realised that she was right – she was a confident driver. He gave himself up to the madness of the moment. What else could he do?

'Take it steady up here,' he warned. 'There was quite a crowd earlier.'

They were still there – the TV crews, the journalists, the reporters, the police. Slowing the vehicle to walking pace, Sky skirted the horde at the gates of the Old Vicarage, where soft lights burned at the end of the drive.

When they were clear, she gunned it up the hill, barely stopping at the junction of the A303. There was no traffic tonight – anyone with any sense was safely cocooned with their loved ones. Shooting straight across the carriageway, she headed towards a small gateway in the fence surrounding English Heritage land. Caine realised that it was one of those narrow permissive tracks that criss-crossed the plains. Soon they were sliding and bouncing along rutted ground between hedges and barbed-wire fences.

This was, and always had been, disputed land. The army. English Heritage. The tourists. Archaeologists. Druids. All of them staked a claim. These had been the promised lands of the travellers back in the Thatcher years, for which Silas had paid such a heavy price.

As sunset morphed to moonlight, the headlights illuminated their path, and Sky hastened across the plain. Caine was grateful for the goggles, as his face was pelted by shards of ice thrown up by the skis of the vehicle. Peering across the silvery desert, he saw the focus of all that rivalry, looming far away beneath the gawking eye of the moon. Silent. Deserted. Draped in snowy splendour. The holy grail of Stonehenge.

***

What Caine did not know was that Shanti was lying there, stretched out on the Altar Stone, with cords tightly bound around her hands and feet.

High above her head, the moon rose full and peachy pink. By twisting her head to the side, she could see the turning area by the Portaloos, where the Druids were assembling.

There was nothing hurried about their preparations – on the contrary, this group of older men and women chatted amiably as they changed into their robes. The men were heavily bearded and tattooed, their rotund bellies revealing a taste for ale. The women cheerily greeted new arrivals, and the GoodGuys security team embraced their fellow Druids.

Shortly after she had been seized on the ridge above Imber, she had lost sight of Troy McAble. The last thing she'd seen was his wild face, demented and raving as he goaded his stallion to rear on its hind legs – suggesting, she surmised, a more unusual ingredient than fermented honey within the Henge Hives Mead.

The slab on which she lay was cold granite. Uncomfortable certainly, but beneath her back, her fingers were busily seeking out sharp edges. Whatever the hell was going on, she was not one to lie back like a maiden in distress.

You had to appreciate Dawn's efficiency. Not only had the tower been dismantled, but every scrap of tape and litter, as well as the stepping plates and the forensics tent, had been removed. The monument had been restored to its brooding simplicity.

The Chief Druid paid Shanti a quick courtesy call to ensure she was as comfortable as could be expected. He apologised for the delay, and assured her that it wouldn't be too long before they were ready to begin the ceremony.

Amongst the parked motorbikes and ex-military vehicles, the Psyche Squad were fully cloaked and hooded now, calmly hunting for a few last-minute items in the boots of vehicles or sidecars. There was something so very English about the scene, Shanti decided. It was as if they were about to play a game of cricket on a village green.

And that would have soothed her, had she not been about to die.

A mile past Stonehenge, the narrow track ended and the snow-mobile swept across the open plain, glowing ultraviolet in the lunar light. As Sky strained the engine to its limits, Caine's face was bombarded with snowflakes.

'I think we're getting close,' yelled Sky. 'Imber is beyond that ridge, up ahead. And according to Finch's sketches, his excavation was around here too.'

It was clear that theirs was not the first vehicle to pass here tonight. Caine could see numerous tracks in the snow – the hooves of horses, and the treads of various vehicles. Including motorcycles, he realised with alarm.

Even more unnerving were the large signs, which reflected the beam of their headlights:

MILITARY FIRING RANGE KEEP OUT
Danger of unexploded ordnance!
No civilian access beyond this point

Caine felt as powerless as a child. Intimidated by the military and driven by a teenager.

'I think we should be OK if we stick to the tracks,' Sky called. 'According to the journal, this is the route that Finch used.'

Caine marvelled at her competence and courage. The kid had lost her father. And here she was heading fearlessly into the unknown.

The idea of unexploded ordnance was terrifying, but he comforted himself with the thought that all these others vehicles had passed this way without harm. Perhaps the warning signs were nothing more than insurance against potential consequences, or a bluff to discourage trespassers.

As if to confirm his theory, he realised that the dark riders had been swerving and criss-crossing the brittle shell of snow, veering in and out as if playing games, like kids on speeding bicycles. Daring each other to perform wilder feats of wheelcraft.

Caine had an aching desire to see Shanti. To know that she was well. The teachings about letting go were all very well, but what could an old Chinese monk know about love?

So why was Sky slowing down? Why was she coming to a halt out here in this emptiness, four miles from Stonehenge, a mile from their destination at Imber? Not engine trouble, surely? That would be unbearable.

'What's the problem, Sky?'

In answer, she put a finger to her lips. 'Listen!'

The snowmobile had stopped completely now. At the handlebars, Sky stood upright, huge eyes staring in wonder. Then she pointed to the ridge a mile ahead.

Caine felt it before he saw it. A rumble under his feet. From somewhere deep beneath the ground. Below the very crust of the earth.

A moment later, he saw it. The first of four apparitions like Jurassic monsters, looming over the hill. Vast ... lumbering ... menacing.

'What is that, Mr Caine?' Sky asked, suddenly a child again.

The behemoths had seen them now. And there was nowhere to hide on this infinite wilderness, beneath the all-seeing moon.

The first creature swung its long proboscis in their direction, paused for a millisecond, then thundered down the slope, rattling and groaning towards them.

'Tanks!' said Caine. 'They're tanks. And they're heading this way.'

'Should I turn back, Mr Caine? What should I do?'

'We'll never outrun them. Listen . . . listen, don't worry . . . I'm sure they don't mean us any harm. We're probably . . . Yes, that's it. We're trespassing on restricted land. They'll make us pay a fine or something. When they realise who I am, and that I'm on a case . . . I'm sure we can sort it out.'

He was rambling. Partly to reassure the girl, partly to reassure himself, but mainly because those four metallic beasts were thundering towards them at an alarming speed, with no sign of slowing.

'OK. Listen, Sky. On reflection, I don't think these people are . . . you know, messengers of love . . .'

'You mean they're not going to stop?'

'It's a bit weird, isn't it? I honestly don't know.'

'Shit. Well I'm not waiting to find out. Come on, Mr Caine . . . let's run!'

The girl leapt from the vehicle and headed barefoot across the snow.

Caine, who had been clear-headed and mindful for most of the day, felt as stunned as the proverbial rabbit in the headlights. Except that this rabbit was alone in the middle of a snowy plain as a convoy of fast-moving tanks approached.

From beyond the hilltop came a terrifying bang, and a flash lit up the horizon. Then another. And another, until the night reverberated with the ear-splitting sounds. They must be flares, Caine thought. Surely no one would fire live ammunition out here, would they?

He had always been too sensitive. As teenagers, his friends had loved war films – the louder and bloodier the better. Sometimes Caine had pretended to laugh at the horrors playing out on the screen, in Vietnam or the killing fields of Cambodia. But in reality he felt traumatised, as if he were there among the persecuted peasants whose villages and families were blown asunder. And this – this insane scene playing out in front of his eyes – was a thousand times more disturbing than any of those movies.

Glancing around, he could not see the girl. That was good, although he had no idea where she could be hiding.

As he watched the approaching tanks, and listened to the distant explosions, he considered his options. Maybe he could delay the tanks for a while, like the man in Tiananmen Square. But what was he thinking? How could he stop a speeding tank? How could he stop four tanks?

And how on earth could he stop these other things . . . these new arrivals? The hulking metallic apparitions that now rose over the ridge? As he gawped in stunned horror, he saw the bellies of two machines twitching overhead like colossal mechanical birds. Clattering, thundering, terrifying . . .

Helicopters!

Their searchlights swept the plains until they picked him out, and Caine stood helplessly exposed, as if every nerve was bare in that deafening, blinding bedlam.

He was defeated. It was as simple as that. Powerless against the machines. The lone peasant on the killing fields. The last Sioux warrior against the Confederate army. With one hand shading his eyes from the glare and the other raised in humble surrender, he waited unsteadily for whatever was to come.

And then he witnessed something so weird and unworldly that the last reserves of will drained from his body.

The command hatch of the leading tank opened, and a figure rose from inside. It was a man. An outlandish man with a large moustache, dressed in camouflage fatigues, who shrieked with glee and wild abandon. It was Major Troy McAble. And on his head was a vast set of stag antlers.

In the seconds before the mighty machine crushed the snow-mobile to smithereens, Caine heard the stag man's exultant howl echoing across the plains and into every ancient niche of Stonehenge.

'YAH! I'M A GOD! I'M A WARLORD! I'M THE DARK LORD OF DEATH!'

Chapter 32

Blood of My Blood

Shanti watched the fireworks out on the plains, with accompanying flashes and whirring sky craft.

Peculiar as that was, her immediate focus was on the Druids, who were chanting now, and dancing in a languid circle around her. Robes and beards. Beards and robes. Women swaying in white dresses beneath the fiery moon.

The Chief Druid stepped forward, dressed in a white gown emblazoned with a dragon. As he approached, the circle parted reverentially.

With ever-building excitement, the coven swarmed and swirled. Above the hypnotic chanting, Shanti heard another vehicle arrive.

'They're here,' murmured the Druids. 'They've arrived at last.'

On the slope by the Portaloos, a vintage Bentley in gleaming maroon pulled up between the motorbikes and other vehicles. The driver's door opened and Shanti caught the sound of cultured voices raised in argument.

A spindly figure emerged, wearing thick-lensed glasses, a trilby hat and a camel-hair coat with a woollen collar. He scurried to the back of the car, lifted out a folding wheelchair and set about the complicated task of kicking and wrestling the thing into shape. When it sprang open, the force dislodged the trilby, revealing a distinctively elongated head with a plunging waterfall of hair. It was Quentin Lovell-Finch. The usurped heir of Lovell Court.

The politician wheeled the chair to the passenger door, from where a willowy figure emerged, in miniskirt, furs and blonde curls beneath a purple hat. The skeletal face, with eyelashes like spiders, was unmistakable. This was Tiggy Antrobus-Lovell-Finch, whose family, Quentin had boasted, had once owned Stonehenge.

Even as Quentin wrapped a tartan blanket around her bony knees and steered the wheelchair precariously up the slope, their bickering did not cease. As the Druids waited patiently, he navigated the chair inside the stone circle, where the Chief Druid bowed deferentially.

There was a short argument about why they were late – each blaming the other. Then, when all was silent, the Chief Druid commenced the incantation. With hands reddened by cold, he offered a chalice to the moon. His words were dragon's breath in the air.

'Friends, we are gathered to mark the passing of the Holly King to the life beyond. Blood of my blood,' he boomed.

'Blood of my blood,' called the assembled ones.

'Bone of my flesh. Flesh of my bone. I will live on within your hearts. Take me now . . .'

'Take me now . . .'

'For to face the Summerlands.'

263

The congregants resumed their mesmeric dancing, with flaming torches held high.

'Help!' called Shanti from the slab. 'Someone help me, please.'

'Is that you, dear lady?' answered Quentin, gyrating at her side. 'I thought I recognised those dulcet norf Lunden tones.'

'For God's sake, help!' shouted Shanti. 'Those bastards have tied my hands.'

'It is her!' shrieked Tiggy. 'The bitch who visited my chamber.'

'Tell me, dear lady, where is your unwashed friend, Detective Caliban?'

'He's . . . he's on his way. He knows exactly where I am.'

'I doubt it. We have policemen amongst our number. The security guards? We own them too. Were you not paying attention when I told you that I am a man of influence? I warned you not to make an enemy of me, dear lady. Did you not hear me mention my contacts in powerful places?'

'You're insane,' shouted Shanti. 'You're completely fucking barmy.'

He turned and stared at her. 'You see, this has been the problem since days of yore. When ignorant masses rise above their station, there is bound to be trouble. Look at the simple people around you. Let them be an example. Like you, they are uneducated, but they know their status. They are therefore useful. You, dear lady, are not.'

'Right. Listen. I demand to use a phone.'

'But we do not allow telephones here. That is part of the fun. Our own little world, where one can play till teatime or beyond. Tell me, who brought you here? Was it McAble? Where is the major? Tell me, who has seen McAble?'

'We gave him medication, sir,' said the Chief Druid.

'He has imbibed hemlock?'

'No, my lord. Merely mead, fortified with psilocybin.'

'You're all mad,' shouted Shanti.

'Well, he *will* be mad,' smirked Quentin. 'The psilocybin grows prodigiously on the plains in the autumn months. Those pretty fungal bodies are shaped like tiny penises, some say. The ancient ones used them to enter a state of trance. To move between this world and the world of the spirits.'

It was as if Tiggy could resist no longer. Throwing the blanket aside, she leapt from her chair and began to jive, stick legs shimmying beneath her tiny skirt.

And at her side, Quentin Lovell-Finch shook his angular frame in a wild pagan dance. Oval occiput swaying. A pink moon on each owlish lens.

Staring in wonder at the belly of the tank, which rose like a house above him, Caine accepted that he and the snowmobile were about to become pizza. An unusual way for a Buddhist to die, but what was death after all?

Above the roar of engines, he heard a scream, and when he looked down, he saw Sky yanking violently at his arm. She physically hauled him off the snowmobile and threw him to the ground.

Then they were rolling, Caine and the girl, over and over in the snow, before plunging into a deep trench in the ground. As he covered his head with his hands, Caine was vaguely aware of a groaning, cracking sound as the snowmobile was pulverised like a cheap caravan at a breaker's yard.

And now, the vast caterpillar tracks of the tank rolled like conveyor belts above their heads, sending a cascade of snow and fragments of metal raining upon them.

As it passed, the sky opened like a trapdoor, and Caine looked straight up at the moon. The moment of calm was transitory. A moment later, the trench was plunged into darkness again as the second tank roared overhead. Then the third. And the fourth.

Finally, to the intense relief of his battered senses, the world became quiet, except for the distant sound of the retreating army – the receding tanks and the thundering of helicopter blades.

At last he was able to take stock. Looking around, he realised that they were crouched inside a deep chalk trench, half covered with a brown tarpaulin.

'Are you OK?' said Sky. 'Let me check you over, Mr Caine. Yeah, we were lucky. I don't think you're hurt.'

'But . . . but what is this place?'

'It must be my father's excavation. Finch saved us.'

'No, *you* saved me, Sky. Another second and I'd have been crushed.'

Sky peered over the trench wall, surveying the landscape.

'They've gone,' she said. 'The tanks are way over there. Heading towards the barracks. They're crazy, aren't they? I think they were actually trying to kill us.'

'I have no doubt about that. But what is all this?' Caine was examining the chaotic contents of the trench. The weight of the tanks had caused the chalk walls to partially collapse, and the tarpaulin, which must have protected the excavation from the elements, lay crumpled at their feet. But there was other stuff here – archaeological artefacts, perhaps, and yet he was confused by how well preserved they seemed to be. Clumps of fur and

animal skin protruding from the strata of the walls. And something else ... something that made his pounding heart stall.
Bones. Broken bones, with flesh and hair still clinging.

Suppressing a wave of nausea, he attempted to hide the grim
sight from the girl. He boosted her out of the trench, then, taking another look at the grisly remains, allowed her to help him
scramble upwards. As he brushed the snow from his coat, he
found that his legs were trembling violently.

Despite the turmoil that had ensued, however, one thing had
not left him – a driving sense of urgency. He and the girl were
alive, but what of Shanti?

'Now listen, Sky. I need to move fast. How do you feel about
walking back to Lovell Court? Would you feel safe?'

'Forget it. I'm coming with you.'

He looked at her and realised that there would be no arguing
with this girl.

They set off at a steady jog, and despite what they had been
through, Sky moved steadily on her bare feet, Caine falling in at
her side. It was good to run. To release the adrenaline and fear
that had built up in his body, almost clogging the arteries. Now
his chest opened and the cold, sweet air of the plains was like
balm on his lungs.

At the top of the ridge, they gazed down at the moonlit
stones. From here, they could make out a cluster of vehicles,
flickering flames and oscillating figures.

'I'm going to pick up speed, Sky. Don't try to keep up, OK?
You follow at your own pace. But for God's sake, keep well away
from the stones. We're dealing with dangerous people – I'm sure
you know that.'

And Caine began to sprint. Faster than he had in years.

Skidding and sliding, leaping over stones buried in piles of snow. But no matter how fast he travelled, the girl stayed on his heels.

As they approached the temple, he bent double to lower his profile against the snow. Damn that moon! But then why else were the Druids here tonight, if not for the cold moon of Yule? By the time Sky caught up, he was darting from one vehicle to the next so that he would not be seen. One car in particular held his attention. A maroon Derby Bentley.

Now they were near enough to see the hooded figures. More than twenty of them, Caine estimated, dancing in the light of flickering torches. The closest thing to the KKK in Wiltshire, Constanza had called them.

And then he saw the figure laid out on the Altar Stone – the woollen hat, the leather jacket. The sacrifice was Shanti.

Shanti was filled with terror, there was no denying it. But alongside the fear was fury. With a little wriggling, she had succeeded in pressing the cords against a knapped ridge on the Altar Stone, so that the sharp edge bit into the nylon strands. It was slow work, but as she shifted her hands from side to side, she could feel the fibres loosening.

They had stopped dancing now, the robed ones, and formed a circle around her stone. They stood so close, she could smell their sweat. She saw heavily muscled arms protruding from white cloth. Glimpses of tattoos, and leather, and chains. If she didn't know it already, it was clear that the Psyche Squad were big and brutal men.

Quite tenderly now, Quentin helped Tiggy back into her chair and wrapped the blanket around her slender knees, wheeling her forward so that she could see what was to come.

At a signal from Quentin, the Chief Druid stepped forward. To Shanti's absolute horror, she saw that he was holding a flint hatchet.

'Who will wield the blade?' he boomed.

An excited whisper circulated like an agitated swarm.

'Who will wield the blade?' he called again.

'I will,' said a tall Druid at the back of the circle. 'I will wield the blade.' Stepping forward, he grasped the hatchet, bowing his head to the Chief Druid.

Shanti looked up at the robed man, and as if in a silent film, her life began to stream past her eyes. She saw again the ones she had loved. Her departed father. Her dear son, Paul. Her mum, Amma, always faithful, always there for her.

And as the dark-faced Druid loomed above her and raised the blade, she thought tenderly of the man named Caine.

Down amongst the motorbikes and military vehicles, Sky saw the lights approaching from the visitor centre. Pulsating blue lights, accompanied by the electrifying *whoop-whoo-ooop* of sirens.

As one, the pagans turned to gaze at the line of squad cars streaming at high speed towards the temple. At the head of the convoy was the distinctive form of Benno at the wheel of his neon Land Rover.

At the sight of the approaching cavalry, robed figures began to scatter across the plains, and immediately a few squad cars swerved off-road to give chase.

'Strike her now,' roared the Chief Druid.

The tall figure with the hatchet knelt at Shanti's side.

'If you roll on your side, I can cut the rope,' he said gently.

'Jesus, Caine,' said Shanti. 'Always late for school.'

269

Chapter 33

The Temple of the Winds

In the timeless arena, the corvids reclaimed their terrain, and the *Kra! Kraa! Kraaa!* of their cries began to recede. Only two of the foolish mortals remained.

'I was so worried about you, Shanti. And I still think you need to be checked over. I wish you'd let Benno take you to the hospital.'

'For God's sake, Caine. It's two o'clock in the morning on Christmas Eve. I've got better things to do than hang about in A&E.'

They sat side by side on the Altar Stone, and for the first time, Caine noticed that the gleaming monoliths of Stonehenge resembled a grove of gigantic stone Druids.

'I'm glad Benno was able to take Sky back to Lovell Court,' he said. 'That girl saved my life, you know. You should have seen her, Shanti. She was extraordinary. McAble was raging. Absolutely off his tree.'

'Troy. Jeez . . . You never liked him, did you?'

'I suppose he can't be blamed for the narcissistic personality disorder. But there's one thing about him that's unforgivable . . .'

'What's that, Caine?'

'The moustache, Shanti.'

Far above their heads, stars were born and died in the crucible of space.

The Druidic robe that Caine had found stuffed in one of the motorcycle sidecars was made of thick linen, and now Shanti pulled it tight around her shoulders.

'I thought Druids were supposed to be peaceful people,' she said.

'Ah, they're not real Druids.'

'I have to be honest, I'm still pretty confused about this case. You've been piecing it together all along, haven't you?'

'I always had my suspicions about Troy. Do you remember being trained to pay careful attention to who is present at the earliest stage of an inquiry? Some killers just can't keep away from the scene of crime. A kind of morbid fascination. They'll even inject themselves into the police investigation.'

'And Troy was at the scene even before we arrived.'

'Exactly. And then late last night, Tull told me something critical.'

'This is fascinating, Caine. But could you save it until the morning? I think my head is liable to explode.'

'Of course. I'm so sorry. You must be exhausted. Would you like to walk up to the roundhouse?'

'You're right, I am absolutely knackered. And unlike Tull, I can't wait to be reunited with my electric blanket. But right now, I don't feel like walking anywhere, and in any case, this place is . . . What's the word?' She looked around at the luminescent temple.

'Magical, Shant?'

'We talked about that adjective. But yeah, that's exactly what it is.'

They sat listening to the weird acoustics – the cackling of the spirit birds in their nests, and a spooky sonic tune created by the wind in the jagged teeth of the sarsens.

'Listen to it,' said Caine. 'You know what Hardy called this place? The temple of the winds!'

'Don't you ever stop jabbering, Caine?'

'Tess of the d'Urbervilles lay down and rested exactly where you are now.'

'I don't blame her. I wouldn't mind a snooze myself.'

Caine brushed the snow from the slab, unbuttoned his coat and laid it out for her.

'You'll get cold, Caine. They forgot to turn the central heating on.'

'Angel Clare stood at her side and guarded her.'

'I can guard myself, thank you very much.'

'You're the strongest person I know.'

She lay back and closed her eyes, and soon he heard her steady breathing. He sat for a long time holding her hand, and all the while he reflected on the strange case of Hector Lovell-Finch, the Holly King, until every last stone of that mysterious case slotted into place.

Although the icy wind crept into his bones, Caine did not move until he noticed a faint streak of light between the pillars – the dawning day at the earth's edge. As the sky began to lighten, the corvids flew from their roosts and goose-stepped amongst the stones.

Caine saw something approaching from the visitor centre.

A mere dot. A Land Rover on the roadway. It came to a halt in the turning area, and after a while, Benno and Masako entered the stone arena.

'Let her finish her sleep,' said Caine quietly.

Benno nodded, and they waited patiently, until a ray of sunlight shone on Shanti's sleeping form and she stirred.

'Have they come for me, Caine?'

'Yes. They've come.'

She stood up and stretched, handing the coat to Caine and the robe to Benno.

'I'm ready,' she said quietly. 'It's time to go home.'

Chapter 34

A Devilish Denouement

In the dazzling morning of Christmas Eve, they sat around a wooden picnic table to hear Caine unravel the enigma of the Holly King.

Shanti and Benno sipped coffee from cardboard cups, while Caine and Masako drank tea. Around the site, dozens of police officers went about their work, and the visitor car park was filled with emergency vehicles. Up at the gates, the crowd of journalists was larger and more frenetic than ever.

'Go on then,' said Shanti. 'This is the bit you love – filling us in on the details. The denouement, isn't that what it's called?'

Caine seemed to be taking just a little longer than necessary to stir a spoonful of Henge Hives Honey into his tea. *It's the bees' knees*, said the legend on the mini jar. Shanti noticed that at some point in the proceedings, he had washed his hair and shaved. Part of her missed the shadowy stubble.

'Maybe we should begin back in 2007,' he said. 'The fourth of August, to be precise, when a young couple from the *Neolithic Neighbours* community set off to forage on the plains.'

'Talin Tull and his Dutch girlfriend,' said Masako.

'Accidentally or deliberately, they strayed onto army land near Imber. As they made love in the heather, the unfortunate couple were hit by a speeding military vehicle, driven by Major Troy McAble. In order to avoid the consequences, he buried them on the spot.'

'Jeez,' said Shanti. 'And only Ned Tull held onto the belief that something terrible had happened to his son.'

'McAble's secret lay undiscovered until a few months ago, when Finch stumbled upon the burial site with his magnetometer. In his journal, he describes how he uncovered knapped flint tools, and thought he had found a Neolithic tomb. Until, to his horror, he unearthed bones with flesh and hair still clinging.

'Troy McAble was out deer-hunting when he came across Finch busily digging up the grave and realised that he was perilously close to revealing his historic crime. McAble became desperate, and sought advice from his old classmate, Quentin Lovell-Finch.'

'Never a good move,' said Shanti.

'Throughout their schooldays, Troy had been mercilessly bullied by Quentin and his upper-class chums ...'

'*Troy, Troy, scholarship boy.*'

'Now Quentin saw a new way to bully McAble, and to reclaim his legacy as the earl of Lovell Court. The first thing he did was to take the story to his mother, Tiggy, at the Once-a-Star Rest Home.'

'This is the part I don't get,' said Shanti. 'When we met Tiggy, she was flummoxed, befuddled and discombobulated.'

'All an act,' said Caine dramatically. 'The terrible stroke that followed her divorce from Finch was in effect the last great role

275

for the declining actress. Her swansong, if you like.'

'I've just remembered,' said Benno. 'At the first team briefing, you suggested that the perp might be someone who was seeking the limelight. A theatrical murder, you said.'

'It was just a guess,' said Caine modestly.

'Someone who wanted to be noticed in the most public way possible,' continued Benno.

'Someone who literally wanted a platform,' added Masako in awe. 'Is it OK if I put this in my thesis?'

'Like a massive extrovert,' recalled Shanti. 'Or the opposite – someone who felt unnoticed or insignificant. And I suppose Tiggy was both those things. Her career was already in decline when Quentin was a boy, and when Finch gave refuge to a group of travellers, it was the final nail in the marriage. Perhaps the stroke started as histrionics, but Tiggy realised that it gave her power.'

'Then her lawyers compelled Finch to cover her extortionate nursing bills,' Caine went on. 'And, I suspect, to cover the cost of silence from her carers.'

'Which gave her all the time in the world to perfect the role of the decrepit invalid,' said Shanti. 'Whilst dreaming of the day when she could return to Lovell Court and take her revenge on Finch and his young Brazilian bride.'

'Are you saying that Tiggy was the murderer?' asked Masako.

'It's a little more nuanced than that,' said Caine. 'Late last night, I remembered something from my school history lessons. Did you ever hear the horrible expression *Krawattennazis und Stiefelnazis*?'

'What the hell does that mean?' said Shanti.

'I think it translates as tie Nazis and boot Nazis,' chirped Masako.

'Exactly,' said Caine. 'Thinkers and thugs. It's been a phenomenon throughout history. The boot Nazis carry out the dirty work for the people in power: the top brass who don't like getting their hands dirty or facing the consequences.'

'So,' said Masako. 'We're talking about a chain of command, right? With Tiggy at the top. Then Quentin, then Troy McAble ...'

'Yes, but you're getting ahead of me,' said Caine with a mystical smile. 'When Quentin came to Tiggy with the story of McAble's desperate need to silence Finch, she realised that her moment had finally come ...'

'And the former Naked Vampire Woman decided that the perfect time and place for maximum melodrama was Stonehenge at the midwinter solstice,' concluded Shanti.

'The apex of the ancient year, in which primal forces roam,' agreed Caine.

'Excuse me,' said Benno, rising to his feet. 'This is all a bit complicated for me. I think they may need help with the detainees inside.'

'I must admit, I feel terrible about Tull,' said Shanti when the sergeant had gone. 'Although I guess he can at least have some closure over Talin now.'

'I'm afraid I also had my doubts,' admitted Caine. 'Whereas Ned was the one who brought me to a moment of awakening.'

'Spit it out then, Caine. You've been trying to tell me Tull's theory all day.'

'It came out of his studies into how Stonehenge was built. He told me that the key word is *teamwork* – Stonehenge was constructed by a team working under the direction of a leader. Under his own instruction, Ned organised a hundred young squaddies to demonstrate how those sarsens of thirty-five tons or more were moved hundreds of miles on wooden sleds or rollers. He believed that Stonehenge was constructed in a similar way by a huge close-knit community working together as a tribe – the family of man, if you like.'

'I don't like,' said Shanti. 'Not everything was made by men. In any case, what has this got to do with Finch's death?'

'The point Ned was making was that the same theory applies here – a complex murder of this nature must have been carried out by a hierarchical team. He convinced me that rather than hunting for a single perpetrator, we should be focusing on a tribe under the direction of a deviously clever leader – the equivalent of a tribal chief. A chain of command, as Masako put it. Ned and I sat up half the night brainstorming all the groups or tribes who operate in this area – the Evolutionaries, the Druids, GoodGuys ... even English Heritage. But the most organised tribe of all ...'

'... is the army,' said Masako.

'Yeah, we all know about your peacenik tendencies, Caine. But I'll have you know that Everkill garrison is renowned for its fundraising work. Wednesday night's dance raised a handsome sum for local charities.'

'It's an important observation,' he said. 'Perhaps you could say that the murder was crowd-funded.'

'A crowd-funded murder?'

'Think about it, Shant – McAble has a reputation as a fundraiser. He also admitted to gambling debts. I'm convinced that he and the Psyche Squad were paid handsomely by Tiggy and Quentin— Ah, look, perfect timing ...'

He nodded towards the sliding doors, where Benno and the team were escorting the prisoners to the waiting vans.

First came the Psyche Squad – a rabble of roughneck rene-gades, struggling aggressively against the restraining officers.

'OK, let me see if I understand,' said Shanti. 'We're talking about a hierarchical tribe, with these guys at the bottom of the chain?'

'Exactly,' said Caine. 'The older ones are ex-cops who were dismissed for gross misconduct after the Battle of the Beanfield. Maybe the ones who beat Silas are among them. And it's ironic that the group they joined included the travellers who were expelled by Finch.'

Like convicts from a Dickensian prison, they shuffled past, some still in Druidic robes with hoods over bleary faces. Others in leathers, with remnants of military attire.

'And some are demobbed soldiers?' asked Masako.

'Who experienced terrible things in war zones,' said Caine. 'It brutalised them, but it also bonded them for life.'

'A band of brothers, isn't that what they say?' said Shanti. 'And I suppose Troy was their contact within the ranks.'

'But these people are from such varied backgrounds,' said Masako. 'Travellers, soldiers, police, a few Druids.'

'Yes, but they have one thing in common,' Caine explained. 'A massive chip on their shoulder. They each feel alienated from society – banished from their respective tribes. I'm sure Ned would tell you that from an anthropological perspective, being cast out is the most terrible thing that can happen to an individ-ual. The loner dies.'

'Or they join a breakaway tribe of outcasts,' said Masako.

'Precisely. A collective of loose cannons. Each of them burn-ing with resentment.'

'And they all shared a grudge against Finch,' said Shanti.

'They despised his anti-war and ecological ideology, and his disdain for uniforms of all kinds. There's no doubt that Finch upset a lot of people over the years.'

'He collected enemies like Tull collected axes.'

'And I guess the motocross games around the monument were a deliberate provocation,' said Caine. 'As was the building they put up to block the solstice sunrise.'

'You could almost describe them as mercenaries,' said Shanti.

As the Psyche Squad were seated in transit vans, a broad-bellied figure was led blinking into the daylight. He had a cumulus of beard around his red face, and his robes were embellished with a fiery dragon.

'The Chief Druid,' said Caine. 'He's an apiarist who makes this lovely stuff – Henge Hives Honey. His company also specialises in mead. I've no doubt he's well acquainted with hemlock and psilocybin too. And by a strange coincidence, his family were evicted from Imber during the war, when Finch's grandfather was the squire. I wonder if there's such a thing as a hereditary grudge.'

Now Troy McAble emerged between two female officers. He was handcuffed and dishevelled, and his moustache hung limp as a dead bird.

As he neared the detectives, he stared contemptuously at Caine. But when he reached Shanti, he stopped, straining against his wardens.

'We could have had fun together,' he said arrogantly. 'I knew you were special the moment I saw you, Shantala. A goddess. And I think you liked old Troy too.'

'Yeah, I've always had a soft spot for controlling sociopaths.'

'That's the spirit I admire. You know, I only have one regret.'

'Oh yes?'

'To use a military term, I regret that you and I never became embedded.'

In her peripheral vision, Shanti saw Caine bristle – unusual for that peace-loving man.

'You'll have plenty of time to enjoy that fantasy, Troy. I've got a feeling your next deployment will be a long one. Take him away, will you?'

They hauled him up the slope to the car park. As the DIs watched, the caged door was closed and firmly bolted.

Maybe he imagined it, but for a brief moment Caine thought that Shanti had shifted a millimetre closer to him.

'I suppose he's good-looking in a superficial sort of way,' he said.

'Never trust a man who doesn't like kids, that's what I say,' said Shanti.

'I love kids,' he told her.

'I know you do, Caine. And for the record, don't ever grow a moustache, unless you want to look like a seventies porn star. But you know, there's still a monumental unresolved mystery. How the hell did they raise Finch's body on top of that trilobite? We've already established he weighed in excess of a hundred and fifty kilos.'

'I think you know the answer.'

'I do?'

'You must have heard them last night.'

'I heard all manner of sounds last night.'

'Apaches.'

'Been on the mead, Caine?'

'Helicopters, Shanti. The afternoon before the solstice, Finch walked with his dogs from Lovell Court to his excavation site near Imber, dressed in his Green Man garb. McAble and his cronies were waiting. They captured Finch and dragged him into the deserted village. While the Druids celebrated Solstice Eve, he was forced to drink mead laced with hemlock. I hope with all my heart that he felt nothing. As the blizzard began to build, they brought an Apache helicopter from Everkill to Imber. The paralysed aristocrat was flown to Stonehenge before dawn, and lowered onto the trilithon. This accounts for the absence of footprints on the snowy ground.'

'Then they raised his beard and his throat was slashed with the flint hatchet, which was covered in Ned's DNA and fingerprints.'

'I'm afraid so. And the ex-cops amongst them knew enough to wipe every trace of real evidence.'

'I suppose it was renegade members of the GoodGuys team who stole the hatchet from Ned's storage space . . .'

'. . . and who later placed it where Dawn would find it.'

'Absolutely brazen!' said Shanti. 'Both Dawn and I felt sure we were being watched. I bet they even joined the search on the plains.'

'Poor old Ned,' said Caine. 'He had already offended the Druids by disparaging their claim to the stones, and he was well known as a master knapper, so they knew we would automatically connect him with the hatchet.'

'You mean *I* would.'

'And because he's a skilled forager, they assumed that the hemlock in Finch's gut would incriminate him further. Ned was set up to take the rap for everything. Like you said – a sacrificial lamb.'

'But what about the dogs?' asked Shanti.

'At some point Ganesh escaped, but they managed to hold on to Albion.'

'Until he was drugged by the GoodGuys crew and placed in Tull's hut as a warning to us, and a further attempt to incriminate the professor. '

'Ah, look who's coming,' said Caine.

'That's a sweet sight, isn't it?' said Shanti.

Two tall men emerged from the visitor centre. One big and burly, the other goggle-eyed and gawkish in a camel-hair coat. One honest as the day was long, one devious as darkness itself. Sergeant 'Benno' Bennett and Quentin Lovell-Finch.

'That's the definition of karma, isn't it, Caine?'

'I don't mean to be pedantic, Shanti, but karma is a Sanskrit word meaning action or work, which is often misinterpreted as revenge or justice. Karmaphala is the fruit of our action. But you're right, there's a strong Buddhist teaching that what you give out, you get back. It coincides closely with the Christian allegory: what you reap, you sow.'

'I think I'll enjoy some nice cold revenge, if it's all the same to you.'

As he approached the DIs, the Honourable Member for the Underworld raised his cuffed hands to remove his trilby. Then he bowed theatrically, so that Shanti looked down at the greased waterfall at the back of his extended occiput.

'It seems victory is thine. *Sic vita est.*'

'Yeah, well, you win some, you lose some, eh, Quinty?'

'For the moment only, dear lady. I have the finest lawyers money can buy. As we speak, they are assembling a watertight case – which, you may care to know, includes a formal complaint about your professional manner . . . or lack thereof.'

'My colleague has acted with the utmost propriety,' said Caine.

'Ah, Inspector Caliban. As raggedy as ever. Do you know the meaning of the phrase *vir prudens non contra ventum mingit*?'

'*Ventum* is wind. *Mingit* is . . . urinate, I believe.'

'Quite so. It means that a wise man does not urinate against the wind, Inspector. Which is a warning to menials not to tangle with their betters, for they shall be rewarded with nothing but damp trisers. My people are confident that I shall be released forthwith, whence I shall set about evicting those hoodlums from the great hise and restoring Lovell Court to its former glory.'

'I'd like to introduce you to Masako,' said Shanti. 'She's a key member of our team. I have a feeling she's going to go a very long way in her career. This week, for example, she has been carrying out a deep dive into your business activities. It makes fascinating bedtime reading.'

Jade eyes jittered behind dense lenses.

'I warn you, I am a man of importance.'

'It's nice to be important, Mr Lovell-Finch . . . but it's more important to be nice.'

'Wonderful phrase,' said Caine. 'I love that.'

'Take him away, will you, Benno?' said Shanti.

'My absolute pleasure, boss,' said Benno, grinning broadly. 'I said you'd get there in the end, you and Vince. You always do. Oh, and by the way, I got a call from the vet to say that Albion has been safely returned, much to the relief of everyone at Evol.'

'Do not employ that ghastly moniker,' shrieked Lovell-Finch. 'Lovell Court! The hise is Lovell Court!'

They watched as Benno led the gangly politician to the car park, where he was placed in his very own cage in the back of a van.

'Here comes our last little jailbird,' said Shanti. 'I wonder if she'll sing.'

A wheelchair was rolled through the doors bearing a svelte girl in a miniskirt and fur coat.

'Tiggy Antrobus-Lovell-Finch,' said Caine.

She stared pitifully at them through spidery lashes, but said nothing.

'You're quiet this morning,' said Shanti. 'Funny that. Last time I saw you, you were partying like it was 1963.'

From beneath the Biba hat came not a word, but as she was wheeled away, Shanti noticed the faintest smile of satisfaction on the tangerine lips of the ancient actor.

'Her final role will be in the theatre of the High Court,' said Caine. 'With an appreciative audience of judge and jury, and reviews in all the papers. I wouldn't be surprised if she didn't relish the attention in some bizarre way.'

'Promise me they won't get off, Caine?'

'I wish I could, Shanti, I wish I could make that promise. But Silas will tell you that the aristocracy have been getting away with murder since time began.'

They watched as the vans drove away in single file through the heavily guarded barriers, where the paparazzi surged forward, cameras flashing, microphones bristling.

'Can we head home now?' said Shanti.

'I think we should. If you drop me in Yeovil, I'll catch the last bus back to Lyme. I should be at the Undercliff before dark.'

For the last time, the pap posse surrounded the Saab as they drove through the barriers. Shanti attempted to creep the vehicle forward, but these people were ravenous for a fat Christmas story with all the greasy trimmings.

'I feel the same as you did at Everkill, Caine. I just can't face this.'

'No worries. It's time I did my share of public speaking.'

'But you'll say weird things.'

'I'm fine. You stay here. Let me handle this.'

He rolled down the window, smiling into a flurry of cameras and frantic questions.

'DI Caine, we've just witnessed upwards of thirty suspects being taken away ... Which of them murdered Hector Lovell-Finch?'

'It's complicated,' said Caine.

'Could you expand on that, Inspector?'

'Let's just drive on, shall we?' said Shanti.

'Bear with me, Shant. I think this could be serendipitous. You know I've been trying to interpret my dream? Well, last night, while you were sleeping at the stones, it finally came to me. I feel I should seize the moment to deliver a message to the world.'

'For God's sake, Caine ...'

But Caine was already easing his way out of the door, sliding between the corpulent newshounds to the front of the car, where he climbed onto the bonnet. With strands of hair and earflaps blowing, he addressed the crowd – and a live audience of millions.

'Thanks for your patience, everyone. I'm sure you won't want me to prejudice any future trial, so I can't address the specifics of the case ...'

'We get that, DI Caine. But surely you can give us something?'

'How did Finch die?'

'How did he get on that stone, Inspector? He was a big geezer.'

'Our audience needs a story . . .'

'Who killed Hector Lovell-Finch, Inspector, that's what we'd like to know.'

Caine centred himself, waiting for inspiration to descend.

'In a way,' he said quietly, 'we all killed him.'

'What's that mean?'

'We all killed him, Inspector?'

They looked at each other and began to laugh.

'*I* didn't kill him.'

'Nor did I.'

'I mean,' said Caine, 'this case is about the fragility of nature. We are all responsible for the death of the Green Man.'

'Not quite following you there.'

'We like to believe that our planet is immortal. That it will endure eternally. We assume that the earth will carry on absorbing everything we throw at it without complaint, as we plunder its resources – razing rainforests, butchering animals, poisoning the oceans . . . But the truth is . . .'

'What is the truth, DI Caine?'

'The earth is small and fragile . . . And the earth is tired.'

Zoom lenses captured two tears that tumbled from his oil-well eyes.

'You been smoking something, DI Caine?'

'I'm fine. Perhaps someone out there will understand what I'm trying to say. If you can hear me, Sky, I know you will. I believe Finch would have understood too. You are the future, Sky. You and your generation will show the way.'

'The way to where, Inspector?'

As the journalists gawped, Caine felt the car move beneath his boots. He lost his balance and tumbled onto the bonnet, grabbing the windscreen wipers and peering in at Shanti as she accelerated firmly through the mob.

Some tried to give chase, but Shanti surged forward with Caine clinging on for dear life. When they reached the junction of the A303, she jerked on the brakes and leaned out of the window.

'Get in, Caine. Now.'

'Of course, Shanti. Are you mad at me?'

'What the fuck were you talking about? *We are all responsible for the death of the Green Man.*'

'But it's true.'

'Caine, can you do one thing for me? Just one small thing?'

'Of course, Shanti. Anything.'

'Nothing, Caine. For once in your barmy Buddhist life, don't do or say anything. Just sit quietly until we get to Yeovil. And if you see anything remotely open, like a garage where I can buy some semblance of Christmas cheer for my son, again, don't say anything. Just wait in the car.'

'Sorry, Shanti, but I do have one thing to say. Remember I told you that Ned made one of his hand-crafted presents for Paul? I put it in the boot for you, alongside your lovely red dress.'

Somewhere in her bag, Shanti's phone vibrated.

'Right, if this is Mum, I am begging you not to tell her that she is responsible for the destruction of the planet, or that her daughter spent half the night as a Druidic sacrifice ... Jesus, where is that phone?'

'I won't interfere, Shanti, I promise. But I'd like to wish her a happy Christmas. Here, I'll put it on speakerphone ...'

Amma's voice filled the car.

'Shanti? Are you finally on your way?'

'Yes, Mum.'

'You must be exhausted, darling.'

'I'm fine.'

'Is Vincent with you? I always feel happier when you're with Vincent. I think you look after each other.'

'Hello, Amma,' said Caine. 'How are you?'

'I'm well. How lovely to hear your voice. Will you join us for something to eat? I know Paul would love that.'

'That's incredibly kind ...'

'Caine has to get back, Mum. He left a meditation half finished. It doesn't keep, you know.'

'Paul's been crying, I'm afraid, Shanti.'

'Oh Jeez. Is he there? Can I speak to him?'

'He won't talk to you.'

'Please, Mum. I'll be home in an hour ... Paul? Paul is that you?'

'What?'

'Paul, listen, darling—'

'You promised. You promised we'd have the best Christmas ever.'

'But Christmas is tomorrow, sweetheart ... Today is only Christmas Eve.'

'You're a rubbish mum.'

'Oh Paul. That isn't fair.'

'Hey, Paul,' interrupted Caine. 'How are you? You wait till I tell you what your mum has been up to. All I can say is a lot of cops think she must have superpowers. You're going to be so proud of her.'

'She promised me the best Christmas ever. Now it's too late to go to Dad's and we won't have Christmas at all.'

'Don't underestimate your mum, Paul. I'm telling you, she's a superhero. If she promised you the best Christmas ever, then that's precisely what you'll get.'

'Really?'

'Trust me, Paul. Trust your mum. Excited?'

'Maybe.'

'Listen, she'll be with you very soon. Now, you need to get everything ready, 'cos she's been working so hard ... just like Santa. Do you think you can make her a superhero cup of tea? Got any mince pies? How about superwoman bubble bath?'

'OK.'

'And don't stay up too late. You know why?'

'Christmas.'

'You've got it. Magic day, right?'

'All right, Vince.'

'Good man, Paul.'

He terminated the call.

'Sorry, Shant. I know I wasn't supposed to speak ...'

'Ah, Jeez, what does it matter? Thanks for trying. He sounded happier, I must admit. You've got a way with kids, I'll give you that. But you don't quite understand, Caine. If you build up their hopes like that, and then let them down, they could be psychologically scarred for life. He'll probably grow up like McAble.'

'He's fine. He's a great lad. You've done an incredible job with him.'

'But what the hell am I going to do tomorrow?'

'Oh, we'll think of something.'

'Think of something? What does that mean? I've left it all too late.'

They entered the empty grey streets of Yeovil. At the corner of Shanti's estate, Caine collected his bag, pulled on the flying hat and stepped onto the slushy road.

Shanti opened the window.

'Wait a minute,' she called. 'You haven't answered the question.'

'Which question, Shant?'

'What the hell am I supposed to do tomorrow? It's Christmas Day, if that means anything to you at all. My entire future relationship with my son hangs in the balance.'

He walked to the side of the car and gazed in.

'Like I say, Shanti, it's pretty simple really . . .'

When he had told her, he went to wait in the shelter on the corner.

And the lonesome Buddhist took the last bus to Lyme Regis.

Chapter 35

Christmas Present

Snow.

Snow fell.

Snow fell softly on the Undercliff at Lyme Regis.

At first a light dusting on frosted trees. Then feathery flakes filled the air. In the small hours before dawn, the Mindful Detective rose from his bed and placed the kettle on the stove.

The slogan on Caine's mug said: *THERE'S NO PLACE LIKE OM.*

When he had washed and shaved, he went to the bookcase to find the volume that old master Tu had given him so long ago. When he had found it, he searched for the verse by Cheng-Li that he had been groping for all week.

There it was. Shorter and more perfect than he remembered. He read it carefully, then placed the book open on the shrine. Taking his seat cross-legged on the zafu cushion, he read it once more. It was about awareness of dukkha, or suffering.

When sad, let go of the cause of sadness.

What was it that made him sad? Police work? Maybe. Shanti? No, she brought more happiness than he could bear.

Closing his eyes, he plunged at last into the ocean of tranquillity that lies beneath words.

And when he rose, the cabin was filled with light.

Caine put on an apron and tidied the cabin, then he began to prepare a meal. More than a meal – a feast. And as he decorated the table with sprigs of holly with beads like blood, he thought with tenderness of a man he had never met – the Holly King, Hector Lovell-Finch.

From somewhere deep in the forest he heard voices approaching, and what sounded like Christmas carols.

With an oven glove, he slid the casserole into the oven and went to the picture window to look at the wonderland below.

On the winding coastal path, three figures approached – two women, and a boy on a hand-crafted sledge.

At Lyme Regis, Shanti, Amma and Paul had watched the sunrise, pink and orange and mauve, over the Cobb that snaked into the sea.

Then they had set off excitedly along the path that meandered through the wild white forest. An hour later, when they reached the place called the Lost Chimney, Shanti looked up at Caine's high cabin, which gazed like the wooden eye of an insect towards the horizon.

'Paul, I can't pull you up the hill,' she said. 'You'll have to leave the sledge here. Park it by that tree.'

'But someone will nick it, Mum.'

'Someone? There's no one here, darling. Not for miles. Not one person except Caine.'

As they began the steep ascent, Shanti noticed something extraordinary. Perched on the turf roof beside the chimney was a huge, solitary creature. A buzzard, which spread its wings and sailed languidly over their heads, letting out a long, lonely call of greeting – *Kreuw-ee-ee-ee!*

The tall man came to the window, dark against the lights of the interior, and looked down at them. When he saw them, his face lit up like the sunrise over the Cobb.

This was dangerous. This was crazy. Caine was her work colleague. And an annoying one at that. Cops didn't dream. And they didn't fall in love.

Paul ran ahead up the near-vertical track to the deck by the cabin door.

Jesus, as if these tree roots weren't dangerous enough, the ice had turned the path into a ski slope. It was a health-and-safety issue for sure. You bet your life Caine didn't have public liability insurance.

And here he was, coming to meet them, hugging and kissing the boy, holding tight to the rope handrail as they hauled Amma upwards, while she huffed and puffed and laughed.

'It's so good to see you,' he said when he got them inside. His voice was actually trembling with emotion.

Amma, who had never visited before, was given a guided tour by Paul.

'And I sleep in the hammock on the deck,' he shouted.

'Not tonight,' said Caine. 'It's way too cold.'

'Oh. Will we have to go home?'

'We could hang the hammock inside,' said Caine. 'Near the stove is good.'

'Can we? Can we? Can we?' sang Paul.

'I must admit,' said Shanti, as she handed Caine her coat, 'it looks cosy in here. Snug.'

'Yeah, and it smells good too,' added Paul.

'Cloves,' said Caine. 'And Christmas lunch. Now sit yourselves down while I finish cooking.'

'I didn't think Buddhists celebrated Christmas,' said Amma, as she settled back with a glass of sherry.

'I hate to say it,' Caine told her, 'but I think the Christians pinched it from the pagans. Almost every culture celebrates midwinter.'

'Well I think it's lovely. A real fire and everything.'

'We have our friends the Druids to thank for the Yule log.'

'He mentioned the D word,' said Shanti.

'Sorry, Shant. But honestly, Druids are wonderful people. Don't forget we have them to thank for the best Christmas tradition of all.'

'Oh yeah. And what's that?'

Caine looked around the cabin.

'Ah, I thought I'd forgotten something. I'll fix it later. Maybe Paul can help. In the meantime, I hope everyone is hungry.'

'Starving!' shouted Paul.

'Jeez, that's quite a spread,' said Shanti cautiously. 'I'm guessing no animal died.'

When they had eaten, twice over in Paul's case, they exchanged presents, which included mugs with slogans, Henge Hives Honey, a signed *Neolithic Neighbours* book and a real flint hatchet (not too sharp) for Paul.

'Shanti is asleep,' whispered Amma. 'I don't think she slept at all on that investigation. Vincent, do you think you could lift her and put her on your bed?'

'I'm fine, thank you very much,' said Shanti, opening one eye.

'But a rest is a good idea,' said Caine.

'Maybe I'll have a quiet read,' agreed Shanti. 'Got any magazines, Caine?'

'Not as such,' he said. 'But I was looking at a wonderful book before you came.'

He handed her the volume from the shrine, then led her into his own room, where the sheets were crisp as snow. Just before she dived into sleep, she realised that everything – the room, the bed and even the funny little book – smelled sweetly and strangely of him: the man named Caine.

'Vincent,' said Amma, when he had quietly closed the bedroom door, 'you are forbidden from clearing up. It will be my pleasure after such a wonderful meal.'

So Paul and Caine pulled on boots and coats and hats, and slid down the track to find the sledge, hand-built by Professor Ned Tull. And it had not been stolen.

Caine towed the boy through the sparkling forest and showed him how the snow is like the page of a book; and the words are animal footprints, which tell the story of the night before.

Lying on his back on the sledge, Paul gazed up through the broken forest roof, where a buzzard soared on outspread wings.

They heard its long and lonesome cry – '*Kreuw-ee-ee-ee!*'

From nests hidden in branches all around, a pack of wild corvids sprang, leaping to peck and harass the majestic bird.

'What are those birds doing, Vincent?'

'The crows are mobbing him. It's their territory. They're chasing him away.'

'But they'll hurt him.'

'No. He's smarter than that ... Watch.'

With Zen-like calm the buzzard caught a thermal, soaring majestically over the precipice, drifting free above the milky ocean.

From the cliff edge, Caine and Paul watched him. To their delight, the lonesome bird was joined by a mate, and the buzzards skated together across the ice-blue sky.

'It's dark outside,' said Shanti. 'Did I sleep a long time?'

He had brought her tea in bed, in a proper cup and saucer.

'You dropped the book, Shanti. What did you think?'

'Couldn't make head or tail of it. But it helped me sleep.'

'The wind has got up again,' he said. 'I'm afraid you won't get home tonight. I hope you don't mind, but I made up a bed for Amma on the sofa. They're both asleep.'

'I couldn't have separated Paul from that hammock anyway. Guess what he said to me earlier, Caine? I could have cried.'

'Tell me.'

'He said that today was the most magical Christmas of all time.'

'I thought that word was banned, Shanti.'

She sipped the tea and listened to the distant sighing of the waves.

'You know I said that cops don't dream?'

'They work, they sleep, they work again.'

'Yeah. Only so much of what happened recently seems like a dream. Last night ... this morning ... whenever the hell it was that I was sleeping on that damned altar ...'

'You looked so beautiful, Shant.'

'. . . did I imagine it, or were you holding my hand?'

'Oh! I'm so sorry. It's unforgivable. I should have asked for consent. I forgot the second precept.'

'The second what?'

'The second precept says you should refrain from taking the not-given. But you were asleep, you see . . . No, that sounds even worse . . .'

'Christ, Caine. I liked it. Now shut up a minute.'

'I brought you something from the forest. A gift from the Druids. Just to show they aren't all bad.'

'Not hemlock, is it? Or psilocybin? Don't fancy that tonight.'

From behind his back, he conjured a sprig – dark viridian embellished with ivory pearls.

'Mistletoe,' she said.

'An ancient midwinter custom. But of course it doesn't mean we have to . . .'

'Have to what, Caine?'

'You know – follow the whole tradition. It's optional, Shanti . . . Everything is optional. Choice is everything.'

To silence him, she slid her fingers behind the long strands at the back of his neck. When her nails made him moan, Caine dropped the book again, where it lay open on the wooden floor, at an ancient text by Cheng-Li.

As she drew him closer, every care and worry fell away. In that moment there was no pain. No suffering. No mourning. No death.

The winds of circumstance blew across emptiness.

And the world was filled with love.

You sentient beings who seek deliverance, why do you not let go?
When sad, let go of the cause of sadness,
When covetous or lustful, let go of the object of desire.
From moment to moment, be free of self.
Where no self is, there can be no sorrow, no desire,
The winds of circumstance blow across emptiness.
Whom can they harm?

Cheng-Li

Newport Community
Learning & Libraries

CRIME AND THRILLER FAN?

CHECK OUT **THECRIMEVAULT.COM**

The online home of exceptional crime fiction

KEEP YOURSELF IN SUSPENSE

Sign up to our newsletter for regular recommendations, competitions and exclusives at **www.thecrimevault.com/connect**

Follow us

🐦 **@TheCrimeVault**

f **/TheCrimeVault**

for all the latest news

Z991800